NOT JUST A

Coolly Remo surveyed [illegible] bed. Then, before his shocked eyes, her corpse came upright.

"I . . . want . . . you," she said slowly. And the hands folded on her magnificent chest began to tear at the front of her dress.

Remo caught them, one hand on each wrist. The wrists struggled in his grip. They were stronger than human limbs should be.

"You don't take no for an answer, do you?" Remo said, straining to keep in control. This Kimberly was no pushover.

Then he smelled a familiar scent—dying flowers, musky womanhood, blood, and other sweet and savage odors. It slammed into his lungs like cold fire.

"Oh, no," he croaked. "Kali."

Kimberly's chest convulsed and strained. Her dress front began to rip and tear away. And a familiar voice that was not Kimberly's snarled, "*You are mine! Mine! Mine!*"

#85

The Destroyer

BLOOD LUST

Created by
WARREN MURPHY & RICHARD SAPIR

A SIGNET BOOK

SIGNET
Published by the Penguin Group
Penguin Books USA Inc., 375 Hudson Street,
New York, New York 10014, U.S.A.
Penguin Books Ltd, 27 Wrights Lane,
London W8 5TZ, England
Penguin Books Australia Ltd, Ringwood,
Victoria, Australia
Penguin Books Canada Ltd, 2801 John Street,
Markham, Ontario, Canada L3R 1B4
Penguin Books (N.Z.) Ltd, 182-190 Wairau Road,
Auckland 10, New Zealand

Penguin Books Ltd, Registered Offices:
Harmondsworth, Middlesex, England

First published by Signet, an imprint of New American Library,
a division of Penguin Books USA Inc.

First Printing, July, 1991
10 9 8 7 6 5 4 3 2 1

PRINTED IN THE UNITED STATES OF AMERICA

PUBLISHER'S NOTE
This is a work of fiction. Names, characters, places, and incidents either are the product of the author's imagination or are used fictitiously, and any resemblance to actual persons, living or dead, events, or locales is entirely coincidental.

For Hector Garrido, who has always painted the Destroyer covers. And we hope always will.

And for the Glorious House of Sinanju, P.O. Box 2505, Quincy, MA 02269.

1

Allison Baynes was very, very worried about little Kimberly.

"It's not drugs, is it?" Norma Quinlan asked, her froglike voice cracking. She winced. Her heart skipped a beat. But inside, she couldn't wait to tell Beverly and Kathleen. She might even start speaking with Ida MacDonough again, just to see the look on her stuck-up face when she told Ida that poor Kimberly Baynes had become a drug addict. She tonged a sugar cube into her tea.

"No, it's not drugs," Allison Baynes said in a hushed and age-quavered voice. Her eyes went to the window, as if the neighbors were listening. In a way, they were. Through Norma Quinlan, the gossip queen of Aurora, Colorado, a suburb of Denver. "I almost wish it were. If it were only drugs, I could send her to Betty Ford."

"Do they take them that young?" asked Norma, deciding that a second sugar cube was called for. She would need her energy for all the phone calls she would be making later.

"Perhaps not," Mrs. Baynes said worriedly. Her plump face wore a motherly frown. She balanced her china saucer in one age-spotted hand. The other held the fine china cup suspended a micro-inch over the saucer, as if both would shatter if they met. She raised the cup to her unlipsticked mouth thoughtfully, frowned, and sipped. The cup returned to its hovering position, and Allison Baynes resumed speaking. "She's only thirteen, you know."

"That young? Why, I saw her only the other day. She looked like a high-school girl in that . . . dress."

"She's wearing lipstick now too."

"I guess she's at the age, then. You know, they become more sophisticated at a much younger age than we did," said Norma Quinlan in a proper voice, shoving into the furthest recess of her mind the half-buried memory of the day she let Harvey Bluestein grope her at the drive-in. That, after all, had been the sixties. The late sixties. People did those things then.

"It is true, isn't it?" Mrs. Baynes said ruefully, looking at the coppery liquid steaming in her cup. Her hair was a silvery-blue halo that might have been spun by a platinum spider. She sighed.

Norma Quinlan reached for a raisin scone, knowing that the moment of truth was almost at hand. The sigh was her clue. They always sighed before unburdering themselves. And she was such an attentive listener.

"She's been gaining weight, you know."

"The dress I saw the other day was a positive tent," Norma said quickly between nibbles of the scone, which was dry. "But her face was so thin. And so pretty. She's very pretty."

"Like a little doll," agreed Allison Baynes with grandmotherly pride. "You know, she adjusted very well. After the unpleasantness."

"Unpleasantness?" asked Norma, masking her interest with an innocent tone. She knew very well about the unpleasantness, but wanted to hear it directly. In case new details slipped out. They often did.

"You know that Kimmo's parents died tragically several years ago."

"I've heard that," Norma said vaguely. "Somewhere."

"Her mother was found strangled in Paris. It was perfectly horrible. They never found the killer."

Norma nodded attentively. She knew that.

"A.H., my son, met a similar fate. They found him dead in his Rocky Mountain vacation home, his tongue sticking out of his mouth. Just like my daughter-in-law."

"No!" said Norma, who knew that too.

Mrs. Baynes contemplated the steam rising from her cup with oracular intentness. "What I'm about to tell you is strictly between the two of us."

"Absolutely," Norma said sincerely, deciding right then and there that she would call Ida, after all.

"They found them both with identical yellow scarves around their necks."

"My God!"

"It's true, I sold A.H.'s place, you know. Wouldn't even step into it."

"Places like that are often haunted," Norma said sagely.

"True."

"Did they ever find the killers?"

Mrs. Baynes sipped delicately. "Never. I think they stopped looking. You see, before they died, A.H. and Evelyn—that was my daughter-in-law's name, Evelyn—joined one of those horrid . . . cults."

"I didn't know that," Norma said, spilling tea on her lap. This was better than she could have imagined. She could hardly wait to get to that phone.

"What kind of a cult?" she asked, her voice steady.

"I was never clear on that," Mrs. Baynes confessed. "And frankly, I have no interest in knowing. Looking back, it seems all so unbelievable. Like something that would happen to common people back East. After all, A.H. was the president of Just Folks Airlines."

"Too bad they went bankrupt like that," Norma said sympathetically. "Their fares were so reasonable."

"I had to sell the company, you know. And the new owners simply ran it into the ground."

Norma nodded. She neglected to mention that Mrs. Baynes had attempted to run the company for a year. Her free-fares-for-senior-citizens offer had put Just Folks into receivership. She was forced to sell her stock. A year later, Just Folks was just a memory.

"So you think they were victims of this cult?"

"They had to be. I think they hypnotized A.H. into joining. He was a graduate of the Cambridge Business School, you know."

Norma made a mental note of that.

"After the funeral," Mrs. Baynes continued, "Kimberly came to stay with me. She was very unstable at first. Forever chanting childish nonsense. I guess she picked that up from the horrid cult environment. But Kimmo came out of it after only a week."

"A week!" Norma clucked. "Imagine that. Children are so resilient. It's really a blessing."

Mrs. Baynes nodded. "A blessing. She hasn't spoken of her mother or father since the funeral. Not even about Joshua."

Norma's teacup quivered in her hand. "Joshua?"

"Her brother. She had an older brother. I buried him with A.H. and Evelyn."

"Not strangled?"

"No."

Relief washed over Norma Quinlan's face.

"He was blown up," Allison Baynes said matter-of-factly, sipping her tea.

"Blown . . . up?" Norma was aghast.

"The cult had a van. Joshua was riding in it with some others. It exploded somehow. The police told me it might have been the work of a rival cult."

"You poor dear! What you've been through! And now this business with Kimberly," Norma said solicitously, steering Mrs. Baynes back to the topic at hand.

"I told you that she's been gaining weight."

"The onset of puberty will do that with some girls."

"I first noticed her developing three years ago."

"And you say she's thirteen?"

Allison Baynes nodded. "At ten."

"I read an article in *Ladies' Home Journal* once that said some girls start developing as early as nine. Or was it eight?"

"My Kimmo blossomed into a tiny woman almost overnight. One day she was playing with dolls, the next she was in a training bra and putting on makeup."

"They grow up so fast. My Calvin enters college next month. Law school. Tulane. I wouldn't let him go to an eastern college."

Mrs. Baynes let the veiled dismissal of Cambridge Business College go by without comment.

"I didn't think much of it at the time," she said reflectively, "but I noticed the statue grew overnight as well."

"Statue?"

Allison Baynes stared into her tea for a thoughtful interval, watching the concentric ripples created by the subtle tremor in her aging hands. Abruptly, she replaced the cup in the saucer and the saucer on the coffee table.

"I shouldn't do this but . . ." She stood up decisively. "Let me show you something."

They tiptoed up the carpeted steps—Mrs. Baynes because she had learned to tiptoe and speak softly in her own home and Norma because Mrs. Baynes was doing it.

Mrs. Baynes led her down a cream-colored hallway to the closed door at its end.

"She sometimes locks it," Mrs. Baynes explained, testing the doorknob. Norma Quinlan took advantage of the stubborn doorknob to peek through the half-closed door to the other bedroom. The expensive damask bedspread lay on the bed as if enameled to it. The open bathroom door, on the other hand, showed a slovenly array of unhung towels. Norma wrinkled her nose as if at an offending odor, but deep inside she was pleased. Allison Baynes put on such airs. It was comforting to see that she was not the world's greatest housekeeper, as some busybodies thought.

The doorknob rattled uncooperatively in Mrs. Baynes's hands and Norma's heart sank. She really wanted to see this statue.

Finally the door surrendered. Mrs. Baynes pushed it in. She looked in with more than a trace of fear on her face, Norma saw. She stepped aside for Norma to enter.

Carefully, still on tiptoe, Norma Quinlan did just that.

She gasped.

"She calls it Calley," Mrs. Baynes said, as if speaking of the family dog.

For once, Norma Quinlan was speechless. The thing in the room was grayish-white, like a weather-beathen skull. It squatted—that was exactly the word for it—on a child's toy chest. It was nearly four feet tall, and fairly broad. The face was a malevolent mask. Norma blinked, realizing there were three faces. Two others framed the central one. But most arrestingly, it had four arms. They were upflung in spidery, arcane gestures. Draped between the lower pair was a yellow silk scarf.

"It's . . . it's . . ." Norma began, groping for words.

"Hideous."

"My thought exactly."

"Kimberly made it. Herself."

"She must be very . . . good with her hands," Norma Quinlan gulped.

"It started as a little Play-Doh figure," Mrs. Baynes explained in a faraway tone. "She made the first one not long after I took custody. It had four arms. But she kept adding new ones. They sprouted from the chest, the legs, even the headdress. Until it made me think of an angry spider."

"I'd prefer a spider myself," Norma said, aghast. So aghast she right then and there decided not to mention the statue to any of her friends. Where would she find the words to describe it?

"One day I mentioned to Kimmo that perhaps she should stop adding arms, that the statue was pretty enough as it was. And do you know what she said to me?"

"What?"

Mrs. Baynes fixed Norma Quinlan with her steady sad gaze. "She said she didn't make the arms. Then she asked for another cat."

"Yes?" Norma said slowly, not seeing the connection.

"It was the fifth cat I had gotten her. The others had all run away."

"No!"

"She cried so much, I brought her a nice tabby. A week later it was gone. I mentioned this to Kimmo and she didn't seem very sad at all. She just asked for another cat. I didn't get her another cat. This time I got her a puppy. They're more stay-at-home."

"Dogs are a sensible pet, I'll agree. I remember when we had our Ginger—"

"The poor puppy wouldn't sleep in her room," Mrs. Baynes continued distantly. "It wouldn't even go upstairs, no matter how much Kimmo tried to coax it. It just sat at the foot of the steps and looked up. *Growling*."

"How odd."

"One night Kimberly came home with a leash and dragged that poor dog up the stairs. The next morning it was gone."

Norma's hand flew to her scrawny chest.

"My goodness. You don't think Kimberly had anything to do with that?"

"I called the dog officer," Mrs. Baynes said. "The highway department. The city. Everyone I could think of."

She stared at the grotesque statue a long time, her hands clutching one another.

"You know," she resumed in a too-calm voice, "they found that poor animal by the side of the road, its tongue hanging out, strangled. There was a yellow scarf around its neck. Just like that one. Just like the ones that killed Evelyn and A.H."

The coincidence registered on Norma Quinlan's thin, witchy face.

"Perhaps we should leave now," she said quickly. "You know how teenagers are about their privacy."

"You're right," Mrs. Baynes said, closing the door. It wouldn't quite shut, so she left it slightly ajar.

They descended the carpeted stairs in uneasy silence.

"More tea?" Mrs. Baynes asked when they were back in the homey living room.

Norma Quinlan hesitated. Their little chat had taken a nasty turn. She felt positively queasy. Gossip was one thing, but this could give a person nightmares.

As Norma debated her answer, the back door banged.

Norma started. Fearfully, her eyes went to the kitchen.

"Is that you, Kimmo?" Mrs. Baynes asked calmly, as if speaking to a normal child, not a strangler of innocent pets.

"Yeah," said a frowning girlish voice.

Norma stood up. "Perhaps I should be going now," she said nervously.

In from the kitchen came Kimberly Baynes. She wore a flowing yellow dashiki that almost matched her fluffy hair. It hung from her small but womanly body like a tarpaulin on a Christmas tree. She stopped when she saw Norma. Her bright blue eyes flashed with veiled danger. That anger went away quickly and in a thin voice she said, "Hi."

"Hello, Kimberly," Norma said, mustering a sweetness that had fled her voice years ago. "Nice to see you again."

"Same thing," said Kimberly casually. "Gramma, any calls for me?"

"No, dear."

The tentlike dress fluttered disquietingly. "Darn."

"What is it?"

"Robby Simpson's cat had kittens and he promised me one," Kimberly explained. "Remember when we used to have kittens?"

"Distinctly," said Mrs. Baynes, her eyes going to Norma. Norma looked as comfortable as an Israeli in Mecca.

"I have to go now," she said quickly.

"I'll see you to the door," Mrs. Baynes said.

Norma beat Mrs. Baynes to the front door by eight seconds. She flung it open herself. Stumbling out onto the walk, she stuttered breathlessly, "Very nice talking to you, Mrs. Baynes."

"We must do it again," Mrs. Baynes called after her. "Soon. There are so many things I haven't told you."

"Oh, please . . ." Norma Quinlan muttered under her breath as she stumbled across their adjoining lawn to the sanctuary of her own home.

Norma Quinlan hurried inside. She tore right past the

telephone and pulled a dusty cookbook off the pantry shelf. She was going to make Fred his favorite dish tonight—Lava Chicken. She hadn't made it for him in years. Not after she put a stop to his little fling with that cheap Calloway hussy. But tonight she would serve him Lava Chicken.

Now that she understood precisely what lived next door, she appreciated him in a new way.

Mrs. Allison Baynes was clearing the living room when Kimberly came storming down the carpeted stairs, her yellow dress fluttering excitedly in symphathy with her agitated arms.

"You've been in my room! How could you?"

"I know you like your privacy, Kimmo," Mrs. Baynes said, unperturbed. "But this is my home too."

"Don't call me Kimmo, you old bag!" Kimberly said with such elemental vehemence that Mrs. Baynes allowed the sterling-silver tea service to slip from her startled fingers. It clattered to the Oriental rug.

"Oh, look what you made me do," she said without rancor.

"And you let that gossip in, too!"

"Mrs. Quinlan is a very nice woman. Could you help me?"

"Why? Why did you let her into my room?"

"Nonsense, Kimberly," Mrs. Baynes said, her voice growing chilly. "What makes you think I would do such a thing?"

"She told me."

"She?"

"And She insists on her privacy."

"I hope you're not referring to that hideous statue. I thought you'd have outgrown it by now."

Kimberly's eyes grew hard and reflective. "Maybe it's the other way around."

"If you won't help me," said Mrs. Baynes, getting down on her hands and knees with difficulty, "then at least take these things into the kitchen as I hand them up to you. I'm not young anymore."

"Maybe She's outgrown this house," Kimberly said, advancing slowly. "Maybe I have too."

"Nonsense. You're only thirteen. Would you take this service into the kitchen for me, please?"

"Sure," Kimberly said lightly. "Glad to."

Ignoring the offered service, Kimberly stepped around her kneeling grandmother.

"What are you doing, Kimberly?" Mrs. Baynes asked.

There was no answer. Only sudden strong hands on her shoulders. Their grip was quite firm.

"Kimmo, what are you doing?" Mrs. Baynes repeated.

"Hold still, Gramma," Kimberly said, pushing down hard.

Alarmed, Mrs. Baynes tried to rise. But the strong hands only pushed harder. They were irresistible.

"Kimberly," Mrs. Baynes said, dread flooding her voice. "Are those hands yours?"

Then there came a tremendous ripping sound, like a sail in a storm. She couldn't imagine what it was. But the remorseless hands on her shoulders shook in frantic sympathy.

That really alarmed Mrs. Baynes. She struggled to regain her feet, the tea service forgotten. It clattered to the rug.

And while she struggled, a flash of bright yellow crossed her field of vision, and she found it increasingly hard to breathe.

She touched her throat. Mrs. Baynes felt something silky, and her thoughts flashed to the yellow scarf that had been in Calley's clay hands.

"Kimberly, this is not funny. I can barely breathe."

The silk constricted. When Mrs. Baynes really, really could no longer breathe, she brought the other hand up to fight the tightening noose. It refused to budge.

She grabbed the cruel, tightening fingers. They were implacable. The edges of Mrs. Baynes's vision began to darken. The roaring sound in her ears reminded her of a seashell sound, but greatly magnified.

"She loves it," Kimberly sang through the growing blood roar. "She loves it."

Allison Baynes tried to tell Kimberly that she didn't in fact enjoy being choked, but since no air could squeeze past her windpipe, speaking was impossible.

And as her mind darkened, Mrs. Baynes was struck by a very odd thought.

If these were Kimberly's hands holding her down, whose were tightening the yellow scarf?

The police found Mrs. Allison Baynes hunched and kneeling in the middle of her living room, nose and forehead pressed into the rug, surrounded by the scattered pieces of her silver tea set. Her eyes bulged in an incredulous death stare. Her tongue lolled out of her mouth, a rich purplish-black. Robin's-egg blue was the color of her face.

Detective Oscar Sale took one look and rushed out of the house.

"We got another one," he called to the medical examiner.

The medical examiner was overseeing two morgue attendants as they rolled a sheet-covered gurney out of the house to a waiting ambulance.

The M.E. fingered one ear forward. "What?"

"Same method—looks like a ligature strangulation."

The M.E. hurried over to the house.

"What?" he repeated.

Detective Sale led the M.E. to the front door, saying, "The door was ajar. No one answered, so I pushed it. That's what I found."

The medical examiner looked in. When he saw Mrs. Baynes, curled in a kneeling fetal position like a hibernating larva, he said, "Jesus, just like the Quinlan woman. Better check every house on the block. We could have a serial killer running loose."

But they never found the killer. Although they did find a large moist spot in an upstairs bedroom whose irregular edges were flecked with bits of a whitish substance that they rushed in evidence bags to an FBI forensics laboratory in Washington.

When the report came back that the whitish substance was common modeling clay, they decided it was not important and focused on finding Mrs. Baynes's missing granddaugter, Kimberly.

All they found of her was a shredded yellow dashiki that looked as if it had been savagely torn from its owner's body. It was found stuffed into a trashcan five houses down the street.

A nationwide alert was posted for a possible sex-maniac killer, but since no one knew what he looked like, all the law-enforcement authorities could do was wait until he struck again.

2

His name was Remo and he wasn't asking for much. Just someone to kill.

"C'mon, Smitty," Remo said testily. "Give me a name. Or an address. Anything." Traffic hummed behind him, exhaust fumes thickening the humid summer air.

"Where are you, Remo?" came the voice of Dr. Harold W. Smith. It was an astringent voice, one that might have been produced by a larynx cured in lemon juice.

"In a phone booth, okay?" Remo snapped. "And I'm running out of quarters. Just give me someone to hit."

"Remo, I think you should come in." Smith's voice was suddenly tender with concern. Now it sounded like a hasp sawing wood. For Dr. Harold W. Smith, director of Folcroft Sanitarium, that unpleasant sound constituted tenderness.

"Smith," Remo said with sudden fierceness, "are you hunched over your computer?"

"I am at my desk, yes," Smith allowed. "I would not describe myself as hunched. I take pride in my posture."

"Take it from me," Remo growled, "you're hunched. Look, you've got a computer full of bad guys. I just want one. I don't care where he is. I don't care who he is. I'll go there. Just give me somebody—anybody—to hit."

"If I do this, will you return to Folcroft?"

"Maybe," Remo said noncommittally.

"That is not a satisfactory answer," Smith returned stiffly.

"It's not a freaking satisfactory world!" Remo shouted suddenly.

Miles away, the earpiece against Harold Smith's ear actually buzzed with the force of Remo's shouting.

Adjusting his rimless eyeglasses on his patrician nose, Smith shouldered the phone closer to his ear so that both hands were free to attack his desktop computer keyboard. As he reached forward, his back fell into a natural stoop.

"What city, please?" Smith asked stiffly.

"Tacoma."

"I have a report of a crack house on Jane Street. Number 334."

"Great!" Remo said joyously. "Just what I need. A crack house. It might take all of thirty minutes to clear it out. Thanks, Smitty. I owe you one."

"Remo, wait!" Smith called urgently.

The click in Smith's ear was final. Harold Smith hung up, and addressed his humming computer. He input a command that would scan all incoming data feeds for reported violence in Tacoma, Washington. He wondered how long it would take until the computer verified that the crack house on 334 Jane Street had been violently cleared of its criminal element.

Of Remo Williams' success, he had absolutely no doubt.

It took one hour and fifty-seven minutes.

It broke down this way: Eight minutes for Remo to hail a cab and be whisked to the target neighborhood. Fourteen-point-seven minutes for the assignment itself, and a total of six minutes for the news of the Jane Street Massacre—as it was subsequently dubbed—to hit the wire services, from which it was conveyed to Harold Smith a nation away in Rye, New York, in the form of luminous green letters on a glareproof screen.

The remaining one hour and seven-point-three minutes constituted the police-response time from the time 911 received the first estimated body count from concerned Jane Street neighbors. That number was five. Before the call was concluded, it was seven. Before it was all over, the death toll was twenty-three.

Soapy Suggs was number five.

He loitered inside the front door to 334 Jane Street unaware of the four bodies sprawled on the sidewalk outside. Not that he would much have cared. They were satisfied customers, passing around a crack pipe in the battered Camaro because they had been in too big a hurry to get high to bother driving somewhere less public. No big deal. In Soapy's line of work, customers had a high mortality rate.

Soapy heard the polite knock on the door and grew immediately suspicious. Nobody knocked polite on his door. Not thrill-hungry uptown yuppies. Not the police. And definitely not the neighborhood.

He bounced off an overstuffed chair, grabbing a Mac-10, which he cocked with a quick, nervous jerk.

Soapy threw open the door, leaning so his gun hand was hidden by the jamb.

A man stood there with his arms folded impatiently.

"Yeah?" Soapy asked. "Whatchu want?" He didn't notice the corpse-filled Camero out on the curb. His eyes were on the man. He was a white dude. Roughly six feet tall, but looking taller because he was so skinny.

"Welcome Wagon," the skinny man said in a chipper voice. "I've been sent by request of the neighborhood to formally welcome you from Jane Street."

"You mean *to*," Soapy suggested.

"My mistake," the man said. "I'm new at this."

"You shittin' me?" Soapy asked, spitting out the words. "You really with the Welcome Wagon?"

"Absolutely," said the man. "May I come in?"

"Not dressed like that, you don't," Soapy said with a raucous laugh. The stress lines in his face melted with his widening grin of relief. "We got standards in this house. Just look at you."

"Oh?" the white guy said with a falling face. It was a strong face, lean with deep-set dark eyes and high cheekbones. He wore his dark hair short. His T-shirt was as black as his flat pupils. His chinos were blacker. He looked like a pool hustler in mourning. "Perhaps you'd like me to come back after I've changed into something more formal," he added good-naturedly.

"Yeah, you do that," Soapy Suggs said, his trigger finger loosening. "You get silked down. And while you're at it, trade in those jivy shoes for some good Nikes or something. Those things look like they'd scratch my floor some."

The white guy looked down at his well-polished loafers.

"These are Italian leather," he complained. "What's wrong with them?"

"They out of style," Soapy barked, spitting on the left shoe. "By about thirty years." Laughing, he drew back to shut the door.

Instead, the polite man from Welcome Wagon gave him a close-up look at the hand-tooled Italian leather.

Splat!

Soapy Suggs swallowed his teeth. His head flew back. His Mac burped reflexively, chewing the wood like a runaway buzz saw.

"Welcome Wagon!" Remo Williams sang out, stepping in and slamming the door behind him.

On the floor, Soapy gurgled as he tried to claw loose teeth from his mouth. He was having inexplicable trouble breathing—inexplicable because everything had happened so fast.

Remo gave him another close look at his very expensive shoes. He pressed one of them into Soapy's eyes.

"These particular shoes are made by diligent craftsmen in Milan," he was saying. "Notice the all-leather soles. The heel is a single piece. Also notice the tasteful absence of neon labels. No factory stamped these out."

Soapy spat up a squirt of blood. A bicuspid danced momentarily atop the red fountain. The squirt died. The tooth slid down Soapy's spasming gullet.

An inner door opened and a long black face peered around its edge.

"Who you?" he asked.

Two more faces looked down from the top of the stairs.

"Yeah," one said gruffly, "and whatchu doing to my man Soapy?"

"Educating him on the fine points of quality footwear," Remo said, trying to sound convincingly like a shoe salesman. "Come on down. This is for all of you. Don't be bashful." Remo wiggled a playful finger at them.

The two black faces at the top of the stairs exchanged dumbstruck glances.

The face at the door crack withdrew cautiously. It asked: "You ain't said who you was yet."

"Welcome Wagon."

"You said that. Don't mean nothing to me." This from the stairs.

"Neither does proper English, it seems. Welcome Wagon is a benevolent organization dedicated to making new neighbors feel a part of their chosen community."

"By steppin' on their faces and making 'em squirm on the floor?" the face at the door asked.

"Oh," Remo said, remembering Soapy under one shoe. "Sorry. I was so engrossed in our highly educational exchange, I forgot about your friend." Remo looked down. He said he was sorry. He sounded sincerely contrite. Then he brought his left heel up and down like a jackhammer. Once. Once was enough. When the foot came away, Soapy Suggs's throat looked like a Tonka toy steamroller had flattened it.

Thus did Soapy Suggs become number five.

Remo put his hands on his hips. He looked up. "Now, where were we?"

"Getting dead," snarled Jarris Jameel, flinging the door open and launching himself out. He carried a combat knife held low. His angry eyes were on Remo's flat stomach.

Remo unfolded his arms. Jarris Jameel drove in, his knife arm out like an uncoiling viper. The knife went through a ghostly afterimage. Jarris kept going.

Remo chopped at the back of his neck in passing. It was a quick, casual chop. But it sent Jarris Jameel's head rolling out the open front door to bounce down the steps. The jettisoned body took two stumbling steps and banged off a wall. It struck a throw rug, raising dust. The spurting neck stump began repainting the fading wallpaper, actually improving it, Remo thought.

"Anyone else?" Remo asked, looking up hopefully.

"One moment," he was told.

"Yeah. We be with you in a mo', Welcome Wagon," the other added.

They retreated. To get weapons, Remo assumed.

Remo went up the stairs like a bouncy wraith. His feet on the rubber runners were silent. He was actually in a good mood. It was good to work again. Really work.

The hallway was long and definitely not designed by a claustrophobic architect. Doors lay open on either side of its narrow length. A variety of odors assaulted Remo's nose. Some were chemical. Others organic. Sanitation did not seem to be a household tradition at the modest two-story frame dwelling that was 334 Jane Street.

Remo gave his abnormally thick wrists a warm-up twist. Then he casually began going from room to room, where people sprawled on beds and couches with vacant expressions.

Most of them were drugged out, which disappointed Remo. He wanted action.

"Hello?" he called, ducking his head into a promising room. "Anyone sentient?"

"Who you?" a sleepy voice asked.

"I answered that already," Remo told the muscular man who quickly pulled a silk sheet over his naked legs. The nude woman beside him lifted a rust-red head off a ridiculously large pillow.

"I ax you a question," the black man snarled, taking a chrome-plated revolver from under his own fluffy pillow.

"And I ax you back," Remo returned, relieving the man of his threatening weapon with a chop of his knifelike hand.

Chuk! Bunngg!

The pistol bounced off the floor, where the attached hand finally shook loose. The man used his remaining hand to grab his bloodied stump of a wrist. He looked from it to Remo with a horror-struck "Why me?" expression.

The expression was so piteous that Remo erased it with the heel of his hand. The gunman fell back on his pillow, his face turning into a massive bruise like a concave prune.

The redheaded woman jerked her head up, saw the blood, and asked a shrill question.

"You don't do womens, do you?"

"You sell drugs?" Remo asked.

"Sell, snort, and swallow," she said eagerly.

"I do women," Remo said, driving her nose flat and riddling her brain with splinters of nose bone. Her head was swallowed by the pillow.

Whistling "Whistle While You Work," Remo moved on to the next room.

It looked empty. But his highly attuned senses detected a heartbeat on the other side of the open door. Remo silently took the doorknob in hand.

"Well, nobody in this room," he said aloud.

He stepped back, pulling the door closed. A man inhaled sharply. A preattack inhalation. Grinning, Remo reversed the door on its hinges.

He used only the strength of his bare right arm, but the door struck the inner wall so hard that the plaster cracked on both sides, fissuring the wallpaper.

Putting a contrite expression on his face, Remo pulled the door back and peered around it.

"Oh, sorry," he said in a small voice as the lumpy body

slid to the floor with the muffled gritty sound of pulverized bone.

In the next room, Remo simply lunged in and started picking up people. They were very obliging. Wherever he flung them, they would go. Quickly. And with hardly a complaint. Through walls. Out windows. And into one another.

Oh, there were a few rattling groans coming from heaps of broken limbs, but Remo took them as praise.

"Only doing my job," he said modestly.

The sound of commotion drew his attention to the remaining rooms. The noise the last bodies had made as they went through the windows had awoken even the most stupefied inhabitant of the house.

The house shook with the rattle of feet pounding on stairs.

Remo rushed out to intercept the escapees. A few made attempts to shoot him down. A weapon burped here. An automatic snapped there.

Remo dodged each bullet as he had been taught so long ago, with lightning ease. The bullets came so fast they cut shock waves in the air ahead of them. Sensing the approaching turbulence, Remo simply shifted out of the way. Even when they came from behind. His body automatically retreated from the warning pressure. He was like a paper kite that gave before the slightest wind. Except Remo wasn't at the mercy of those breezes. He gave before them, only then cutting away from the deadly bullets he could not always see coming.

Chuk! Chuk! Chuk! Chuk!

Holes chopped through wallboard where he had been. Remo kept moving.

Four men were pounding down the stairs. Remo went to the top runner and, bending at waist and knees, drove straight fingers into the wood. The staircase collapsed like a linchpin had been removed.

The quartet found themselves groaning and squirming in an astonishingly abrupt pile of splinters, like victims of a bombing.

"Did I mention the termite problem on this street?" Remo asked.

Someone tried sneaking up behind him. The sound of a

clip driving home gave him away. Remo whirled, taking hold of the would-be assailant's gun arm with both hands.

Naturally, the man opened up with his automatic weapon. Remo let him empty the clip, first making sure the muzzle was pointing down the nonexistent steps where four men groaned. Bone and meat spattered the walls. The groaning in the broken runners trailed off into dying gurgles.

The gunman added a stricken "What'd I do?" to the cacophony.

"I think you got the termites," Remo told him, bright-voiced.

The gunman spat an unintelligible curse. Remo showed him how deadly even an empty pistol can be when it strikes one's own belly muscles with pile-driver force. *Whump!* Behind his ridged abdomen, the gunman's stomach burst like a balloon.

With a careless toss, Remo sent him into the pile.

Crasshh!

He was number eighteen.

Remo Williams made a final sweep of the rooms. They were empty. But warm beds and a chair seat told him there were more unaccounted-for occupants. The closet gave up only one. A fat ball of blubber with a ring on every finger and one through each nostril.

Crouching on the floor, he tried diving out between Remo's legs. Remo faded back and used his head for a walnut. The slamming door and jamb were the nutcracker.

Cruunch!

Remo put his head out into the hallway.

"Come out, come out, whereever you are," he invited. His voice was cheerful.

Stealthy movement came from over his head.

"Ah-hah!" Remo said softly. "Naughty little children. They're hiding in the attic."

Reaching up, Remo felt the ceiling plaster. A slight but visible bowing told him of a foot coming to rest. Using both hands, Remo followed the man's progress. He was creeping to a definite spot in the attic.

As if walking with his hands, Remo followed the creeping feet to another room, where a drop ladder hung down from a square well. The man was creeping to the well.

Dropping his hands, Remo beat him to the ladder.

Remo waited, his face just under the square black hole. His grin widened. He flexed his thick wrists.

Presently a wide-eyed face came into view, a pistol close by. He looked around. His eyes locked on Remo's.

"Boo!" Remo said.

"Yahh!" the man returned, whipping down his weapon.

Remo reached up and pulled him bodily down the steps, making sure his face hit every rung. After the man had collapsed on the floor, Remo took pains to shatter his spine in three places.

Then he yanked the ladder away and stood back as someone spanked the trapdoor back into place. Feet stampeded.

Folding his arms. Remo listened.

"He got Derrick!" a voice wailed. He was one of the top-of-the-stairs guards who had retreated earlier.

"He gonna get us too," the other said. His missing companion. "Why'd we had to move into this damn neighborhood in the first place? I told you it was no damn good. Ain't no malls for three miles!"

"You shut up!" the first voice said tensely.

While they were arguing, Remo zeroed in on their exact location. He reached up and rapped once on the plaster with his fist, asking, "Anybody home?"

"That crazy guy! He's right under us. Shoot the fool!"

A spurt of bullets rained down, creating a salt-shaker-lid effect in a circle of ceiling plaster.

From a safe corner, Remo watched the plaster dust and Spackle rain down.

"You get him?" a muffled voice wondered.

"I ain't sure."

"Better check," the other said cautiously.

"I ain't gonna check! How am I gonna do that?"

"Try putting your eye to one of the holes," Remo called up helpfully.

"He ain't dead! You missed!"

Another *bratt* of sound chopped bits of plaster the length of the ceiling, peppering the floor. Remo faded out into the hall while the air cleared of settling white dust.

"Try again," Remo suggested. "You almost got me that time."

Two weapons opened up next. They fired as the gunman backed away, Remo's keen eyes spotting the imperceptible trail of bulges on the plaster. Obviously the attic floor wasn't well-shored with timber.

He maneuvered around the chewing bullets to a point where the steady track of bulges seemed to head.

When one pair of footsteps came close, Remo drove a hand up through the crumbling plaster. He took hold of an ankle. He yanked.

An Air Jordan athletic shoe came down through the crumbly hole. So did a howl of fright.

"He got me! Motherfuck got my ankle!"

"He's gonna get both your ankles," Remo warned. "And then your legs. And then your throat."

"He's gonna get my throat!" the man wailed.

Footsteps pounded up. Remo knew what was coming. He let go of the frantic ankle and slid over to one side, ready to dodge in any direction.

The storm of lead doubled the size of the ceiling hole that framed the jerking ankle. The entire leg started to slide down. An exploding kneecap punched through the plaster.

Syrupy red blood began dripping down. The leg quivered briefly as if shaking off a cramp. Then it simply relaxed.

"Oh, sorry, Darnell. Sorry, man," the last remaining voice said. "I was just tryin' to get the dude."

Remo got under the pitiful sounds of contrition and sent both fists through. The plaster heaved up. Scabby sections fell. The man ran around, screaming and firing wildly.

"You ain't gonna get me, asshole!" he howled furiously. "I ain't coming down!"

Bullets peppered the ceiling all around Remo. He wove between the spurts, taking care not to trip over the splintery holes that were collecting in the polished pine flooring.

Upstairs, the gunman was replacing clips frantically. He must have had an arsenal up there because he seemed never to run out of ammunition. Every so often he paused as if listening.

Remo encouraged him to continue wasting his ammunition with a taunting, "Nope, I'm not dead yet," in a mordant voice he had once heard in an old cartoon. "Try again."

Each time, the gunman obliged him with blistering return fire.

Soon the ceiling stopped being a ceiling. Instead, it was

now an upside-down moonscape of pocked holes and shattered plaster.

When the holes became as big as portholes, Remo shot the man an encouraging wave.

The man shot Remo back the bird. Then he opened up on the spot where Remo had been.

Remo wasn't there anymore. He had taken up a position directly under the island of plaster on which the man stood.

While the gunman was frantically replacing a clip, Remo reached up and grabbed him by both ankles.

"Yee-ahh!" The shriek was fearsome.

Remo encouraged his terror by mimicking the *Jaws* theme.

"Duh-duh-duh-duh-duh," Remo mocked ominously.

The replenished weapon began chattering again. Gouts of plaster exploded all around Remo. The floor sprouted holes. But Remo remained intact. Which was more than could be said for his opponent's state of mind.

"You won't take me! You won't take me alive, motherfuck!"

"Done," said Remo, breaking the man's ankles with swift jerks of his thick-wristed hands.

He stepped back.

The gunman was slow to realize what had happened. He began tottering. His jaw dropped. His eyed bugged like white grapes. His nerve-dead feet refused to make allowances for his sudden lack of equilibrium.

Pitching forward, the gunman fell like a big black tree. His head went through an isle of plaster.

Remo caught his face.

"One moment," he said, supporting the man by his twisting head. The gunman hung almost upside down while Remo stomped out a hole in the bullet-riddled floor. A section crashed away.

"Okay," Remo said, stepping back, "you can fall now."

The man went through the hole as if it was made for him. His crazily disjointed feet disappeared last.

Konk!

Remo looked down. The man had landed on his head. He looked dead. His feet angled one way, his broken neck the other.

"Happy now?" Remo called down. And getting no answer, decided his work was done.

Remo floated over the debris that was all that remained

of the staircase, like Tinker Bell treading fairy dust. He landed back in the living room.

He gave the broken-necked, snap-footed body a final glance and said, "Baby makes twenty-three."

His acute hearing told him that his own heart was the only one working in the entire house. His work was done. Jane Street belonged to the neighborhood once again.

Remo took time out to scribble a note on a pad by the telephone.

Welcome Wagon was here while you were out, he wrote. *Sorry we missed you.* Then, whistling contentedly, he sauntered down the porch steps.

Turning right, he shot a cheery wave to the man sitting stiff-spined behind the wheel of the red Camaro. The man declined to wave back. He stared out the windshield as if off into eternity. In a way it was.

He had been number one.

3

Kimberly Baynes paraded through Washington National Airport dressed in a flowing yellow dress, her blond hair worn high over her fresh-scrubbed face and tied in place with a bright yellow scarf.

She balanced with difficulty on her black high heels, as if walking on heels was new to her. Stepping off an escalator, she steadied herself momentarily, swaying like a tree worried by a warm summer wind.

"I'll never get used to these things," she muttered in a pouty voice.

Her predicament attracted the attention of more than one male traveler who, upon seeing her heavily made-up face and yellow fingernails, jumped to a natural conclusion.

Cosmo Bellingham was one of those. A surgical-appliance salesman from Rockford, Illinois, Cosmo had come to Washington for the annual surgical-equipment convention, where he hoped to interest Johns Hopkins in his new titanium-hip-joint-replacement line, guaranteed not to "lock, balk, or shock," as the company brochure put it so poetically. Cosmo had lobbied to have the motto stamped into each unit, but had been overruled. Cosmo did not believe in hiding one's light under a bushel.

Seeing the petite young woman floating through the maze of terminals, her bright eyes as innocent as a child's, Cosmo veered in her direction.

"Little lady, you look lost," he chirped.

The blue eyes—wide, limpid, somehow innocent and daring simultaneously—grew brighter as they met Cosmo's broadly smiling face.

"I'm new in town," she said simply. Her voice was sweet. A child's voice, breathy and unsure.

Cosmo tipped his Tyrolean hat. "Cosmo Bellingham," he said by way of introduction. "I'm staying at the Sheraton. If you haven't a place to stay, I recommend it highly."

"Thank you, but I have no money," she said, fingers touching her yellow scarf. "My purse was with my luggage. Just my luck." Her pout was precious. A little-girl-lost pout. Cosmo calculated her age as eighteen. A perfect age. Ripe. Most *Penthouse* centerfolds were eighteen.

"I'm sure we can work something out with Travelers Aid," Cosmo said. "Why don't we share a cab to my hotel?"

"Oh, mister, I couldn't. My grandmother taught me never to accept rides from strangers."

"We'll put the room on my American Express card until we figure something out," Cosmo said, as if not hearing.

"Wellll," the girl said, glancing about like a frightened deer. "You have a nice face. What could happen?"

"Splendid," said Cosmo, who right then and there decided that he wouldn't be shelling out for a too-polished Washington call girl this year. He was going to have warm fresh-from-the-oven meat. He offered his arm. The girl took it.

During the ride to the hotel, the girl said her name was Kimberly. She had come to Washington to look for work. Things were tough back in North Dakota.

"What kind of work you got in mind?" Cosmo asked, missing completely her Colorado accent. He had never been west of Kansas City.

"Ooh," she said dreamily, gazing out at official Washington passing by, "something that involves people. I like working on people."

"You mean *with* people," Cosmo teased.

"Yes, I mean that." She laughed. Cosmo joined in. The back seat of the cab filled with light, promising mirth.

They were still giggling when Cosmo Bellingham magnanimously checked Kimberly Baynes into the Sheraton Washington.

"Put the little lady into a room next to mine," Cosmo said in a too-loud, nervous voice. He turned to Kimberly. "Just so I can keep an eye on you, of course. Heh heh heh."

Kimberly smiled. She crossed her arms tightly, accentuating her small breasts. As the fabric of her long but attractive dress rippled, Cosmo noticed how thick around the middle she was.

He frowned. He preferred an hourglass shape. His wife was pretty thick around the middle. How could a pretty young thing with such a sweet face have such a tubular body? he wondered.

As the elevator took them up to their rooms on the twelfth floor, Cosmo decided beggars couldn't be choosers. After all, this ripe little plum had practically fallen into his lap.

He cleared his throat noisily, trying to figure out what kind of pickup line an innocent eighteen-year-old would fall for.

"Are you all right?" Kimberly asked in her breathy sweet voice.

"Little something caught in my throat," Cosmo said. "I'm not used to riding elevators with such a pretty thing as you. Heh heh heh."

"Maybe," Kimberly said, her voice dropping two octaves into a seductive Veronica Hamel contralto, "we should stop so you can catch your breath." One yellow-nailed hand lifted, tapping the heavy red stop switch.

The elevator stopped with an unsettling jar.

"I . . . I . . . I . . ." Cosmo sputtered.

Kimberly pressed her warm perfumed body close to Cosmo's own. "You want me, don't you?" she asked, looking up through thick lashes.

"I . . . I . . ."

"I can tell," Kimberly said, touching his pendulous lower lip. "*She* wants you too."

"She?"

"She whom I serve." Kimberly's finger ran down his chin, to his tie, and continued south, not hurrying, but not slowly either.

"Huh?"

And in answer, Kimberly removed her yellow scarf with a sudden flick, causing her bound-up hair to cascade downward. Meanwhile, her traveling finger coasted over his belt buckle to the tongue of his zipper.

Cosmo Bellingham felt his zipper slide down as his manhood swelled, rising, behind the loosening prison of cloth.

Oh, my God, he thought. She's gonna go down on me right in the elevator. Oh, thank you, Lord. Thank you.

Cosmo's attention was so centered around his crotch that he barely felt the silken scarf encircle his throat.

For two butterfly delicate hands had taken his stiff member. One was squeezing it rhythmically. The other raked its yellow nails along its entire throbbing length, softly caressing.

Eyes going closed, Cosmo gritted his teeth in anticipation.

The yellow scarf began to tighten slowly, imperceptibly. Okay, he thought, she had a few kinks. He could go along with that. Maybe learn something new to take back to the wife.

Cosmo became aware of a problem when he suddenly couldn't breathe.

The realization that he was being throttled occurred simultaneously with the odd thought.

Who the hell was strangling him? She had both hands on his gearshift, for Christ's sake. And they were alone in the elevator.

Cosmo Bellingham's body was discovered later that afternoon when a hotel maintenance man, responding to an inoperative-elevator call, forced open the doors on the tenth floor, exposing the grease-stained elevator roof. He frowned. The car had come to a stop level with his knees. He was surprised to find the trap door already open. Lugging his toolbox, he stepped onto the cable-snarled platform.

On his hands and knees, he looked down the open trap.

A body lay sprawled below, faceup. Pecker up, too.

The elevator repairman hastily called the front desk.

"Murdered?" the nervous desk clerk sputtered.

"Well," the repairman said dryly, "if he was, he got a hell of a charge out of the experience."

The body was taken out the back way by the ambulance attendants and hustled into the waiting vehicle to spare street traffic the spectacle of a body whose shroud tented up in a place where dead people usually didn't.

Across town, Kimberly Baynes returned to her Capitol Hill hotel, where she quietly paid her next week's hotel bill in advance. In cash.

She was pleased, upon entering the room, to see that the clay image squatting on the dresser had grown a new arm. This one protruded from its back. It had grown so fast—as fast as it had taken for Cosmo Bellingham to expire—that it had right-angled off the wall like a tree branch veering away from a stone wall.

Kimberly had left a newspaper lying at the statue's feet. Now it lay scattered about the floor as if a furious reader had gone through it for a misplaced item.

One soft white hand clutched a torn piece from the classified section. Another had the upper portion of the front page. Kimberly recognized the photograph of a man who had been in the news almost daily.

"I know whose blood you seek, my lady," Kimberly murmured.

Plucking the other item free, she read it. It was an advertisement.

"And I know how I shall reach this man," she added.

Kimberly Baynes changed clothes in the privacy of her room. Even though she was on an upper floor, she drew the drapes before she disrobed.

When she left the hotel, she was wearing a yellow sheath dress that accentuated her lean waist, lyre-shaped hips, and size-thirty-eight bust.

With the remainder of Cosmo Bellingham's billfold contents she had bought a fresh yellow scarf for her naked throat. The purchase made her feel so much better.

For today, she intended to apply for her first job.

4

No American ever cast a vote for Dr. Harold W. Smith.

It was doubtful that had Smith ever shown up on a ballot, very many people in this age of television campaigning would have voted for the aging bureaucrat. He was a thin Ichabod Crane hank of man with skin the unappetizing color of a beached flounder. His hair was as gray as his face. His eyes yet another shade of gray. And his three-piece suit—definitely not selected with an eye to pleasing the modern voter—was still another neutral gray.

As he sat at his worn oak desk, gray eyes blinking through his rimless spectacles, this gray man unknown to over ninety-nine percent of the American electorate quietly exercised more power than the executive, legislative, and judical branches of the U.S. Government combined.

For nearly three decades, since a promising young president tragically cut down a thousand days into his only term had appointed him to his lonely post, Harold Smith had held forth in his Folcroft Sanitarium office, guarding America and its constitutional form of government from subversion. Under cover of Folcroft, Smith headed CURE, a supersecret government agency that officially didn't exist. Created in the sixties, when the fabric of American society began to burst at the seams, Smith was invested with the awesome responsibility of protecting America through extralegal means.

In order that Smith might uphold the Constitution, his job called for him to violate it as if it were a dishwasher warranty. Where the law stopped, Smith was sanctioned to proceed. When the Constitution was perverted to shield the guilty, Smith was empowered to shred it to punish them.

For the last twenty of those thirty years Smith had relied

on a human weapon in his ongoing war. One man, long believed dead, who, like CURE, officially didn't exist. And now that person, the assassin he had code-named "Destroyer," was ranging the forty-eight contiguous states as if he could single-handedly stamp out all lawless elements.

Not that he wasn't making a dent, Smith thought ruefully.

His aged fingers tapped clicking keys. Bar graphs appeared, their data fluctuating like a sound-system spectrograph registering volume. It was late. The benighted expanse of Long Island Sound sparkled behind Harold Smith like a restive bejeweled giant. In Rye, New York, Harold Winston Smith was working overtime.

There had been no reports of Remo Williams since the Tacoma incident. This was not good. Smith had hoped that if he fed Remo assignments on demand, his lone enforcement arm would soon grow bored with a string of inconsequential hits and return. Remo had always complained about the small assignments. Now he seemed to relish them.

The graphs were keyed to major American cities. They charted something unusual: raw violence. Smith's massive computers culled this data from ongoing scans of news reports and quantified them. Most cities charted between twenty and forty on the violence scale.

Smith was studiously looking for fifty-plus. Anything that high would mean either an armed incursion from foreign forces or Remo on a tear.

To his profound disappointment, nothing higher than a thirty-seven-point-six registered. That was a street riot down in Miami.

Smith leaned back in his ancient cracked leather chair, his lemony frown souring further.

"Where the hell is Remo?" he said aloud. It was an unusual breach of decorum for the Vermont-born Smith. He seldom swore. And speaking aloud the name of a man who had ceased to exist long years before—even in an empty office—was not in character.

But these were not normal times. Everything had been turned upside down. Death had struck the inner circle of CURE.

As the hour approached midnight, Smith reluctantly pressed a concealed stud under his old desk.

The desktop terminal began to sink into the oak, its

keyboard folding back politely. The device disappeared from view. A scratched section of desktop clicked back into place. No seams showed.

Harold Smith got stiffly to his feet. He retrieved his battered briefcase from atop a gunmetal file cabinet and locked his office behind him.

He took the stairs to the first floor because he needed the exercise. It was one flight down.

Nodding to the night guard, Smith walked to his reserved space, his shoulders stooped. Thirty years had taken a toll on the ex-CIA bureaucrat who had neither asked for nor wanted the incredible weight placed on his rail-thin shoulders.

Smith tooled his battered station wagon through the lion's-head guarded gates of Folcroft Sanitarium, his briefcase bouncing on the passenger seat beside him.

The summer trees—poplars and elms—filed by like a towering eldritch army on the march. The fresh sea air rushed in through the open windows. It revived Smith's logy brain.

As he coasted into the center of Rye, New York, Smith searched for an open drugstore. His stomach had started to bother him. Some antacid would help. He looked for a chain store. They usually had the generic brands at the cheapest prices.

The briefcase beside him emitted an insistent buzzing. Smith pulled over to the curb and unlatched the case carefully, so as not to trigger the built-in detonation charges.

The lid came up, exposing a portable computer and a telephone receiver. Smith picked this up.

"Yes?" he said, knowing it could only be one of two people, the President of the United States or Remo.

To his relief, it was Remo.

"Hiya, Smitty," Remo said distantly. "Miss me?"

"Remo! Where are you now?"

"Phone booth," Remo said. "One of the old-fashioned ones with a glass door and the rank bouquet of passing winos. I thought they had all been put to sleep—or whatever they do to antique phone booths."

"Remo, it is time you returned home."

"Can't go home." Traffic sounds almost smothered his quiet reply.

"Why not?"

"It's haunted."

"What did you say?"

"That's why I left, Smitty. Everywhere I looked, I saw . . . him."

"You cannot run from the natural grieving process," Smith said firmly. He would be firm with Remo. There was no point in coddling him. He was a grown man. Even if he had suffered a great loss. "Confronting the loss is the first step. Denial only prolongs the pain."

"Smith," Remo said with sudden bitterness, "I want you to write down everything you just told me."

"I will gladly do that."

"Good. Then roll the paper up and cheerfully shove it up your constipated ass."

Smith made no reply. His knuckles whitened on the receiver. He adjusted his striped Dartmouth tie. The hand then drifted to the briefcase computer. He logged on.

"I can't go back to that place," Remo said tightly. "I keep seeing Chiun. I wake up in the middle of the night and he's staring at me, pointing at me like Marley's freaking ghost. I couldn't take it anymore. That's why I left."

"Are you saying that you literally *saw* Chiun?" Smith asked slowly.

"In the ectoplasm," Remo returned grimly. "It's like he's haunting me. That's why I'm hopping all over the map. I figured if he doesn't know where I am, he can't haunt me anymore."

"And?"

"So far, it's working."

"You can't keep running forever," Smith warned.

"Why not? Before we bought that place, Chiun and I lived out of hotels. We never stayed in one place long enough to break in the furniture. I can get used to the vagabond life again."

"What about the house itself?"

"Sell it," Remo said morosely. "I don't care. Listen, Smitty," Remo added, his voice dropping to a hush like a junkie begging for a fix. "Got anyone you need hit?"

"You promised me you would return after the last . . . er, hit," Smith pointed out as he slowly, carefully input commands into the silent mini-computer.

"I will, I will. I just need something to get me through the night. I'm not sleeping like I used to."

"And you promised you'd return after the hit before that."

"Sure, sure, but—"

"And the one before *that*," Smith said pointedly.

"How about Mad Ass?" Remo asked suddenly. "I caught him on the late news. He's just begging for it."

"We've been through this," Smith said with a trace of weariness. "That person is off-limits. At least until the President orders otherwise. Our hope is he will be overthrown by internal discontent."

"I could do him so it looks like an accident," Remo said eagerly. "There won't be a mark on him. I swear."

"Too risky. A palace coup would serve American interests in the region much more elegantly."

"I'll organize one," Remo said quickly. "How hard can it be to motivate those camel jockeys?"

"No." Smith's voice was frigid. "The President himself has declared CURE on stand-down in the Irait situation."

"We both know the President doesn't have the power to order you around," Remo said in a wheedling tone. "He can only suggest assignments. Or order you to shut the organization down."

"Which he may do if he learns that CURE's enforcement arm is unwilling to return for debriefing," Smith warned.

"If I do it right, the President will never know it was us." Remo's tone was hopeful.

Smith's retort was flat. "No."

Silence clung to the open line. Smith continued manipulating buttons. Soon he would have a back-trace. In the meantime, he would have to stall for time.

"Remo, are you still there?" he asked in a forced tone.

"What's it to you?" Remo said sourly. "All these years I worked for you, you can't find me a few people worthy of the boneyard."

"My computers are full of them," Smith said. "Regrettably, you caught me as I was driving home."

"Sorry. It's still light here."

Smith smiled tightly. Remo was in either the Pacific or the Mountain time zone. He hoped the back-trace program would not take much longer.

"You know what next Thursday is?" Remo asked, low-voiced.

"No, I do not."

"Chiun's birthday. His hundredth birthday. I had no idea he was so old. He was eighty when I first met him. I always thought of him as being eighty. I expected him to live forever." Remo paused. His voice cracked with his next words. "I guess I wanted him to be eighty forever."

Smith's eyes flicked to his computer screen. Why was it taking so long?

"You still there?" Remo asked suddenly.

"Yes, I am. I was distracted by a—"

"You're not trying to trace this call, are you, Smitty?" Remo asked in a suspicous growl.

Before Smith could answer, he heard a second voice coming over the line.

"Gotta use the phone," it said insolently.

"I'm in the middle of talking to my mother, pal," Remo shot back. "Take it down the street."

"Got to use the phone," the voice repeated, going steely with intent.

Smith's gray eyes narrowed. The screen began signaling "TRACE COMPLETED." The location code was about to appear.

"Smith," Remo said quickly. "Gotta call you back. I think I've found someone to while away a few minutes with."

"Remo, wait!"

The line went dead. It didn't click. It simply went dead.

The back-trace program winked out without reading off the all-important location code.

Frowning, Harold W. Smith closed his briefcase and went into the nearest drugstore. Hang the expense, he thought. He needed a roll of the best antacid tablets money could buy. And he would pay well for it.

Even if it meant spending more than a dollar.

Remo yanked the telephone receiver out by its coaxial cable and offered it to the impatient man with the scraggly Fu Manchu mustache.

"Here," he said, flashing the man a just-trying-to-be-helpful grin.

The man's frown became a glower. He had been hanging around this phone booth, glancing at his watch, for ten minutes. When his pocket pager went off, he impatiently accosted Remo. Since he wore a black silk running suit with red stripes and sniffed as if it were cold, Remo had him pegged as a drug dealer. A lot of them did their business through pay phones and beepers these days.

"You dumb shit!" the man bellowed. "What'd you do that for? I need to use the phone."

"So use it," Remo said nonchalantly. "I'll bet if you twist it right, it'll go right up your nostril. Plug that nasty drip. Of course, you'll need two. And this is the only phone booth for miles around. I checked."

The man stared at the dangling steel cable with eyes going mean. One hand snaked to the small of his back. It started back clutching a wicked knife. It went *snik!* A blade popped out.

"You gonna cut me?" Remo wondered.

"No," the man returned, "I'm gonna disembowel you."

"Thanks for the clarification."

Casually Remo reached up for the man's face.

"Here's a trick I'll bet you never saw before," Remo said.

His splayed fingers took the man by the face, thumb and little finger attaching themselves to the man's cheekbones, the other fingers resting lightly on the forehead. Remo simply crooked his fingers slightly.

Then he brought his hand away.

Mauricio Guillermo Echeverry heard the crack of a sound.

It surprised him. The Anglo's hand was in his face so suddenly he hadn't time to react. The crack sounded very near.

Then the hand went away.

Mauricio staggered, clutching the folding glass phone-booth door. Something was wrong. He dropped his knife, as if instinctively understanding it would not help him. Something was very wrong, but he wasn't sure just what. Had the Anglo guy palmed a blackjack and belted him in the face? He hoped no bones were busted. That crack sounded *muy* serious.

The skinny Anglo stepped back, holding something limp up to the fading light.

Mauricio would have blinked, but lacked the necessary equipment. As a red film fell over his staring eyes, the skinny Anglo made a few passes over the limp thing in his hands. Like a cornball stage magician trying to make an egg disappear.

"Notice there's nothing up my sleeve," the Anglo said in a really irritating tone.

"You ain't got no sleeve crazy guy," Mauricio snarled, his voice sounding funny because he couldn't get his lips to work.

"Just sticking to my act," the Anglo said. "No need to get upset. Here, watch the birdie."

Then he turned it around.

"Look familiar?" the skinny Anglo wanted to know.

Mauricio was surprised to recognize his own face. His closed lids were strangely flat and sunken. He was a little droopy around the lips too, and his handsome Latin face was kind of hangdog. But it was his face. Of that there was no question.

The question was, what was the Anglo doing with his face? And why wasn't it hanging off his own head where it belonged?

"Shall I repeat the question?" the Anglo asked.

Mauricio Guillermo Echeverry didn't respond. He simply leaned forward and fell square on his mush. Which was the sound he made.

Mush.

Remo tossed the flaccid skullbone-and-skin mask on the quivering owner's back and walked into the Salt Lake City twilight, humming contentedly.

He felt better. He was doing his share to keep drug use down. He could hardly wait until next month's Department of Justice crime statistics. Just by himself, he was probably responsible for a four-percent drop.

He just wished he could get the Master of Sinanju's anguished old face out of his mind.

5

The Iraiti ambassador to the United States was having a ball.

"If this is Tuesday," he sang to himself as he entered the Irait consulate on Massachusetts Avenue, Washington's consulate row, "I must be on *Nightline*."

He beamed under his thick mustache to the guard at the gate. The identically mustachioed guard grinned back. He passed on. All was good. All was well. True, his nation had been condemned by every government except Libya, Albania, and diehard Cuba. It lay under a punishing blockade. Down in Hamidi Arabia, the largest deployment of U.S. troops since World War Two were poised to strike north and liberate occupied Kuran.

War talk had it that soon—very soon—the U.S. would rain the thunder of world indignation down on the outlaw Republic of Irait.

But that was of no moment to Turqi Abaatira, the Iraiti ambassador. He was safe in the U.S. More important, he was a media star, and had been ever since his home government had rolled its Soviet-made tanks down the Irait-Kuran Friendship Road and annihilated the Kurani Army and police force and driven its people into exile as Iraiti forces literally stripped the tiny nation like a hot car, carrying every portable item of value back to the ancient Iraiti capital, Abominadad.

His smiling, good-humored face had been appearing for months on television news shows. Daily, limousines whisked him from broadcast studio to broadcast studio. As the Iraiti Army clamped down on hapless Kuran, Abaatira reassured the world of Irait's peaceful intentions in a soothing, unruffled voice.

Almost no one called him a liar to his face. The one exception—an indignant journalist who demanded to know why Iraiti troops had emptied Kurani incubators of their struggling infants—had been fired for "violating commonplace journalistic standards." Yes, it was wonderfully civilized.

Climbing the marble steps, Abaatira strode confidently into the consulate.

"Ah, Fatima," he said smilingly. "Who has called for me on this glorious summer day?"

"The U.S. Department of State," he was told. "They wish to denounce you in private once again."

Abaatira lost his good-humored grin. His face fell. His thick mustache drooped. It resembled a furry caterpillar that had been microwaved to a crisp.

"What is their problem now?" Abaatira asked dispiritedly. Lately the State Department had been interfering with his personal appearances. It was most inconvenient. Had the Americans no sense of priorities?

"It is over our President's latest edict."

"And what is that?" Abaatira asked, taking a long-stemmed rose from a glass vase and sniffing delicately.

"That all Western male hostages—"

"Guests under duress," Abaatira said quickly. "GUD's."

"That all guests under duress grow mustaches in emulation of our beloved leader."

"What is so unreasonable about that?" Abaatira asked, slipping the rose into his secretary's ample cleavage. He bent to bestow a friendly kiss on her puckering brow. "The edict does say 'males.' Insisting that women and children do this would be unreasonable. When were we ever unreasonable?"

"We are never unreasonable," the secretary said, adjusting the rose so the thorns didn't break her dusky skin. She smiled up at the ambassador invitingly. She despised her lecherous superior, but she did not wish to be shipped back to Abominadad with a poor report. The President's torturers would break not just her skin.

Abaatira sighed. "Perhaps I should have you accompany me to the State Department. I am sure that at the sight of your Arab beauty they would wilt like oasis flowers in the midday sun."

The secretary blushed, turning her dusky face even darker.

Ambassador Abaatira tore his avid eyes off that happy rose with a darkening expression of his own.

"Very well, please inform them that I am on my way for my daily spanking."

Turning on his heel, Turqi Abaatira stepped smartly to his waiting car. He instructed the driver. The car pulled away from the curb like a sleek black shark speeding toward a meal.

In the gilded State Department conference room, Turqi Abaatira used a silk pocket handkerchief to conceal a yawn.

The undersecretary of state was truly wound up this time. The poor overworked man was beside himself, pounding the table in his fury. He was not getting much ink these days, Abaatira reflected. No doubt it rankled. He could understand that. Not so many months before, he himself could not get a choice table in the better restaurants.

"This is an outrage!" the man was raging.

"You said that yesterday," Abaatira replied in a bored voice. "And last week. Twice. Really, what can you except me to do?"

"I expect," the undersecretary of state said, coming around the table to tower over the ambassador, "that you act like a civilized diplomat, get on the damned horn to Abominadad, and talk sense to that mad Arab you call a President. The whole house of cards in the Middle East is about to come tumbling down on his head."

"That, too, I have heard before. Is there anything else?"

"This mustache thing. Is Hinsein serious about this?"

Abaatira shrugged. "Why not? You know the saying, 'When in Rome, do as the Romans do'?"

"Abominadad is not Rome," the undersecretary snapped. "And if your people don't watch their step, it might just become the next Pompeii."

"As I was saying," Abaatira continued smoothly, "when in Abominadad, one should respect the great traditions of the Arab people. In my country, there is a law stipulating that all men should emulate our President in all ways, especially in regard to facial adornment. If we expect this of our own people, should we not also ask it of our honored guests?"

"Hostages."

"Such an overused term," Abaatira said, stuffing his handkerchief back into his coat pocket. "So like calling everyone who disagrees with you a latter-day Hitler. Really, sir. You ought to change your record. I believe it is skipping."

The undersecretary of state stood over the Iraiti ambassador, clenched fists trembling.

He exhaled a slow, dangerous breath. Words came out with it.

"Get the hell out of here," he hissed. "And communicate our extreme displeasure to your President."

"I shall be delighted," Abaatira, said, rising. At the door, he paused. "He finds my cables outlining your outbursts hugely entertaining."

Returning to his limousine, Ambassador Abaatira picked up the speaking tube.

"Never mind the consulate," he told the driver. "Take me to the Embassy Row Hotel."

Then, getting on the car phone, he made two calls. The first was to reserve a room at the Hotel Potomac.

"Just for the afternoon," he told the front desk.

Next he put in a call to the Diplomatic Escort Service.

"Hellooo, Corinne?" he asked cheerfully. "This is Turqi. How are you, my dear?"

An unfamiliar voice said, "Corinne is indisposed. May I assist you in some way?"

"I truly hope so. Is Pamela available for a few hours?"

"I'm sorry, but she is indisposed."

"Hmmm. I see. How about Rachel?"

"Rachel is out of town."

Abaatira frowned. They were passing the White House. A protest group was assembled outside the east lawn, shouting, "Food, not bombs! No blood for oil!" They waved placards: "U.S. OUT OF HAMIDI ARABIA." His frown melted. His heart gave a little leap of joy. Such a civilized country.

"I will tell you what," he said magnanimously. "I am feeling adventurous today. Why not send over a selection of your choosing? Hotel Potomac. Room 1045."

"Kimberly is available. You'll like her. She's a fresh face. Very, very good with her hands. And blond."

"Yes, I like the sound of that. Kimberly will do nicely."

Ambassador Abaatira replaced the receiver. He leaned back in the tooled leather seat, folding his hands on his stomach and closing his eyes. He thought pleasant thoughts. Of blond-as-daffodils Kimberly.

"Ah," he murmured, "Washington is so restful in the summer."

At the office of the Diplomatic Escort Service, Kimberly Baynes put down the phone.

She stood up, her yellow silk dress shifting in the light. It was a sheer ankle-length dress cut in the Chinese pattern. A slit showed most of one shapely leg. Above the waist, it thickened and billowed around her ample bosom.

Taking her purse from the desk, she went to a door and opened it a crack, revealing a bare closet.

On the floor, Corinne D'Angelo, founder of the Diplomatic Escort Service, lay in a heap, a yellow silk scarf twisted around her neck. Her tongue lolled out like a black snail extruding from its shell. Her eyes were open, but only the whites showed.

Because she was still quivering. Kimberly knelt down—careful not to split her dress seams—and wrapped spiderlike fingers around the ends of the tight scarf.

She gave a hard, fast jerk. The quivering stopped. A faint gurgle escaped past the swollen black tongue. Another came from deep within her, and the sudden stink of released bowels filled the closet's narrow confines.

"Oh, yuk," Kimberly said recoiling. She hated it when they let go like that. She slammed the door sharply on her way out of the office suite.

On her way to the elevator, she bumped into a redhead wearing a white knit dress through which her black lace brassiere and panties showed like playful black cats in a heavy fog.

"Oh!" the redhead said. Stepping back, she looked Kimberly up and down frankly. "You're new, I suppose." Her tone was appraising, a little cool. "I'm Rachel."

"Corinne's expecting you," Kimberly said quickly.

"Good. I could use a few bucks. Catch you later."

Rachel brushed past. Kimberly tugged a long yellow silk scarf from her neck while the redhead rattled the office doorknob with growing annoyance.

She was knocking on the panel when Kimberly came up behind her, holding the yellow scarf in both hands.

"You have to lean into it," Kimberly said. "It's stuck."

Rachel's long-lashed eyes flickered in her direction. Taking in the scarf, she said. "You should get another color to go with that dress. Yellow on yellow is so tacky. Try white or black."

"That's a good idea," Kimberly said. "Maybe you should take this one."

"No, thanks," Rachel said, rapping on the door. "Yellow isn't my color."

"Oh, no," Kimberly said sweetly, lowering the scarf around the redhead's neck. "I insist."

"Hey!" Rachel said, flailing. Then: "Ugh! Ukk Ukk Ukkkkk."

"She loves it!" Kimberly cried. "Can't you tell?"

Rachel's knees buckled. Face bluing, she slowly collapsed into a heap of warm white knit flesh.

Holding Rachel's head off the floor by the yellow scarf, Kimberly Baynes unlocked the door. She dragged Rachel by the neck. Rachel protested not a bit as she was hauled into the well of the reception-room desk. When Kimberly let go of the scarf, Rachel's head went *boink!* She jammed her cooling limbs in.

Kimberly left her to decompose in private.

Ambassador Turqi Abaatira changed into a dressing gown in the privacy of his hotel room. As he waited patiently, he watched CNN, his eyes going often to his gold wristwatch, which he had set on the nightstand by the bed.

A reporter was engaged in a carefully worded report of U.S. troop deployment in faraway Hamidi Arabia.

"Since we are forbidden by military censors to report our location," the reporter was saying, "I can only say that I am reporting from a place near the Hamidi Arabia–Kuran border, where forward units of the Twenty-fourth Mechanized Infantry Division are dug into the shifting sands. Rumor has it that only a few kilometers north of here, Hamidi frontline troops are busily erecting a top-secret weapon, described only as a kind of modern Maginot Line they say will neutralize any gas attack the Iraitis dare launch. Operation Sand Blast commanders have so far refused all comment on the exact nature of this breakthrough. . . ."

Abaatira smiled. Let the Americans have their spy satellites, which cost billions of dollars and could read a license plate from orbit. The Iraiti Revolting Command Council had a superior tool. The American media. Under the banner of freedom of the press, they were daily feeding all sorts of valuable intelligence directly to Abominadad. And all for the price of a satellite dish. Who needed spies?

The knock at the door was sudden and inviting.

Abaatira hit the remote unit and bounced off the bed in one motion.

He padded to the door, his spirits soaring. With a grand flourish, he flung the door open.

She was, if anything, lovelier that Abaatira had expected.

"Ah, and you could only be the unrivaled Kimberly," he said, eyeing her yellow silk gown. A flash of thigh showed like a tantalizing dream.

"May I come in?" Kimberly asked demurely.

"Of course." She entered with a languid grace. Abaatira closed the door after her.

She stepped around the room, casually placing a small yellow purse on the nightstand by the bed. She turned. Her smile was red and inviting.

"And what would you like today?"

"I have been under a certain tension," Abaatira said. "I seek relaxation. And relief."

Kimberly perched on the edge of the bed. She patted it. "Come. Join me."

Abaatira obeyed with alacrity. He rolled onto the bed.

"Lie back," Kimberly purred, leaning over to whisper into his ear. "Let Kimberly soothe you."

"Yes, soothing," Abaatira sighed. "I need soothing. Very much."

"I have brought love oil with me. Would you like me to use it?"

"Yes, that would be fine," Abaatira said, feeling his loins stir in response.

"Close your eyes, please."

Abaatira did as he was told. His ears were alert. Something else was coming to attention too. As he waited, delicate fingers tugged at the sash of his robe.

He felt himself being exposed. The coolness of the air conditioner passed over his stiffening member. He folded his hands on his bare stomach, swallowing with anticipation.

A hand took firm hold of his root, steadying his quivering tool. The sound of a small cap being unscrewed made his heart beat faster. He hoped this Kimberly would take her time. Abaatira preferred thoroughness in these matters, something he had stressed to Corinne D'Angelo when he had first explained his needs, many Kimberlys ago.

The cap was set down. There was a tantalizing drawn-out moment. Then the warm thick liquid began to pour. It slid over the tip of his Arab maleness, running down the shaft like warm, gooey syrup. A delicious scent tickled his nostrils. He sniffed curiously.

"Raspberry," Kimberly whispered naughtily.

"Ah, raspberry," Abaatira breathed. "Allah is just." He trusted that meant she would use her mouth. There was no rush. Eventually.

Then the other hand joined the first, and together they began kneading and manipulating him in clever, surprising ways. . . .

When Turqi Abaatira woke up, the first thing he noticed was that his erection was as proud as ever.

He blinked. This was unusual. He could distinctly recall climaxing. In fact, under the discreet manipulations of the girl named Kimberly, he had experienced the most nerve-satisfying climax of his life. It was also, oddly, the last thing he could recall.

He must have fallen asleep. It sometimes happened after he spent himself.

But there it was, proud and undaunted by its recent exercise.

Abaatira blinked again. There was something strange about his tool. It wasn't the yellow scarf that seemed wound rather loosely around the root of his intromittent organ. It was the color of the column of upright flesh towering above.

It looked rather . . . blackish. Or was it green? No, greenish-black, he decided. He had never before seen himself turn that unlovely color. It must have been quite an orgasm to cause him to turn such a remarkable hue.

"Kimberly?" he called.

No answer. He tried to sit up. Then it was he noticed that his feet were lashed to the baseboard. By two yellow scarves identical to the one coiled on his belly.

"I did not ask for this," he muttered darkly.

He again attempted to sit up. His arms refused to move. He looked up. His wrists, too, were lashed to the bedposts.

"I definitely did not ask for this," he said aloud. Raising his voice, he called, "Kimberly, where are you, my apricot?"

Then he noticed his watch sitting on the nightstand. It said four o'clock. Much later than he had thought.

His eyes happened to alight on the tiny window that displayed the day of the week. They went wide. The red letters said: "THURSDAY."

"Thursday?" he gulped. "But this is Tuesday." Then the cold, mouth-drying realization sank in. His hot, dark eyes went to his defiantly inexhaustible manhood.

Ambassador Turqi Abaatira did the only thing he could do under the circumstances.

He screamed for his mother.

6

The Master of Sinanju was dead.

Remo stared up at the cold stars wheeling overhead and tried to make sense of it all.

He could not. Nor had he been able to make sense of it in all the bitter months since the tragedy.

It had been, after all, a nothing assignment. Well, maybe not nothing exactly, but not as important as some. Looking back on it, Remo decided that he simply had underestimated what he and Chiun had gotten into.

It had started with a poison-gas attack on a failing northeast Missouri farm town. Remo had already forgotten its name. La Plume or something. Overnight, the town had been wiped out. Remo and Chiun had been out of the country when it had happened. No sooner had they returned to the States than Harold Smith had put them on the trail of the unknown culprits.

In Missouri they had collided with a strange group of characters, including a bankrupt condominium developer, a college girl with a no-nukes message, plus a working neutron bomb and an environmentalist group known as Dirt First!! The bomb had been stolen and, jumping to the conclusion that it had been the work of the Dirt Firsters, Remo and Chiun had gone after them. A mistake.

The neutron bomb had been stolen by the condo developer, Connors Swindell, whose grandiose visions of reversing his slumping business caused him to gas one town and plan on nuking another so that after the bodies were hauled off, he could scoop up the distressed real estate on the cheap.

"A frigging real-estate scam," Remo reflected bitterly. He lay in the coarse gravel of the Newark high-rise roof. He had lived here in the days after he had left St. Theresa's

Orphanage. The day when, as a young Newark cop, he had opened up his draft notice, he had taken a bottle of beer up to this roof and lain back on the biting gravel to count the stars as he daydreamed of what Vietnam would be like.

Tonight, Vietnam seemed a thousand years distant. Tonight, his cop days were a receding memory, as were the cruel months he'd spent on death row, framed for the murder of a drug pusher he had never even laid eyes on. It had all been a gigantic scam engineered by Harold Smith and Conrad MacCleary, the one-armed ex-CIA agent who had seen Remo Williams in action in some forgotten rice paddy. MacCleary had mentally filed Remo away for possible future use. And when CURE had been sanctioned to kill, MacCleary had told Smith about a former Marine sharpshooter whom the Twenty-first Marines had nicknamed "The Rifleman."

Remo took a swig on a bottle of mineral water. His beer-drinking days were long behind him. So were his meat-eating days. So was the simple life of Remo Williams of Newark, New Jersey. These days his highly refined metabolism subsisted on rice, fish, and duck.

He had been electrocuted up at Trenton State Prison. They had strapped him in, sweating, frightened but outwardly cool. *Zap!* And he was gone.

The swimming darkness of oblivion gave way to the apple-green sterility of Folcroft Sanitarium and CURE.

Officially dead, his face recut into unrecognizable lines by plastic surgery, Remo found himself pressed into service for his country. As CURE's one-man killer arm. And he had taken the job—just as MacCleary and Smith had known he would. Remo Williams was, after all, a patriot. Besides, the cold bastards were ready to dump him into a shallow grave if he told them no.

In the spacious Folcroft gym, they had introduced him to the eighty-year-old Master of Sinanju, Chiun.

That meeting, Remo recalled as if it had happened last Friday.

MacCleary—a bluff, hard-drinking Irishman—had entered the Folcroft gym and engaged Remo in a seemingly pointless conversation. Remo was anxious to get out into the field. He had been well-trained in weapons handling, codes, disguise, poisons, infiltration—all things that soon became irrelevant. MacCleary had told him he wasn't yet ready, making his point with hand gestures that set his stainless-steel hook flashing under the shaky fluorescent lights.

The big double doors opened. Conn MacCleary turned.

"Ah, here he comes now," MacCleary had said.

Remo's suspicious face went to the door. They separated as if actuated by a photoelectric beam. And framed in the open door, his hands tucked into the wide sleeves of a white kimono so that Remo had wondered who had opened the heavy doors for him, stood a tiny, pathetic figure.

He was approximately five feet tall from his whispering black sandals to the crown of his bald yellow head. Straggly wisps of pale hair floated over each ear. Like a bleached tendril of seaweed clinging to a rock, more ancient hair clung to his chin. His face was a calm mask of papier-mâché wrinkles.

As he padded toward him, Remo saw that the slanted eyes were an unexpected clear hazel color. They were the only thing about him that did not look old, frail, and weak.

MacCleary had explained to Remo that the old Korean was called Chiun and he was going to be Remo's teacher.

Chiun had bowed formally.

Remo had stared blankly, saying, "What's he going to teach me?"

"To kill," MacCleary had replied twenty long years ago. "To be an indestructible, unstoppable, nearly invincible killing machine."

Remo had laughed, causing a dark shadow of anger to cross Chiun's eyes like stop-motion storm clouds scudding by.

Suppressing his amusement, MacCleary had offered Remo a night away from Folcroft if he could tag the Korean called Chiun. MacCleary then handed him a hair-trigger .38.

Sighting coolly, Remo lifted the sights to the Korean's sunken chest. It was easy. All he had to do was pretend the old gook was a Vietcong. Inwardly he decided that this was a test of his ability to kill on command.

Remo fired. Twice. A faint smile seemed to gild the old Korean's face. It was still there when the reverberations of the shots ceased echoing. Holes popped into the padded tumble mats.

But the frail little man flashed, unscathed, through the gym. He slid sideways with nervous, geometrically angular motions. He faded here. He danced there. Annoyed, Remo continued trying to nail him as the sweat came to his forehead.

And when the last chamber contained only a spent, smoking cartridge, Remo angrily threw the weapon at the older man's head. Missing completely.

The Oriental came up on Remo so cleverly that he never saw him. Remo was thrown to the hard floor with such force it blew all pain and air from his surprised lungs.

Impassively the old Oriental had stared down into Remo's face. Remo glared up at him.

"I like him," Chiun had said in a high, squeaky voice. "He does not kill for immature or foolish reasons."

Remo later learned he was the Master of Sinanju, a martial-arts form old when Egypt's sands were new.

And on that day Remo started down the difficult path to becoming a Master of Sinanju himself, Chiun's heir, and now, Reigning Master. The first white man in a five-thousand-year chain of consummate assassins.

Long ago.

The last time Remo had seen the Master of Sinanju alive, Chiun had been arguing with him in the California desert near Palm Springs. They had located the stolen neutron bomb. It had been armed, with no way to disarm it. The digital timer was counting off the final minutes of life for the only person Remo had ever thought of as family.

With the real-estate crazy named Connors Swindell and the bomb's inventor, they had barreled out into the desert, racing against that silently screaming timer display, trying to put Palm Springs behind them and out of the kill zone—even as they carried the kill zone along with them.

It was a doomed effort. Chiun had pointed this out, with his usual uncompromising wisdom. One of them would have to bear the bomb out into the desert alone. Or all would perish.

"I'll do it," Remo had volunteered.

"No. You are the future of Sinanju, Remo," Chiun had said stiffly. "I am only its past. The line must continue. So I must do this."

They had been feuding in the days before the end came. Remo didn't even know the reason, until Chiun had reluctantly explained that he was approaching his one hundredth birthday—something Remo had no inkling of. Tired of arguing, concerned for Chiun's advancing years, Remo had cut short the argument to get possession of the bomb in a cruel way. He had ridiculed the Master of Sinanju.

"Cut the martyr act, Chiun," Remo had said. "It's old. You're good, sure, but you're not as fast as me. I'm younger, stronger, and I can get further faster. So stuff your silly Korean pride and face reality. I'm the only one for this job, and we both know it."

The memory of Chiun's stung face was one that seemed to burn behind the stars above.

His soft, "So, that is how you feel about me," still echoed in Remo's ears.

Remo remembered reaching for the neutron bomb. Then the world went black. Chiun. Getting in the last word.

He woke up in the speeding car. It was careening back toward Palm Springs, away from the kill zone. He realized what must have happened. He had only time to look back.

The neutron bomb ignited with a heart-stopping vomiting-up of boiling black smoke and hellish red fire.

Remo had raced back into the rising hell. But the spreading zone of deadly radiation forced him back.

Months later, when it was safe, he had returned to the desert, finding only a capped-off underground condo site and a fused glass crater. Not even the Master of Sinanju's body had survived the blast.

But out there in the remorseless desert, the spirit of the Master of Sinanju had appeared to Remo. Wordlessly it had attempted to indicate what could not be communicated otherwise. By pointing at Remo's feet. Then it simply vanished.

Remo's existence had become an aimless one since then. What Chiun had commanded him to do was to confront the choice he knew he would one day face. He was now the inheritor of the line. It was as Chiun had said. The line had to continue. The House of Sinanju had to go on. The village had to be fed. And the village had always been fed by the work of the Masters of Sinanju.

Now Remo wasn't so sure. Could he continue the tradition? He was an American. The people of Sinanju were a bunch of ungrateful parasites. They knew nothing of the hardships Chiun had endured to feed them. They would care nothing if they had known.

Remo had put off returning to Sinanju to break the terrible news. It was not long after that that Chiun had reappeared to him, spectrally pointing a ghostly finger, commanding him to obey.

"I'll get to it," Remo had said that second time.

But weeks later, when Chiun reappeared, Remo had reverted to the old days of their bickering relationship.

"Get off my back, will you?" he had said heatedly. "I said I'd get around to it!"

Chiun had raised his drawn, stricken face to the ceiling and faded like so much unscented smoke, leaving Remo feeling bitter and ashamed.

After that, he had closed up the house and hit the road. He felt torn between two worlds. He had outgrown America. Yet he was not of the blood of Sinanju. The line that stretched back five thousand years had nothing to do with him. He was a latecomer, a mere pale piece of pig's ear, as Chiun had so often said.

That left only CURE. But to Harold Smith, Remo was a tool. If compromised, he would be abandoned, disavowed—even terminated. Chiun had loved Remo, and Remo had grown to love the Master of Sinanju as a son loves his father. But between Remo and Harold Smith there was only a cool working relationship. Grudging respect. Sometimes, annoyance. Often anger. Who knew, but with Chiun out of the way, Smith might have some prearranged plan to reclaim Remo for the organization. Smith was no fool. He had long ago come to understand that Remo belonged equally to the village of Sinanju.

Suppose Smith decided to reprogram Remo? The cold bastard had tried it once before. Only Chiun had rescued Remo's sorry ass that time.

"What the hell do I do with the rest of my life?" he asked the stars. "Where do I belong? Who do I turn to?"

The stars poured down cold twinkling light that had no answer.

Remo sat up. Draining the last of his water, he tossed the empty bottle straight up. It ascended seventy feet, poised as if frozen by a snapshot, then began its tumbling return to earth.

Remo leapt up and snapped out with the heel of his foot. *Pop!* The glass shattered into a thousand gritlike pieces that sprinkled the roof with no more sound than hail falling.

Remo walked to the roof's edge, thinking how he always seemed to be drawn back to his old neighborhood in times like these. There was nothing for him here anymore. St. Theresa's Orphanage had been razed long ago. The neighborhood had fallen victim to the junkies and the pushers and the inexorable eroding of the American inner city. It was a lawless wasteland—the very thing Remo Williams had been erased from all records to prevent.

Now, lower Broad Street looked like Inner City Nowhere. A tight-skirted hooker lounged against a dirty brick wall. The needle tracks on her arms were like a connect-the-dots Amazon River. Two men passed sandwich-bag packets between them. Drugs. A battered pickup drew up to a red light. A man came out of an alley carrying a VCR still in its cardboard box. He dropped it into the bed of the truck and accepted a roll of bills from the driver. The transaction was accomplished without a word spoken.

"Ah, the hell with it," Remo growled.

He had made his decision. He stepped off the parapet edge.

Using the bricks for steps, Remo walked down the side of the building. His heels stepped from brick to brick, taking tiny jerking steps. Upright, his balance perfect, his bleak dark eyes looking out over the Newark skyline, he might have been descending a steep art-deco staircase.

No one noticed his impossible descent. And no one accosted him as he stepped onto the sidewalk and made his way out of the place he had sprung from and which was now as alien to him as the mud flats and fishing shacks of Sinanju, half a planet away.

Harold Smith picked up the dialless red desk telephone on the first ring.

"Yes, Mr. President?" he said crisply, no trace of fear in his voice. In fact, he was quite scared.

"The FBI aren't cutting it," the President said in a careworn voice that muted his vaguely New England twang. "I am turning to you."

"I presume you are referring to the missing Iraiti ambassador?" Harold Smith asked.

"Abominadad is claiming we've taken him hostage," the President snapped, "and we can't prove otherwise. Personally, I wouldn't mind if the smug son of a gun were found floating facedown in the Potomac, but I'm trying to avoid a war here. This kind of escalation could trigger it. I know you've lost the old one—what was his name?"

"Chiun," Smith said stiffly. "His name was Chiun."

"Right. But you still have your special guy, the Causcasian. Can he cut it alone?"

Harold Smith cleared his throat noisily as he mentally framed the news he had been keeping from the chief executive.

"Mr. President—" he began.

Then another phone rang. The blue one. It was the line through which Remo reported.

"One moment," Smith said quickly, cupping the mouthpiece to his gray vest. He grabbed the other phone like a life preserver. He spoke into it.

"Remo," Smith said harshly. "The President has a critical assignment for you. Will you take it? I must have your answer. Now."

"Assignment?" Remo asked in a taken-aback voice. "What kind?"

"The Iraiti ambassador is missing."

"Why should we care?" Remo demanded.

"Because the President does. Will you accept this assignment?"

The line was silent for nearly a minute.

"Why not?" Remo said breezily. "It should kill an afternoon."

"Hold, please," Smith said, no trace of the relief he felt sweetening his lemony voice. He switched phones, hugging the blue receiver to his chest.

"Mr. President," he said firmly, "I have our enforcement arm on the other line. He is prepared to enter the picture."

"Fast work, Smith," the President returned. "I'm pleased with your efficiency. Damn pleased. Go to it."

The line went dead. Smith hung up the red telephone and lifted the blue one from his vest.

"Remo, there is no time for details. Fly to Washington. Contact me once you get there. I hope to have operational details for you by then."

"On my way," Remo said. "Maybe Mad Ass had him assassinated," he added hopefully.

"I doubt that."

"I'd give anything for a crack at that Arabian nightmare."

"Official policy is hands-off. Now, please, go to Washington."

"Keep the line free. The next voice you hear will be yours truly."

7

Turqi Abaatira listened with attentive straining ears as the gorgeous blond vixen he knew only as Kimberly sat on the edge of the bed and lectured him on the causes and pathological symptoms of gangrene.

"When blood flow is cut off," she explained in a breathy voice like a schoolgirl reciting from a book, "oxygen is also restricted. Without oxygen, the tissue becomes starved for nourishment. It begins to decay, to become corrupt."

Kimberly reached over and gave the bulging tip of his male organ a friendly pat. It quivered. Abaatira couldn't feel a thing. This alarmed him.

It fascinated Kimberly enough to deviate from her lecture.

"Do they always act rubbery like that? When they're not gangreny, I mean."

She removed the gag from his mouth.

"You do not know?" Abaatira gasped. "You, a professional call girl?"

"I'm new at this stuff," Kimberly said, gazing into her high-polished yellow fingernails. "Actually, you're my first customer."

"I refuse to pay you until you release me," Abaatira said hotly. The gag was replaced.

"Tissue death usually signals itself by a slow change in color," Kimberly went on absently. "Healthy pink skin turns green, then black. When it is completely black, it's dead. Amputation is usually the only remedial procedure." She paused. "I think this black goes very well with yellow, don't you?" she added, adjusting the yellow silk scarf that had strangled the blood flow from Abaatira's upright penis.

Ambassador Abaatira gave his head a violent shake. He tried to give vent to his anger, his rage, most of all to his fear, but an identical yellow silk scarf stuffed into his mouth prevented this. A third one held it in place.

Kimberly had stuffed the one into his mouth after he had first started to cry out, carefully tying the other at the back of his head.

"It's been two days," she went on pleasantly. "I would say that another, oh, twelve to fourteen hours from now, it's gotta go. Bye-bye, Black Peter. Of course, the surgeons might not have to cut it all off. Every last inch, I mean. Perhaps they can save some of it. The tip would definitely go. It's pretty black right now. But you might end up with a kind of stump."

"Mumph—mumph!" Abaatira squealed through the silk gag.

"It wouldn't come in very useful during an orgy," Kimberly went on, "but you could tinkle with it. Maybe enough could be salvaged that you could still point the stream where you wanted it to go. Otherwise, you'd have to sit down like us girls."

Abaatira shook his head violently. He strained at the yellow bonds.

"What's that?" Kimberly asked, leaning closer. "You say you don't want to sit like a girl when you tinkle?"

Ambassador Turqi Abaatira changed the direction of his madly shaking head. Up and down instead of side to side. He poured a great deal of enthusiasm into it. He wanted no ambiguity. None at all.

"I might be persuaded to help you out," Kimberly offered.

The up-and-down shaking became even more manic. The entire bed shook.

Kimberly brought her pretty face up to Abaatira's sweat-soaked one. She smiled invitingly as she whispered, "You're in touch with Abominadad every day?"

Oh, no, Abaatira thought to himself. A spy. She is a CIA spy. I will be executed for allowing myself to fall into her brazen toils.

But since his overriding concern was to leave this room with all his body parts a healthy pink, he kept nodding yes.

"If you tell me everything I want to know," Kimberly said, rolling her shoulders against the digging weight of her bra straps, "I might be willing to untie that pretty silk scarf." She ran a yellow nail down his cheek. "You *would* like that, would you not?"

Abaatira hesitated. His English was impeccable—he was a Harvard man—but this was a critical point. His mind raced. Should he answer the "You would like that?" Or the "Would you not" part. Or were they the same thing? The wrong reply could have grave consequences.

Abaatira shook his head yes, and the treacherous, diabolical call girl leaned over to untie the encircling yellow ribbon. She then plucked the yellow wad of silk from his mouth.

Ambassador Abaatira tasted the dryness of his own mouth.

"Water?" he said thickly.

"Answers first."

"You promise?"

"Yes."

"You swear to Allah?"

"Sure, why not?"

"What do you wish to know?" he croaked, his eyes going from the fresh pink face hovering near him to the ugly greenish-black mushroom that he could barely recognize as a cherished part of his anatomy.

"The intentions of your government."

"President Hinsein will never relinquish Kuran. It is our long-lost sister state."

"Whose army you crushed and whose property you carried back to Irait, including the streetlights and cars, and even a giant roller coaster. Not to mention all the rapes."

"You are not a Kurani, by any chance?" Ambassador Abaatira asked with a sudden flare of fear deep in his naked belly.

"No. I serve She who loves blood."

"I love blood too," Abaatira pointed out. "I would love it to circulate more freely through my body. To every needy part."

Kimberly patted his damp hair. "In time, in time. Now, tell me about the plans your government has for war."

"What about them?"

"Everything. I wish to know everything about them. Under what circumstances you would go to war. The provocations necessary. The thoughts of your brave leader, who must love blood, for he spills so much of it. Tell me about his personal life. I want to know everything. About his family, his peccadilloes, his mistress. Everything."

Ambassador Turqi Abaatira closed his eyes. The words

came tumbling out. He told everything. And when he ran out of secrets to reveal, he repeated himself.

Finally, dry of mouth and spent of spirit, he put his head back on the pillow and gasped for breath.

"That is everything you know?" asked Kimberly, the Mata Hari of barbaric Washington, where not even a diplomatic media star was safe from torturers.

Abaatira's gasp could only mean yes.

"Then it is time for me to fulfill my part of our little bargain," Kimberly said brightly.

This brought Abaatira's sweat-sheathed head back up. Eyes widening, he watched as those hateful tapered yellow fingers reached for the deadly yellow silk scarf that seemed so loosely tied, but which had brought him such terror.

He steeled himself, for he knew that the restored blood flow would bring with it horrible pain as the starved nerve endings came back to life.

The fingers tugged and plucked, and with tantalizing slowness they pulled the silk away. A trailing end caressed Abaatira's naked body as it retreated.

With a sudden wicked flick, it was gone.

Childish laughter, mad and mocking, seared his ears.

Ambassador Abaatira's eyes bulged stupidly. He threw his head back and screamed.

For he had seen half-buried in the greenish-black root of his manhood the slick gleam of copper wire—and knew that he had betrayed his country for nothing.

The yellow scarf went around his throat, and his scream became an explosion of choking that trailed off in a frenzy of gagging.

8

Marvin Meskin, manager of Washington's Potomac Hotel, thought he was having union problems.

"Where the hell is that maid?" he roared, slamming down the front desk phone. "That was another guest on the tenth floor, wondering if we charge extra for changing the sheets and towels."

"Let me check," said the bellboy helpfully.

"Yeah, you do that," Meskin muttered, wondering if the entire hotel wasn't going to hell. For two days, maids had been disappearing in the middle of their shifts. They just walked off the job, leaving their service carts behind. The first one had quit on the ninth floor. Her replacement had quit two hours later. Her cart was found on the seventh floor.

But that was not the odd part. The odd part was that the carts were always found on floors that had been completely serviced.

Somehow, the maids never seemed to quite finish the tenth floor.

Meskin had complained to the Hotelworkers' Union, but they claimed it wasn't a job action. The union sent over another replacement, a Filipina named Esmerelda. She spoke even less English than the last one.

The desk phone rang. It was the bellboy.

"I'm on the ninth floor," he said. "I found her cart. No sign of . . . what was her name—Griselda?"

"I thought it was Esmerelda," Meskin said bitterly. "And who the hell cares what her name is? They come and go faster than the damn guests. I think this is a union plot or something."

"What should I do, Mr. Meskin?"

"Keep searching. I'll call every room from nine up and see who needs linen."

Wearily Marvin Meskin began the process. As he went about this irksome task, the lobby elevator door dinged open. His quick eyes went to it, hoping it might be that lazy Esmerelda. He couldn't understand it. Everyone said Filipina help was top shelf.

The woman stepping off the elevator was not Esmerelda. Meskin's eyes followed her through the lobby anyway. She walked with a kind of loose-hipped undulation that wiped Meskin's mind free of his cares. He had never seen such a set of boobs on someone that young. She was quite a piece of work in her tight yellow skirt and yellow fingernails. Like a voluptuous banana. Meskin wondered what it would be like to peel her.

Someone picked up the line, breaking into Meskin's banana-flavored fantasy.

"Yes, this is the front desk," he said. "I was just wondering if you've gotten fresh linen for today. No? Well, I am very sorry. We seem to be having a busy day. I'll get right on it."

Thirty calls later, Marvin Meskin put down the desk telephone to find a man was hovering only inches away. He had not heard him approach the front desk.

"Yes? May I help you in some way?" Meskin asked, his nose wrinkling at the man's all-black ensemble. If a T-shirt and slacks could be called an ensemble.

"I'm looking for a guy," the man in black asked.

"I'll bet you are," Meskin said dryly.

It was the wrong thing to say, and on an ordinary day Marvin Meskin would never have allowed those insolent words to escape his lips, but he was in a bad mood and the man in black was not dressed like a traveler. In fact, he looked as if he had slept in his clothes.

But he had said it, and the wrongness, the utter and complete boneheadedness of the comment was brought home forcefully to Marvin Meskin when the skinny guy in black lifted his thick-wristed hands and clamped first one on Meskin's shoulder and then the other on his throat.

That was all. There was no other sensation. Not of floating. Not of flying. Not even of dislocation.

Yet somehow Marvin Meskin found himself on the other side of the front desk, his back crushing the deep-pile royal-blue lobby rug and his left arm straining to come out of its socket.

Way up there where the oxygen was, the skinny guy was calmly and methodically using one terrible hand to slow-twist Meskin's going-numb left arm. His other hand rested on his hip. One of his feet—Meskin had no idea which—was planted irresistibly in his windpipe, restricting the flow of air.

"Gasp," Marvin Meskin gasped. "Hack! Hack!"

"You'll have to speak up. I didn't hear the answer to my question."

Meskin could not recall a question being put to him, but he signaled with his flailing free hand that he would be delighted to answer.

"Let me repeat it," the skinny guy was saying. "The Iraiti ambassador was dropped off at the Embassy Row Hotel two days ago. The front desk there told the FBI that he never checked in. I double-checked, and what do you know, it was true. Since the FBI understood he was in the habit of being dropped off at the Embassy, according to the ambassador's driver, that means he was pulling the old duck-and-dodge—something that should have occurred to the FBI, but didn't. Your establishment is the closest to that one. Ergo, your establishment goes to the top of the list."

This made perfect sense to Marvin Meskin, so he nodded in agreement. The action scratched the man's shiny shoes. Meskin's five-o'clock shadow appeared around noon. He hoped the desecration was not noticed.

"Okay," the guy in black was saying, "now I ask you if you'd know the Iraiti ambassador if you saw him." And the shoe withdrew.

"I'm a faithful watcher of *Nightline*," Meskin said hoarsely. He started gulping air in case the shoe returned. It did not.

"He check in two days ago?"

"Yes, he did."

"Check out?"

"I'd have to examine our records."

At that moment the bellboy stepped off the elevator. He started at the sight of his employer being held down on the royal-blue rug.

"Mr. Meskin, should I call the police?" he asked from behind a potted rubber plant.

"Say no," the skinny guy said flatly.

"No," Meskin said, really wanting to say yes. But those deep-set eyes promised certain death if he disobeyed.

"Did you hear that?" the skinny guy asked, directing his deadly eyes toward the bellboy.

"I don't work for you," the bellboy said bravely.

"Go look for that maid!" Meskin yelled.

"I found her. I found all of four of them. In the storage room."

"All? What the hell are they doing—playing strip poker?"

"No, sir, they appear to have been strangled."

"Did you say strangled?" the skinny guy demanded.

"Union dispute," Marvin Meskin said quickly. "Nothing for you to concern yourself with. We run a discreet hotel."

The skinny guy frowned. "I'd say this is more than union trouble. Let's look into the ambassador first. I see dead bodies all the time."

"I'll bet you do," Marvin Meskin said as he was hauled by one arm to his feet. Weak-kneed, he stumbled back behind the counter and went to the computer. The skinny guy followed close behind him.

"There's something wrong with this computer," Meskin said, trying to call up the name. The amber screen was misbehaving. The letters and symbols were wavering as if written in disturbed water. "I can't get it to straighten out," Meskin complained, banging the terminal.

"Just a sec," the man said, stepping back.

The amber letters reformed, readable once more.

Meskin looked over his shoulder. The skinny guy stood, his bare arms folded, about twelve feet away.

"Hop to it," he said.

And Meskin hopped to it.

"We have an Abdul Al-Hazred in Room 1045," Meskin called out.

"So?"

"So that's the name the Iraiti ambassador uses whenever he takes a room here."

"He do that often?"

"Quite often. Usually for only an afternoon, if you know what I mean."

"I know. What floor is 1045—tenth or forty-fifth?"

"Tenth," Meskin said, "the same floor we've been having trouble with. Oh, my God," he croaked, his own words registering in their full impact.

The skinny guy came back. The amber screen broke apart like water that had been disturbed by an idly swirling stick. He took Marvin Meskin up by the scruff of his neck and on the way to the elevator collected the bellboy.

"Are we going to be killed too?" the bellboy asked as the elevator shot up to the tenth floor.

"Why?" the skinny guy asked while Meskin felt his stomach contents turn acidic.

"Because I'd like to call home and tell my mother good-bye," the bellboy said sincerely.

"Tell her good-bye over dinner tonight," the skinny guy growled. "I'm in a big rush."

Stepping out into the corridor, Meskin recalled that he had forgotten to bring along a passkey.

"No problem," the skinny guy said, releasing them on either side of Room 1045. "I brought my own."

"You? Where did you get . . . ?"

The question was answered before it was completed. The skinny guy answered it when he took hold of the knob, flexed one monster wrist, and handed the suddenly loose knob to Marvin Meskin.

It was very, very warm, Meskin found. He tossed it from hand to hand, blowing on his free hand by turns.

The door fell open after the man tapped it.

Marvin Meskin was shoved in first. The bellboy stumbled in, propelled by the skinny guy, who had such an irresistible way about him. They collided.

While they were picking themselves up, the skinny guy went for the bed, where the late Iraiti ambassador, Turqi Abaatira, AKA Abdul Al-Hazred, lay spread-eagled, his dark manhood dominating the decor like an overripe banana.

Ambassador Abaatira made a very colorful corpse. His body was a kind of brownish-white, his natural duskiness bleached by his lack of circulation. His tongue was a purplish-black extrusion in his blue face. His manhood was at full mast, a corpsy greenish-black.

The skinny guy looked over the body with a dispassionate eye, as if used to seeing corpses that were lashed to hotel beds by yards of yellow silk. He seemed most interested in the late ambassador's throat. The cords and muscles of his thick neck were squeezed by a long yellow silk scarf.

"Was he into bondage?" the skinny guy asked, turning

from the body. His face was two degrees unhappier than before.

"We do not pry into our guests' affairs," Marvin Meskin sniffed, averting his eyes from the ugly but colorful sight. They kept going back to the swollen member in a kind of mesmerized horror. The bellboy was on his knees in front of the wastepaper basket. From the sounds he made, he was straining hard to throw up—but not hard enough. All he did was hack and spit.

When he at last gave up, the bellboy found himself being hauled to his feet by the tall skinny guy.

"Let's see those maids," he ordered.

The bellboy was only too happy to comply. On the way out of the room, the skinny guy paused to shove Marvin Meskin back.

"You," he said in a no-nonsense voice. "Mind the dead guy."

"Why me?" Meskin bleated.

"Because it's your hotel."

Which somehow made perfect sense to Marvin Meskin. Meekly he went into the bathroom and closed the door.

Remo Williams let the nervous bellboy lead him to the storage room.

"I found them in a corner, behind some stacked chairs," the bellboy was saying. "They . . . they were just like that dead guy."

"If they were, medical science is going to have a field day with them. Not to mention the *National Enquirer, Hard Copy, Inside Edition,* and *Copra Inisfree*."

"No, I didn't mean *exactly* like him," the bellboy protested, his face actually reddening with embarrassment. Looking at him in his tight-fitting hotel uniform, Remo decided he would be embarrassed too. "I meant they were killed the same way. Strangled," he added in a hushed voice as he unlocked the storage-room door.

The room was a dark forest of stacked chrome-and-leather chairs and great round folding tables. The bellboy led Remo to a dim corner.

"This was a smart place to hide them," the bellboy was saying. "All the damaged chairs and broken tables are stashed in this corner. Here."

He stepped aside for Remo to get a good look.

The maids were seated on the floor, their legs straight out, facing one another as if posed in a game of pat-a-cake. Their heads lolled drunkenly off the shoulders of their starched blue uniforms and their arms hung down off their drooping shoulders, elbows and wrists folded stiffly.

Their faces were almost—not quite—the same delicate blue as their starched uniforms. A few stared glassily at nothing.

Each maid was marked by a purplish bruise at the throat. Something had been tied around their necks very, very tightly. Tight enough to seemingly force their tongues from their open mouths. Tight enough to cause at least one of them to defecate into her underwear.

Remo went among them, kneeling at each body, making certain they were gone. They were. He stood up, his high-cheekboned face grim.

"What do you think, sir?" the bellboy asked, getting the idea that the skinny guy was not a dangerous maniac, but something much, much more.

"I don't like that yellow scarf upstairs," he muttered.

The cryptic comment called for no response, so the bellboy offered none. He stood there feeling angry and helpless and wondering if there was something he should have seen or done or heard that might have averted this tragedy.

Then it struck him.

"You know," he said slowly, "I saw a girl walking around the hotel yesterday who wore a scarf like the one we saw."

"Yellow scarves are pretty common," the man said, regarding the bodies dispassionately.

"She also wore a yellow dress. And yellow fingernail polish."

The skinny guy looked up suddenly.

"Did she look like a hooker?" he asked.

"I got that impression, yeah. More like a call girl, though. This is a classy place. The manager doesn't let streetwalkers in."

"If he lets the Iraiti ambassador frolic in the afternoons," the skinny guy said, walking off, "you shouldn't feel so damn proud of this fleabag."

"Should I call the police?" the bellboy called after him.

"No," the skinny guy said. "Wait here."

And even though he never returned, the bellboy obeyed.

He was still standing watch over the bodies when the FBI came in en masse and sealed off the hotel.

The bellboy didn't get a chance to see his mother that night, but he was allowed to call her to say that he'd be home after the debriefing. He made it sound important. It was. Before it was all over, the world would edge toward the brink of a sinkhole of sand from which there was no return.

9

Harold Smith accepted Remo Williams' telephone report without any expression of regret. The loss of the Iraiti ambassador was not exactly an affront to humanity. But the political fallout could be significant.

"If it wasn't for all the strangled maids," Remo was saying grimly, "I'd say it was a kinky lovers' tryst gone bizarre."

"The ambassador was quite a ladies' man," Smith was saying in a half-audible voice that usually meant his attention was divided between his conversation and his computer.

"Who do you think this girl in yellow is?" Remo wondered.

"The possibilities are endless. A Kurani spy out to avenge her homeland. An Isreali Mossad agent out to send a message to Abominadad. Even the U.S. CIA is a possibility, but highly unlikely. If this were sanctioned, I would know about it."

"The bellboy had her pegged as a call girl."

"That is my thought as well. I am checking my file on Ambassador Abaatira even as we speak. Yes, here it is. He is known to prefer the services of the Diplomatic Escort Service."

"Good name," Remo quipped. "You know, you might have mentioned this before."

"I hadn't thought the ambassador's sexual appetites would play a role in this."

"Believe me, Smitty," Remo said airily, "sex was uppermost in the guy's mind when he cashed out. He had a ringside seat to his last hard-on. In fact, if you get to see the morgue photos, you'll notice he had his eye on the ball right to the bitter end."

Harold Smith cleared his throat with the low, throaty

rumble of a distant thundercloud. "Yes . . . er, well, those details are unimportant. Listen carefully, Remo. The FBI is going to suppress this entire matter. For the moment, the Iraiti ambassador is still on the missing-persons list. His death would cause who-knows-what reaction in Abominadad. We cannot afford that."

"Screw Abominadad," Remo snapped. "After all the hostages they've taken, how much of a stink can they raise over one *flagrante delicto* diplomat?"

"The stink I am thinking of," Smith said levelly, "is not diplomatic. The stink I fear is the stink of nerve gas in the lungs of our servicemen stationed in Hamidi Arabia."

"Point taken," Remo said. "I still say you should let me cash out Mad Ass. I'm sick of seeing his face every time I turn on the TV."

"Then do not turn on the TV," Smith countered. "Investigate the Diplomatic Escort Service and report on what you find."

"Could be an interesting investigation," Remo said with relish. "I'm glad I brought my credit cards."

"Remo, under no circumstances are you to procure the services of—"

The line clicked dead.

Harold Smith returned the receiver to its cradle and leaned back in his ancient executive's chair. This was worrisome. This was very, very worrisome. It would be better—although not good—if the Iraiti ambassador had fallen victim to a common criminal, or even a serial killer. If this had an intelligence connection, no matter what nation was involved, the unstable Middle East was about to become even more precarious.

Remo Williams found a yellow police-barrier tape in front of the office building that was the base for the Diplomatic Escort Service. It was the same yellow as the silk scarf around the late Ambassador Abaatira's neck, he noticed without pleasure.

"What's going on?" Remo asked the uniformed cop who stood by the main entrance.

"Just a little matter for the D.C. detectives," the cop returned without rancor. "Watch the evening news."

"Thanks," Remo said. "I will." He continued on his way,

slipped around the corner, and looked up at the dingy facade.

The side of the building wasn't exactly sheer. But it wasn't a ziggurat of brick and gingerbread, either.

Remo walked up to the facade, placing his toes to the building's base as Chiun had taught him so long ago. Raising his arms, he laid his palms flat against the gritty wall.

Then, somehow, he began ascending. He had forgotten the involved theory, the complicated movements, just as he had his old fear of heights. He had mastered ascents long, long ago.

So he ascended. His slightly cupped palm created an impossible but natural tension that enabled him to cling and pause while he shifted his footholds and used his steel-strong fingers to obtain increasingly higher purchase.

Remo wasn't climbing. Exactly. He was using the vertical force of the building to conquer it. There was no sensation of going up. It felt to Remo as if he were pulling the building down, step by step, foot by foot. Of course, the building wasn't sinking into its foundations under Remo's practiced manipulations. He was going up it.

Somehow, it worked. Somehow, he found himself on the eighth-floor ledge. He peered into a window. Dark. He walked around the six-inch-wide ledge with a casual grace, pausing at each grimy window—sometimes scouring pollution particles from the glass the better to see inside—until he found the office window he wanted.

The medical examiner was still shooting pictures. He was shooting into a closet. Remo could smell, even through the glass, the odors of death, sudden perspiration, now stale, bodily wastes, both liquid and not. But no blood.

He took that to mean the bodies—there were at least two because the M.E. turned his camera toward the hidden desk well—had been strangled.

Remo listened to the idle talk of the M.E. and two unhappy detectives.

"Think it's a serial creep?" the M.E. asked.

"I hope not. Damn. I hope not," one detective said.

"Face it. Johns don't happen to walk around with a pair of yellow kerchiefs, lose their cool, and strangle two hookers—"

"Call girls," the first detective said. "These were high-priced broads. Look at those clothes. Designer clothes for sure."

"They smell just like dead hookers to me," the other grunted. "Worse. Like I was saying, no one happens to strangle two hookers with identical scarves. If it was a crime of passion, he'd have cut or bludgeoned one. No, this is a kinky hit. The worst kind. Who knows what this guy had eating away at him to do all this?"

"You think it's a guy?" the M.E asked, changing a flashbulb.

"I know it is. Women don't do serial killings. It's not in their nature. Like lifting the toilet seat when they're done."

"We don't know it's a serial thing yet."

"This is the fourth corpse wrapped this way in less than a week. Trust me. If we don't find more like these in the next few days, it'll be because whoever did this ran out of yellow silk."

Deciding there was nothing more he could learn, Remo started back down, taking the side of the building in hand and using gravity to return him to the sidewalk.

As he walked away, he thought about yellow scarves.

And he thought about how much he missed Chiun, and wished more than ever that the Master of Sinanju were still around.

If the yellow strangling scarves and the cold feeling deep in his stomach meant anything, Remo needed the Master of Sinanju as he had never needed him before.

But Chiun was gone. And Remo walked alone. And there was no one to protect him if his worst fears proved true.

10

Remo walked the humid streets of Washington, D.C., with his hands crammed into his pockets and his sad eyes on the endless pavement unwinding under his feet.

He tried to shove the fear into the deepest recesses of his mind. He tried to push the ugly memories back into some dark corner where he could ignore them.

"Why now?" he said, half-aloud.

Hearing him, an alley-dwelling wino lifted a paper-bag-wrapped green bottle in salute. "Why not?" he said. He upended the bottle and chugalugged it dry.

Remo kept walking.

It had been bad before, but if what he suspected was true, Remo's life had just taken a turn toward catastrophe. He considered, then rejected, calling Smith. But Smith would not understand. He believed in computers and balanced books and bottom lines. He understood cause and effect, action and reaction.

Harold Smith did not understand Sinanju. He would not understand Remo if Remo attempted to tell him the true significance of the yellow silk scarves. Remo could not tell him. That was that. Smith would only tell Remo that his story was preposterous, his fears groundless, and his duty was to America.

But as Remo's feet carried him toward the Capitol Building, he thought that his responsibilities were also with the inhabitants of Sinanju, who, when the Master of Sinanju failed them, were forced to send their babies home to the sea. Which was a polite phrase for infanticide. He owed Smith only the empty grave somewhere in New Jersey. To Chiun, and therefore to the Masters of Sinanju who had preceded him, Remo owed much, much more.

Were it not for Chiun, Remo would never have achieved the full mastery of his mind and body. He would never have learned to eat correctly, or to breathe with his entire body, not merely his lungs. He would have lived an ordinary life doing ordinary things and suffering ordinary disappointments. He was one with the sun source of the martial arts. For Remo, nothing was impossible.

He owed Sinanju a lot. He had just about made up his mind to go back to the village when Smith had called. Now he had more reason than ever to head for Korea.

In Korea, he might be safe.

But if he returned, would it be because he was too afraid of the yellow scarves? Remo wasn't sure. In twenty years of working for CURE, Remo had known fear only a few times. Cowardice he had tasted once. Years ago. And even then, he had not feared for his own safety, but for others'.

And now the terrible unknowable power that had once made of Remo Williams an utter slave to its whims had returned.

Remo found himself on the steps the Pantheon-like National Archives Building. On an impulse, he floated up the broad marble steps and into its quiet, stately interior. He had been here before. Years ago. He glided on soundless feet to the great brass-and-glass repository housing the original Constitution of the United States in a sandwich of inert gas.

It was, of course, where he had last seen it. Remo stepped up to the encircling protective guardrail and began reading the aged parchment paper that struck him as looking a lot like one of Chiun's scrolls, on which he faithfully recorded the history of Sinanju.

A guard came up to him after only a few minutes.

"Excuse me, sir," the guard began in a soft but unequivocal voice, "but we prefer that tourists not loiter here."

"I'm not loitering," Remo said testily. "I'm reading."

"There are brochures available out front with the entire text of the Constitution printed on them. In facsimile."

"I want to read the original," Remo said, not turning.

"I'm sorry, but—"

Remo took the man by the back of the neck, lifting him up and over the guardrail until his surprised nose was jammed up against the breath-steamed glass.

"According to this, it's still a free country," Remo snarled bitterly.

"Absolutely," the guard said quickly. "Life, liberty, and the pursuit of happiness is what I always say. Always." As a reward, his feet clicked back on the polished marble floor. The hand at his collar released. He adjusted his uniform.

"Enjoy your reading, sir," the guard said. He faded back toward a doorway where he could keep his eye on the strange tourist in black, yet still stay out of reach of his strong hands.

If the guy made any weird moves, he would trigger the alert that would cause the Consitution housing to descend by scissors jack into a protective well in the marble flooring.

Then he would get the hell out of the building. The guy's eyes were as spooky as an owl's.

Remo finished reading in silence. Then, turning hard on his heel, he left the Archives Building and glided down the stairs like a purposeful black ghost.

Harold Smith picked up the blue telephone, frowning.

"Yes, Remo?"

"Smitty? I have some good news for you and some bad."

"Go ahead," Smith said in a voice as gray and colorless as his apparel.

"I'm quitting CURE."

Without skipping a beat, Smith asked, "What is the good news?"

"That is the good news," Remo returned. "The bad is that I can't quit until I finish this assignment."

"That is good."

"No, it's bad. I may not survive this one, any more than Chiun survived our last one."

"Come again?" Smith asked, his voice losing its studied neutrality.

"Smitty, you gotta get those computers of yours replaced. They blew it. Big-time."

"Come to the point, Remo."

"If they're still working—which I doubt—you're going to get a report on a couple of strangled call girls found in the offices of the Diplomatic Escort Service."

"I trust you interrogated them before you strangled them?"

"Nope. I didn't strangle them. My guess is our happy hooker did."

Smith paused. Remo could hear the hollow clicking of his computer keys. "What did you learn from the office?"

"That Washington is in the grip of a strangulation flap—something your computers should have picked up, if they were working."

"I am aware of only two homicides by strangulation other than those you have reported," Smith said. "A medical-supply salesman named Cosmo Bellingham and an insurance adjuster by the name of Carl Lusk. One was found in the elevator of the Sheraton Washington Hotel. The other in an alley near Logan Circle."

"And that didn't ring any bells?"

"Two strangulations. Statistically within the norm for an urban center like the District of Columbia."

"Well, counting the two call girls, four hotel maids, and the late ambassador, we have nine. How statistical is that?"

"Are you saying that all of these homicides are connected?"

"You tell me," Remo said acidly. "Does your computer tell you what they were done away with?"

More clicks. "No."

"Silk scarves," Remo said. "*Yellow* silk scarves."

"Like the ambassador?" Harold Smith croaked. "Oh, my God. Are you certain?"

"The cops I overheard at the escort service say it's the killer's trademark. Now, think. Who do we know who strangles with yellow scarves?"

"The Thuggee cult," Smith said hoarsely. "But, Remo, you wiped that group out long ago. It was the work of that pirate who ran Just Folks Airlines, Aldrich Hunt Baynes III. He's dead. The cult was smashed. Even the airline is out of business now."

"Tell me, Smith, were those two salesmen traveling when they got it?"

"Let me check." Smith's fingers attacked his keyboard like a feverish concert pianist. Presently, expanded versions of the wire-service reports on both homicides appeared on the screen as side-by-side blocks of text.

"Bellingham was killed shortly after checking into his hotel," Smith reported. "The other man died before reaching his."

"Travelers. Same M.O., Smitty," Remo pointed out. "They always hit travelers. Make friends, get their confidence, and when they're lulled, wrap the ol' silk scarf around their throats. Then walk away with their wallets."

"The two men were also robbed," Smith said. "But, Remo, if we smashed that cult, how could this be?"

"You forget, Smith. It's just updated Thuggee. It was around long before Just Folks tried to scare up some new customers by scaring passengers away from other airlines. And it'll probably be around long after. Besides," Remo added, his voice going soft, "we smashed the cult, not Kali."

"Beg pardon?"

"When we wrapped that one up," Remo admitted slowly, "there were a few things Chiun and I left out of our debriefing."

Smith clutched the receiver until he was white-fingered. "Go on."

"It wasn't just Baynes and the others. It was Kali herself."

"If I recall my mythology," Smith said aridly, "Kali was a mythical Hindu deity."

"Who lusted for blood and who the original East Indian thugs worshiped. Hapless travelers were sacrificed to Kali. The whole cult thing was triggered, believe it or not, by a stone statue of Kali that somehow exerted an influence over its worshipers."

"Influence?"

"According to Chiun, the spirit of Kali inhabited the statue."

"Yes," Smith said. "I recall now. The cult revolved around the idol. The Master of Sinanju believed that it possessed magical properties. Pure superstition, of course. Chiun comes from a tiny fishing village without running water and electricity."

"That just happens to have produced a line of assassins who worked for every empire since the paint on the sphinx was still wet," Remo retorted. "So backward that when the United States—the greatest nation on the face of the earth anytime, anywhere—needed someone to pull its chestnuts out of the fire, it turned to the last Master of Sinanju."

Smith swallowed. "Where is that statue now?" he asked.

"When we tracked down Baynes," Remo answered, "he had it. I grabbed it. It grabbed back. We struggled. I broke it into a zillion pieces and threw it off the side of a mountain."

"And?"

"Obviously," Remo said in a distracted voice, "the spirit of Kali went somewhere else."

Smith was silent.

"Strictly for the sake of argument," he asked at last, "where?"

"How the hell do I know?" Remo snapped. "I just know that without Chiun, I don't think I'm strong enough to beat her this time."

"But you admitted that you threw it off a mountain."

"Thanks to Chiun. He made it possible. Until he rescued me, I was its slave. It was awful, Smitty. I couldn't help myself." His voice sank to a reedy croak. "I did . . . things."

"What things?'

"I killed a pigeon," Remo said with thick-voiced shame. "An innocent pigeon."

"And . . . ?" Smith prodded.

Remo cleared his throat and looked away guitily. "I laid it before the statue. As an offering. I would have gone on to wasting people, but Chiun gave me the strength to resist. Now he's gone. And I have to face Kali alone."

"Remo, you do not know this," Smith said sharply. "This may simply be a serial killer with an affinity for yellow scarves. Or a copycat."

"There's one way to find out."

"And that is?"

"If this killer is targeting travelers, throw her some tourist bait," Remo suggested.

"Yes. Very good. The other victims were apparently picked up at the Washington National Airport. That is where you should start."

"Not me, Smitty. *You.*"

"I?"

"If it is Kali, I may not be able to resist her scent. That's how she got to me last time. But you might. She has no power over you. We could set up a trap. You play the cheese and I'll be the trap. How about it?"

"The field is not my place. It is yours."

"And I have a responsibility to Sinanju now. I *am* Sinanju. I have to go there and see if I can hack it as Reigning Master. But I gotta close the books on Kali before I go. It's the only way."

"You are serious about leaving CURE?" Smith asked quietly.

"Yeah," Remo said flatly. "That doesn't mean I wouldn't take the odd job here and there," he added. "But nothing small. It's gotta be worth my time. Otherwise you can just send in the Marines. I'm out of it. What say, Smitty?"

The line hummed with the silence between the two men.

At last Harold W. Smith spoke.

"As long as you are with the organization," he said coldly, "you will do as instructed. Go to Washington National. Allow yourself to be picked up by this woman. Interrogate her, and if she is the sole cause of these strangulations, liquidate her. Otherwise, call for further instruction. I will await your report."

"You gutless bas—"

Harold Smith hung up the phone on Remo's reply. If there was one thing he had learned in his many years as an administrator, it was how to motivate employees.

Whatever he had become under Chiun's tutelege, Remo Williams was still an American. He would heed his country's call. He always had. He always would. That was why he had been selected in the first place.

11

"Screw you, Smith!" Remo shouted into the dead receiver. "You're on your own."

Remo slammed the phone on its hook. The hook broke off, taking the receiver to the floor with it.

Remo started away from the pay phone. Outside, he hailed a Checker cab.

"Airport," he told the driver.

"Dulles or Washington National?" the cabby asked.

"Dulles," Remo said, thinking no sense tempting fate. He had been willing to go to the mat one last time for Smith, but only if Smith would do it his way. He had been doing it Smith's way for too damn long. No more.

"Going anyplace interesting?" the cabby asked.

"Asia," Remo said, cranking down the window against the heat of the warm July day.

"Asia. That's pretty far. Better there than the Middle East, huh?"

Remo perked up. "What's going on there now?"

"The usual. Mad Ass is rattling his scimitar. We're rattling ours. But nothing happens. I don't think there'll be a war."

"Don't count on it," Remo said, thinking that what went on in the Middle East wouldn't matter much to him once he was back in Sinanju. Hell, he wouldn't be surprised to find a job offer from Mad Ass himself waiting for him. Of course, he wouldn't take it. He was going to be particular about who he worked for. Unlike Chiun, who would work for anyone as long as their gold took tooth marks.

The ride to Dulles was short. Remo paid the driver and entered the main terminal. He went to the Air Korea booth, bought a one-way ticket to Seoul, and then went in search of his gate.

As he approached the metal-detector station, he noticed the blond woman loitering outside the ladies' room.

The first thing Remo noticed was that she had the largest chest he had ever seen. It projected out like a triangular form straining to burst the yellow fabric of her dress. He wondered how she kept from tipping forward.

Evidently they were quite a burden, because she picked at her brassiere straps with careless fingers.

Remo noticed her yellow nail polish. His eyes flicked to her throat.

"Uh-oh," Remo said, his pupils dilating at sight of the tastefully tied yellow silk scarf.

Remo ducked into the men's room. Bending over a sink, he splashed water onto his face. He patted himself dry with a paper towel. Had she been waiting for him?

"Maybe she won't be there when I get back," Remo muttered. He went to the door. With a single finger he eased it open a crack. She was still there, leaning against a white wall, her eyes darting to the line of passengers coming down the walkway, laden with luggage and shoulder bags.

Remo swallowed. She looked very young. Not dangerous at all—unless she fell on top of you and crushed you with her sharp chest, Remo thought with forced humor.

Words the Master of Sinanju had told him long years ago echoed in Remo's ears.

"Know your enemy."

Remo took a deep breath and stepped out onto the walkway. He went directly to the girl in yellow. His legs actually felt rubbery. He sucked in a double lungful of oxygen, held it in his stomach, and released it slowly, releasing also the tension in his chest and the fear in his belly.

He was in control enough to smile as he approached the blond.

"Excuse me," he said.

Her head turned. Her blue eyes fell on Remo. They were curious. Almost innocent eyes. Maybe he had been mistaken. "Yes?" she said in a sweet, breathy voice.

"Are you Cynthia?" Remo asked. "The office said they'd send a gorgeous blond named Cynthia to meet me."

Her red mouth parted. Thick brows puckered tentatively. "Yes, I'm Cynthia," she said. "You must be—"

"Dale. Dale Cooper."

"Of course, Mr. Cooper." She put out a hand. "Nice to meet you."

Remo smiled. She had taken the bait. "Call me Dale."

"Dale. Let's get your bags together."

"Sure," Remo said. He let her lead him to the luggage carousel, where he made a pretense of picking his luggage from the revolving conveyor.

"This is mine," Remo said, grabbing a brown over-the-shoulder bag and a black leather briefcase. "Shall we go?"

"Yes. But we'll have to take a cab."

"You don't look like you have much driving experience," Remo remarked lightly.

"Oh, I'm older than I look. Much older."

She led him to the first cab waiting in line. The driver got out and opened the trunk. Remo saw that he was the same driver who had brought him here.

"What happened to Asia?" the cabby asked gruffly.

"Search me," Remo said, forcing a smile. "Last I heard, it was still in the Pacific."

The driver scratched his head as he jumped back behind the wheel.

"Where is the office putting me up this time?" Remo asked.

"The Watergate Hotel," the girl who answered to the name of Cynthia said quickly.

"Watergate it is," the driver muttered. To Remo's relief, he was silent during the rest of the ride.

Remo made small talk as he took stock of "Cynthia." Seen closer, she struck him as younger than he had thought. Her body was certainly mature. But her face, under expert makeup that included a purplish-yellow eye shadow, seemed girlish. She had that dewy look.

"Yellow must be your favorite color," Remo suggested.

"I worship yellow," Cynthia said, fingering her scarf. "It's so . . . eye-catching." She laughed. Even her laugh sounded pure. Remo wondered how someone with that kind of high-school laugh could strangle ten people.

He would remember to ask her that—before he took her out.

At the Watergate lobby, Cynthia turned to Remo and said, "Why don't you relax? I'll check you in."

"Thanks," Remo said, putting down his luggage. He watched her saunter over to the front desk. She had a nice walk. A little slinky. She walked in her high heels as if driving tacks with them.

As Remo watched, she leaned over the counter, startling the clerk with her ample bosom. "Any messages?" she whispered.

The clerk's "No" was a croak. His eyes were on her bosom as if it snarled and snapped at him like a pair of pit bulls.

Cynthia thanked him and palmed a key from her yellow purse as she turned.

Remo smiled tightly. His acute hearing had picked up the exchange. And the palming, though slick, was made obvious by Cynthia's body language.

She was taking him to a room she had preregistered. Either her own, or to one that was a convenient dumping ground for victims.

Either way suited Remo Willams just fine. If she was an acolyte of Kali's, he'd soon know where his mortal enemy was hiding. He could decide whether to run or strike, depending on the answer.

Cynthia joined him. "I don't see a bellboy," she said, frowning. A bellboy hovered out of sight. Obviously paid to ignore anyone Cynthia brought in.

"I can carry my own bags," Remo said quickly.

"Great. I hate waiting."

Once they stepped on the elevator, the mood changed. Cynthia stared at the ceiling, lost in thought. Her yellow-tipped fingers went to her neck scarf. This time they plucked at the fabric nervously. The loose knot slipped apart. When Cynthia brought her hand down, the scarf floated with it.

This time Remo suppressed his smile completely.

The elevator came to a stop.

"After you," Cynthia offered, her voice cool and tight.

Remo picked up his bags. This was the critical moment. His hands were encumbered. Would she take him before he stepped off the elevator, or wait until they were in the room itself?

He stepped out into the corridor, feeling Cynthia's warm presence trail after him. Her body heat registered on the back of his bare arms. A temperature change of only a few degrees would indicate an impending attack.

But the attack didn't come. Instead, Cynthia got in front and opened the door for him. It was pitch-dark inside.

Remo slipped in, tossing his bags down. He snapped on the light switch. Before he could turn, it snapped off again. The door slammed. The room went totally black. He was not alone.

Remo skipped the mock protestations. He shifted to one side as his visual purple adjusted to the blackness. As a Master of Sinanju, he could not exactly see in the dark, but he could detect shadowy motion within the blackness.

In the dark, he grinned in fierce anticipation.

And in the dark, the yellow scarf settled over his throat with a silken snap.

Casually Remo reached up. A supersharp fingernail raked the smooth fabric. The scarf tightened. It parted with an angry snarl.

"Sorry," Remo said. "Yellow isn't my color."

A hiss answered him, low and feline.

Remo snagged a soft, thin wrist. He gave it a twist.

"Oww! You're hurting me!" It was Cynthia.

"Not what I had in mind," Remo said, collecting the scratching fingers of Cynthia's hand in one fist. He pushed the hand back, exposing the wrist.

With his other hand, Remo found the girl's wrist and tapped it once, sharply.

"Oh!" said Cynthia. It was a very surprised "Oh." Remo tapped again. This time her exclamation was dreamy and moist.

As he tapped, Remo drew Cynthia to the light switch. He nudged it with an elbow, without breaking the building rhythm of his manipulations.

In the light, Cynthia looked up into Remo's dark, obsidian-chip eyes. There was no anger there. No hate. Just a kind of wondrous fear that caused her pink lips to part. She ran a deeper pink tongue over her lips, moistening them further.

"They call this the thirty-seven steps to bliss," Remo explained in a low, earthy growl. "How do you like it so far?"

"Oh," said Cynthia, as if impaled on a delicious pin. Her eyes went from Remo's cruel face to her wrist as if trying to fathom how this ordinary man could reduce her to squirming helplessness with only one intermittently tapping finger. "I don't understand," she said in a surprise-twisted voice. "What are you doing to me?"

"Let's start with your name."

"Kimberly. It's Kimberly," Kimberly said, panting a little. She squeezed down as if cramping. Her thick eyebrows gathered together, forcing her innocent blue eyes into narrow slits of bright cerulean.

"Good start. This, by the way, is only step one."

Kimberly's eyes popped open. "It is?"

Remo's smile was arch. "Honest. Would I kid a blond that had just tried to throttle me in the dark?"

"I don't . . . know."

"I wouldn't. It's such a rare experience. So, tell me. Why'd you waste the Iraiti ambassador?"

"She told me to."

"She?"

"Kali."

"Spell that."

"K-a-l-i."

"Damn," Remo muttered to himself. It was true. Now he would have to take this to the bitter end.

"Take me to Kali," he said harshly.

"I only take offerings to Kali."

Remo tapped once more, then stopped. "No introduction, no happy finger action," he warned.

"Please! It hurts when you stop."

"But it will feel so good when I start up. So what's it gonna be? Do I finish the job or do I leave you here to play with yourself? It won't be half as much fun. Trust me on that."

"Finish me!" Kimberly pleaded. "I'll do it! Just finish me!"

"For a pro," Remo said, bringing his finger to bear again, "you're not very collected about this stuff."

"This is my first time," Kimberly gulped. Her eyes were worried and inward-looking.

"That's a laugh. Is that what you told the Iraiti ambassador?"

Kimberly was no longer listening. She rested one steadying hand on Remo's hard bicep. The other, trapped in Remo's immovable fist, squeezed harder and harder as her eyes squeezed tighter and tighter. The tapping finger continued to strike the sensitive point she had never suspected existed there. A tear leaked out of one eye as her pretty face gathered together, reddening, twisting, apprehensive.

"Something's happening!" Kimberly cried sharply.

The shudder started in her face. It rippled down her neck

and convulsed her entire body. Her breasts seemed to actually throb. Remo had never seen breasts throb before.

"Oh Oh Oh Oh . . . uuuuhhh," she cried, uncoiling like an old spring from a sofa. She swayed this way and that. Then all the life seemed to escape her body.

Remo caught her.

"If you give as good as you get, you're probably worth every dime," he said, carrying her to the bed. He set her down, noticing that her chest seemed almost an inch bigger than it had before. The damn thing looked like it was trying to strain free of her dress front.

Kimberly lay on the bed, zoned out, as Remo checked the room. The closet and bathroom were both empty. There were no personal items. It was a setup room.

"Where is she?" Remo asked.

"I will never betray her," Kimberly said softly, her eyes fixed on the ceiling.

Remo collected her purse from the rug. He went through it. Deep inside, he found a brass key. It was stamped with the hotel's crest and a room number two floors down.

"Never mind," he said, tossing the purse on a bureau. "I think I can handle it from here."

Remo drifted over to the bed and, with two fingers, closed Kimberly's dreamy eyes. Then he took her trembling chin in hand.

"You're going to kill me." It was a realization, not a question.

"That's the biz, sweetheart," he said, breaking her neck with a quick sideways twist. When he removed his hand, Remo saw no mark. Chiun would have been proud.

He left the room in silence, thinking that maybe this wouldn't be so difficult after all.

The key fitted the lock on Room 606, two floors down.

Remo paused, his heart rising in his chest. He wasn't sure what to expect. Another idol? A portrait? Kali in the flesh?

Whatever, he knew he would have to hit hard and fast, if he wanted to survive. Remo placed an ear to the door. He heard no organic noises. No breathing or heartbeat. No gurgling of bowels.

He turned the key.

The door eased inward. In the harsh hallway light, Remo

caught a flash of maroon drapes. He pushed the door open some more.

The light caught something white and spidery, with too many upraised arms.

Remo hit the light switch, plunging into the room. He flashed for the white outline. One hand out and open, he drove for its vulnerable neck.

Too late, he realized his mistake. His stiffened fingers made contact. The outline shattered into repeating images. The white thing was a mirror reflection.

"Damn!" Remo whirled in place, dropping to a protective crouch, as he zeroed in on the white many-armed thing.

It squatted on a dresser, pale legs crossed, three faces—one looking out, the other two facing east and west—fixed in identical malevolent expressions. The eyes were closed, however. A necklace of flat skulls draped over its pendulous breasts.

Without hesitating, Remo floated up to it. He detected no odor. The last time, it was the hellish scent that had gotten him. There had been no odor clinging to the girl. And this statue was equally sterile.

It was clay, Remo saw. It possessed four normal arms, but other, smaller limbs stuck out from different points in its torso. These lesser limbs were thin and withered.

Remo would dismember the gruesome thing first, he decided.

As if the thought had triggered something deep within the clay idol, its eyelids snapped open. The gash of a mouth writhed in a silent snarl like a Claymation illusion, and a cloying sickly-sweet scent billowed toward him. And the familiar, dreaded waves of psychic force pushed toward him.

Remo struck. A slashing hand slipped through the shoulder area, cleaving two arms and bending others. The clay was soft, Remo found. It would be easy.

Remo drove a fist to the head. He knocked the triple face half off its neck. It gave like soft separating excrement.

The hands came to life. Remo batted them back. Somehow animated, they were still but moist clay. He slapped them back without effort. Clay hands flew from clay wrists. Clay nails raked his face, leaving only slimy whitish trails and clay crumbs.

"Must be the heat," Remo mocked. "You're positively melting."

The psychic waves abated, the dreaded scent grew no stronger. An unhearable voice screamed in defeat.

Grinning with relief, Remo plunged his fingers into the thing's thick white torso. On the floor, the triptych of faces howled in silent protest as Remo kneaded the clay out of shape. His steely fingers constricted. Clay oozed out from between them. He flung clods of the heavy stuff in all directions. Some of it stuck to the walls. The clay make gushy noises as Remo pulled and pushed and separated the heavy white stuff, reducing the ornate body of the thing to a lump of heavy inactive matter.

When he was done, Remo looked around the room. A clay hand was quivering on its back. Remo nudged it with a toe. It flopped over and, finding its fingers, began to scuttle away.

Laughing, Remo brought his foot down on it. The fingers spread out and died.

"Not so tough now, are you?" Remo taunted.

He looked for another hand. He found one, writhing as if in its death throes. Reaching down, Remo brought it up to his wild-eyed face.

The fingers made a futile stab for his face. Remo laughed again as he calmly began pulling the fingers off, one by one.

"She loves me . . ." he sang. "She loves me not."

When he plucked off the thumb, he said, "She loves me," and flushed the maimed palm down the toilet.

There were no other intact hands, Remo was disappointed to see. He looked around for the head. Not finding it, he frowned.

"Here, kitty," he called, for want of a better term. "Here, kitty, kitty."

When that produced no response, Remo got down on hands and knees and spied under the furniture.

"Not under the dresser," he muttered. Shifting, he saw the head wasn't beneath the writing table either. Nor was it hiding under the chairs.

"That leaves . . ." Remo began, reaching down for the hem of the bedspread.

". . . Under the bed. *Boo!*"

The head beneath the bed reacted to the sudden light and the sight of Remo's face with horror. The clay mouth formed an O that was echoed by its mates. The opaque white eyes went round too.

"Well, if it isn't Mrs. Bill," Remo said, reaching in for the head. It bit him. He laughed. The teeth were soft clay. It could do nothing. Kali was the goddess of evil, but he was the Reigning Master of Sinanju. He was invincible.

Getting to his feet, Remo carried the protean head to the window. Brushing aside the drapes, he employed one fingernail to score a circle in the glass. The sound was like a diamond-tipped glass cutter at work.

"Don't you just *hate* that screechy sound?" Remo asked the head, lifting it so its many eyes could see the whitish circle in the pane and the city lights it framed.

"Guess what happens next?" Remo asked the head of Kali. The six eyes closed. And Remo smacked the face into the glass.

It stuck there, the center face mashed flat. The side faces, however, continued their fearstruck contortions.

"Next time, come back as something a little stronger. Like balsa wood," Remo suggested, giving the back of the head a gentle tap.

The glass gave a *crack!* The circle fell outward. It carried the clay head down eight stories to the pavement below.

Upon impact, the glass circle shattered. Remo looked down.

A matronly woman stopped dead in her tracks before the flat white blob on the sidewalk that was surrounded by a litter of glass shards.

"Sorry," Remo called down. "Temperamental artist at work." Then he laughed again, low and raucously. He hadn't felt so good in years. And he had been so scared. Imagine. Over a stupid clay statue. So what if it was imbued by the spirit of the demon Kali? According to Chiun, Remo was the avatar of Shiva the Destroyer. Remo had never believed that. What the hell would Shiva be doing come back to earth as a Newark cop?

But if he was Shiva, obviously Shiva was mightier than Kali.

Remo left the hotel room laughing. He was free now. Really free. He could do whatever he wanted. No more CURE. No more Smith. Hell, he didn't even have to listen to Chiun's carping anymore.

"Free. Free. Freeee," he sang with drunken joy.

12

Remo Williams whistled as he rode the elevator to the lobby.

The cage stopped at the second floor, and a well-dressed man stepped aboard, a copy of *The Wall Street Journal* tucked under his summer jacket.

"Nice night, huh?" Remo said.

"Indeed," the man said dryly.

"On a night like this, you really understand what life is all about."

"And what is that?" The man sounded bored.

"Winning. Taking care of your enemies. Squeezing their soft doughy guts through your fingers. It doesn't get any better than that."

Eyeing Remo nervously, the man edged over to the safety of the elevator control panel. He pretended to finger a spot on the brass panel that was greasy with skin oils. His hand stayed close to the alarm button.

Remo resumed his whistling. He wasn't going to let some stiff who didn't understand what a glorious night this was ruin his good mood.

The cage deposited Remo in the lobby, where he found a pay phone and dropped a quarter in the slot.

"Mission," Remo said after Harold Smith picked up, "accomplished. Surprise. Surprise. Bet you thought I had deserted you."

"I knew you would not," Smith said without pretense.

"Sure, sure," Remo said. "You probably want my report, huh?"

"The target has been neutralized?" Smith asked cautiously.

"Sleeping the sleep of the dead," Remo said, humming. "And I got the statue."

"You did?" Smith said in an odd voice.

"It too has been neutralized, to use your quaint expression. In fact, to coin one of my own, I would say it's been mashed to a crisp."

"I am glad your mind is free of worry," Smith said, dismissing the matter of magical statues with his brittle tone, "but what about the target?"

"I told you—dead as a doornail. Where did that expression come from, anyway? I mean, what the heck is a doornail?"

"It is the metal attached to a knocker," Smith said. "One strikes it with the knocker."

"Is that so? Imagine that. Smith, I'm going to miss your dictionarylike personality. Your encyclopedic wit. Your—"

"Attention to details. Who was your target? What was her goal?"

"I think she had a grudge against Irugis."

"Iraitis. Irug is another country entirely."

"Irait. Irug. Irun. It's all the same. Except Irun. That's what I'm going to do now. Run. I don't know that I can take more than a week in Sinanju, but at least I gotta break the bad news to the villagers. If I'm lucky, they'll throw me out and I won't have to put up with them anymore either."

"Remo, who was this woman?"

"Called herself Kimberly. Had a mean way with a yellow silk scarf, too."

"And her last name?" Smith asked patiently.

"We never got that personal, Smitty. It's hard to get a complete biography when the target's trying to throttle you."

"She must have had personal identification."

Remo considered. "She did have a purse."

"Please, Remo, we have a dead Iraiti ambassador to explain. I must know who this woman is."

"Was. Dead as a doorknob now. But I'll admit she looks good. Natural, as the embalmers like to say."

"Remo, are you drunk?"

"Smitty," Remo clucked, "you know better than that. Alcohol would upset my delicate constitution. I'd end up on the slab next to poor Kimberly. Of course, a hamburger would do that. So would a hot dog. Even a good one."

"You sound unlike yourself."

"I'm happy, Smith," Remo confessed. "Really happy. I was scared for a while there. Scared because I was going up against something I didn't think I could handle alone. But I did. Kali was putty in my hands. So to speak. Damn. Should have used that line on her. Too late now."

"You are really happy?"

"Really," Remo said, scratching his initials in the pay phone's stainless-steel acoustical shield.

"Even with Chiun dead?"

Silence clogged the wire. Remo put a finishing flourish on the W for "Williams." His open, carefree expression froze, then darkened. Lines appeared. They etched themselves around his mouth, his eyes, his forehead.

"Smith," he said in a small voice, "you know exactly how to rain on my life, don't you, you cold-blooded son of a bitch?"

"That is better," Smith said. "Now I am speaking to the Remo I know."

"Fix this moment in your memory, because it may be the last," Remo warned. "I'm officially off the payroll."

"One last thing, Remo. The woman's identity."

"All right. If it's so important that you'd wreck my good mood, I'll root around in her purse."

"Good. I will remain here." Smith disconnected.

"Bastard," Remo muttered, hanging up the phone.

But by the time he returned to the eighth floor, he was humming.

Remo dug out the hotel key and used it. The door opened to the touch of his fingers. He hummed. The tune was "Born Free."

The moment he stepped across the threshold, the sound trailed away on a puzzled note.

Kimberly lay on the bed just as Remo had left her. Except her hands sat folded under her pyramidlike chest. He hadn't arranged her hands that way.

"What the hell?" Remo muttered.

He hesitated, his ears reaching for any telltale sound.

Somewhere, a heart beat. Remo zeroed in on the sound.

It was coming, he was more than astonished to realize, from the bed.

"Impossible," he blurted. "You're dead."

Remo glided across the rug, his heart beating a little high in his throat. His ebullient mood had evaporated. This was not possble. He had used an infallible technique to shatter her upper vertebrae.

Remo reached for the folded hands, intending to feel for a pulse. One wrist felt cool.

The indrawn breath came quick and sharp, sending the pyramid-sharp chest lifting. The innocent blue eyes snapped open. But they were not blue. They were red. Red from the core of their fiery pupils to the outer white, which was crimson. The orbs looked as if they had been dipped in blood.

"Jesus!" Remo said, jumping back reflexively.

Bending at the waist, the cool thing on the bed began to rise, yellow-nailed hands unfolded like poisonous flowers opening to the sun.

Remo watched them, mesmerized. And while his shocked brain registered the impossible, the corpse came upright.

The head swiveled toward him. It hung off to one side, as if from a neck crick. Her features were milk pale, the yellow eye shadow standing out like mold. The legs shifted to a sitting position.

"If you're auditioning for *Exorcist IV*," Remo cracked nervously, "you've got my vote."

"I . . . want . . . you," she said slowly.

The hands flashed up, reaching for her chest. The nails began tearing at the yellow fabric.

Remo caught them, one hand on each wrist.

"Not so fast," he said, trying to control a mounting fear. "I don't remember promising this dance to the girl with the bloodshot eyes. Why don't you—?"

The quip died in his throat. The wrists struggled in his unshakable grip. They were strong—stronger that human limbs should be. Remo centered his hands and let their opposing force work against itself. The wrists made circles in the air, Remo's hand still tightly attached. Every time they pushed or pulled, Remo carried the kinetic energy to a weak position. The result was a stalemate.

Still, the thing that had been Kimberly persisted, its angry red eyes fixed sightlessly on Remo, head tilted to one side like a blind, curious dog. The cool spidery fingers kept gravitating to its heaving chest.

"You don't take no for an answer, do you?" Remo said, trying to figure out how to let go without exposing himself to danger. Kimberly was no pushover.

The question stopped being important a moment later

when a familiar scent insinuated itself into Remo's nostrils like groping gaseous tentacles.

It smelled of dying flowers, musky womanhood, blood, and other impossible-to-separate odors commingled. The stuff slammed into his lungs like cold fire. His brain reeled.

"Oh, no," he croaked. "Kali."

And as his thoughts whirled between attack and escape, Kimberly's chest began heaving spasmodically. It convulsed and strained, and deep in the panicky recesses of Remo's mind an image appeared. It was a scene from an old science-fiction movie. He wondered why it jumped into his mind.

And then the front of Kimberly's yellow dress began a fury of rending, tearing cloth and Remo's horrified eyes went to the things that were breaking free.

And a familiar voice that was not Kimberly's snarled, *"You are mine! Mine! Mine! Mine!"*

13

Harold W. Smith waited an hour before he began worrying.

After two hours, he became concerned. It should not take Remo this long to go through a dead woman's purse.

Smith reached into his right-hand desk drawer and stripped foil from a sixty-nine-cent roll of antacid tablets, causing two tablets to drop into his waiting palm. He put them in his mouth and went to the office mineral-water dispenser. He thumbed the button. Cool water rilled into a paper cup. Smith swallowed the bitter tablets, chasing them with water. After checking for leaks, he returned the paper cup to its holder. It hadn't started to decompose from repeated use yet. He might get another month out of it.

Smith returned to his desk as the phone rang.

He reached for the blue phone, realizing his error when the ringing repeated itself after he lifted the receiver.

It was the red phone.

Smith switched the blue receiver to his other hand and snatched up the red one.

"Yes, Mr. President?" he said with muted embarrassment.

"The lid has come off," the President said tightly. "The Iraiti government wants to know where their ambassador is."

"This is not my area, but I would suggest you arrange a plausible accident."

"It may be too late. They've taken a hostage. A big one."

"Who?" Smith asked tightly.

"That anchorman, Don Cooder."

"Oh," Smith said in a tone of voice that didn't exactly convey relief, but certainly wasn't concerned.

"I won't miss him either," the President said, "but dammit, he *is* a high-profile U.S. citizen. We can't let these repeated provocations go unpunished."

"The decision to go to war rests with you, Mr. President. I have no advice to offer."

"I'm not looking for advice. I want answers. Smith, I know your man did his best to find the ambassador alive. The FBI tells me he was already cold before we left the gate. So that's that. But what the heck is behind it?"

"The ambassador appears to have fallen victim to a serial killer, who I am pleased to report was . . . ah . . . removed from the scene only within the last hour."

"Who, Smith?"

"A woman I am now trying to identify."

"You mean this wasn't political?"

"It does not appear to be," Smith told the President. "Naturally, I will reserve judgment until our investigation has been completed. But from all accounts, the perpetrator seems to have been affiliated with a dangerous cult that was all but neutralized several years back. Other, similarly strangled bodies, have turned up in Washington. Identical yellow scarves wound around the necks of each of the victims."

"A cult, you say?"

"A single woman, who is now dead. There is no reason to believe the cult is active."

"In other words," the President of the United States pressed, "we don't have any live scapegoat to hang this on?"

"I am afraid not," Smith admitted. "Our task is enforcement, not arranging subterfuges."

"No criticism was intended or implied."

"I know."

"Keep working, Smith. I'll get back to you. I'm convening an emergency cabinet meeting to discuss our response to the Iraitis."

"Good luck, Mr. President."

"I don't need luck. I need a goddamned miracle. But thanks anyway, Smith."

Harold Smith replaced the red receiver. He noticed he was still holding the blue one tightly in his other hand. It began emitting the off-the-hook warning beep. Smith replaced it hastily, thinking that he never used to be so absentminded. He hoped it was age, not Alzheimer's. For if his twice-yearly medical exam should ever reveal such a judgment-clouding prognosis, Harold Smith would be forced to make a call to the President of the United States informing him that CURE could no longer function as a secure arm of executive-branch policy.

It would be up to the commander in chief to decide whether Smith would have to be retired or CURE must shut down. If the latter, it would be up to Smith to close down the organization, wiping clean the massive data banks of the four computers hidden behind false walls in the Folcroft basement and taking a coffin-shaped poison pill that he carried in the watch pocket of his gray vest. For only three living persons knew of CURE. And to publicly admit that it even existed would be to admit that America itself didn't work. When the time came for the organization that didn't exist to vanish, all traces—human and technological—would also have to be obliterated. Only a grateful President would remember.

As for Remo Williams, the human superweapon Harold Smith had created, Smith had several ways of retiring him.

If Remo hadn't already abandoned America forever, which was a growing suspicion in Smith's mind.

His weak gray eyes went to the silent blue telephone.

He felt a vague apprehension, but not panic. There had been so many near-disasters in his thirty years as director of CURE that Smith could not summon up any panic. Perhaps, he thought, that was a bad thing. Fear had motivated him in the past, forcing him to go to superhuman extremes to fulfill his mission. Without fear, a man was too prone to let the tides of life swamp him. Smith wondered if he hadn't simply lost the fire in his belly and if that wasn't reason enough to make the termination call to the White House. . . .

14

"Mine! Mine! Mine!"

Two grasping hands exploded for Remo's throat like pale spiders with yellow feet, a banana-colored silk scarf strained between them.

Fighting the clogging miasma in his lungs, Remo released Kimberly's wrists. Or what he thought were her wrists.

He didn't know what to think. In the instant of time in which his mind was paralyzed by impossibility, his Sinanju-honed reflexes took over.

He got one attacking wrist, clamped hard on it. It felt solid. Whipping away the scarf, the opposite hand snapped it at his eyes. Remo ducked instinctively. He snared the other wrist by feel, and twisted it against the natural flex point.

That hand was solid too. Not illusionary. His furiously working brain had begun to question their reality.

A snarl blew hot breath into his face. And as Remo tightened his death grip, two more yellow-nailed hands snatched up the falling scarf and slipped it over his head.

It was happening faster than Remo could comprehend. He had had Kimberly by the wrists. Yet her hands had exploded toward him. He had grabbed them, and now the others were back, the phenomenon repeating itself like a nightmare record skipping. And an absurd thought welled up in his brain.

How many hands did Kimberly have, anyway?

"You will never escape me, Red One," the voice snapped.

"Wanna bet?"

Pivoting on one leg, Remo launched into a Sinanju Stork Spin, taking the girl with him.

Kimberly's feet left the floor. Her legs lifted from centrifugal force. The silken noose tightened around Remo's throat. He ignored it. This would take only a minute.

His eyes fixed on the spinning figure, Remo watched the room blur behind it. Kimberly was helpless in his grip, her body practically perpendicular to the spinning floor. He had her wrists for sure.

The trouble was, she had another pair of arms that were busily engaged in the serious task of throttling him.

Her eyes were hot orbs of blood. Her mouth contorted in a mirror image of the Kali statue's writhing snarl.

She hissed like a burst steam value.

As Remo watched, the wet scarlet color drained from her eyes.

That struck Remo as a cue, so he simply let go.

The silken noose around his neck jerked, and ripped free.

Threshing wildly, Kimberly struck the far wall with a spasmodic twitching of many white limbs. She collapsed to the rug like a broomed scorpion. Her eyes shut slowly, the red hue fading to a bald white like shelled eggs.

Remo moved in fast, ready to deal the coup de grace with a demolishing snapkick to the temple.

He stopped dead in his tracks.

The sight of Kimberly's now-tattered dressfront did it. It looked as if her brassiere had exploded, spilling white lace and heavy support wiring. Her breasts, pale and pink-nippled, hung from the torn bra. They were very small, practically breastlets.

Remo gaped stupidly, but not at the breasts that had proved to be almost nonexistent. Just under them, lying across her lap, was Kimberly's right arm. Remo registered its existence, noting the banana nail polish.

What made his jaw drop was a second right arm that lay straight out, cradling her crazily angled blond head.

A matched pair of left arms splayed over her left side like puppet limbs after the strings had been cut.

"Jesus Christ!" Remo exploded. "Four arms! She's got four frigging arms."

Hovering just out of striking range, as if before a venomous jungle insect, Remo eyed the bizarre collection of arms. The hidden pair was rooted just below the normal set. All twenty fingernails were painted banana yellow. They were otherwise ordinary arms. Obviously the lower set had been crossed inside her oversize brassiere, clutching the hidden scarf.

The sight made Remo shiver and think of the multiple-armed Kali statue and the terrible unearthly voice that had snarled up from Kimberly's throat.

Years ago he had first heard that voice. In his mind. Kali's voice. And it was Kali's scent in the room. It had been overpowering but even as it faded, Remo shook inside with an unreasoning fear of it. The thing with four arms had been Kimberly. And Kimberly had died. Then it had been Kali. Somehow the spirit of the statue had entered her dead shell and reanimated it.

Still, it was dead now. That was certain. Remo forced himself to approach, fascinated as if at the sight of a dead sea creature flung up on an ordinary beach. But no earthly ocean had spawned the thing that was Kimberly.

He knelt, lifting one bruise-yellow eyelid. The revealed pupil was slack, dilated as if in death.

"Funny," Remo muttered. "I thought they were a lighter blue."

His sensitive fingers felt no pulse of life, no hum of blood, no sensation of life coming through the lifted lid.

Kimberly was definitely dead.

"Little girl," Remo said with relief, "you've had a busy day."

The pupil imploded with life, iris turning cerulean blue to deep violet like splashing paint.

"It's not over yet!" Kali's hateful voice ripped out, and the overpowering smell shot into Remo's lungs like poison gas.

As if through a yellow haze, Remo fought back. But the hands were everywhere, in his face, at his throat, grabbing his wrists, pulling him down, overwhelming him, smothering him.

And in the haze, something was wrapped around his throat, something slick and slippery. And even though Remo Williams dimly understood what that was, and the danger it represented, he was helpless to resist it because the scent of Kali was stronger than his will.

"Who is putty now!" Kali mocked.

When Remo woke up, he was nude.

The dawn light was coming in through the chinks in the closed hotel-room drapery. A ray of sunlight fell across his eyes. He blinked, shaking his head, and tried to throw one arm across his face.

The arm hung up. Craning his neck, Remo saw the yellow silken fetters around his thick wrist.

His startled eyes went immediately to his crotch.

To his horror, he saw the encircling yellow scarf, and an evilly gleaming spot of red at the tip of his erect manhood. He was not greenish-black like the late Iraiti ambassador, but closer to purple.

Remo ripped one arm free. He pulled the other loose. Silk thread smoked and parted. He sat up. The yellow scarves around his ankles were anchored to the bedposts.

They snapped with a single rip of complaint when he retracted his legs.

Remo drew himself into a seated position on the bed. His eyes were bleary, and the ugly scent was like old mucus in his nostrils. Compressing his lips, he blew out through his nose, trying to force the detestable odor from his lungs, his senses, his very essense.

As he did so, he untied the yellow scarf at his crotch and revealed a deeply wound copper wire.

Breathing hard, centering his rhythms, Remo concentrated. His face turned red with exertion, his chest heaved as he forced the blood from every extremity to his solar plexus and from there downward.

His manhood quivered and quaked, expanding until the gleam of copper fell into shadow.

And the copper wire slowly, agonizingly, reluctantly parted, falling away under the inexorable flow of blood.

It was then that Remo looked more closely at the moist red blot he thought was a drop of blood. He saw that it was unmistakably in the shape of a woman's lip print. Lipstick.

And then he remembered how it had been. . . .

Remo jumped from the bed, calling her.

"Kimberly! Kimberly!"

No answer.

Then, louder, anguished, "Kimberly!"

He plunged into the bathroom, flung open the closet door. The hallway was empty as well. He grabbed up the room phone and dialed the other room, the one he had ransacked.

"Come on, come on," Remo said as the ring repeated itself like a mantra of bells. Getting no answer he slammed down the receiver. He scooped it up again and got the front desk.

"The woman in Room 606. Has she checked out yet?"

"Two hours ago," he was told.

Remo resisted an urge to go from room to room in a blind, futile searching for her. She would not be there. Her last words came back to him, echoing in his ears. The words he had heard after sinking helpless and spent into a languorous postcoital slumber.

"We are mated once more, Lord Shiva. You are mine forever. Seek me in the Caldron of Blood, and in blood we shall together revel, dancing the Tandava that crushes the bones and souls of men as one under our remorseless feet."

Putting his back to the hotel-room door, Remo looked down at himself. He was still erect. And it came to him why.

He wanted Kimberly. Yet he hated her, with her spidery arms that made his skin crawl. But those same hands had given him more pure pleasure in one night than all the women he had ever known combined.

He had been drugged by her sexual odor, manipulated by her cruel ways. And the very thought of her, the sight of her lipstick brand on him, made him harder, even as he felt his gorge rise in disgust.

Remo plunged into the shower and turned the water on full blast. He soaped himself clean, and when the smell seemed to have gone away, he switched to cold water.

When he stepped from the shower, he was nearly back to normal, his male tool swinging in normal repose.

He looked around the room. The bed was a mess. His clothes lay in a pile. He went to them, pulling on his pants, drawing his black T-shirt over his head. It was torn, as if by an animal. Remo remembered how they had fought to remove it in their fury of lovemaking, his hands and hers. All six plunging into passionate, unholy caresses.

When his shoes were back on his feet, Remo Williams started to leave. Something stopped him. He looked back at the bed. The urge to crawl into it, to wait for Kimberly's return, was growing. The urge to smell her horrible sexual scent was irresistible. He shut his eyes, trying to force the kaleidoscopic memories of their perfect orgy from his brain.

"Damn," Remo muttered. "What did she do to me?"

He returned to the bed and snatched up one of the yellow silk scarves. He pushed it under his nose and inhaled greedily.

The smell hit Remo's brain like a drug. He grabbed a wall for support.

And under his black pants, he could feel his erection return.

Remo stuffed his pockets full of yellow silk and stumbled from the room to the elevator. He walked with one hand hovering over his crotch to conceal the bulge.

Down in the lobby, a fortyish woman carrying a Scottish terrier under one arm was getting on as he was stepping off the elevator. She looked to his strategically placed hand and smiled.

"If you still have that problem around lunchtime, drop on by," she breathed. "Room 225."

"Screw you," Remo muttered.

Her laughing "Exactly what I had in mind" came through the closing steel door.

The cabby was very understanding of Remo's predicament. He asked if Remo had a destination in mind, or was he just planning to play with himself in the back seat?

"Because if you are, the fare's triple," he said. "I know this is Washington, but for that kinda consideration I gotta charge more."

"Airport," Remo said, pulling a length of silk from his pocket and holding it up to his nose.

"I know this place where they specialize in bondage," the cabby suggested as he pulled away from the curb, his eye on the rearview mirror and Remo.

Remo dug his fingers into the heavy mesh of the backseat partition. He squeezed all five fingers.

Grunk!

When he took his hand away, the mesh had a in it like a holed cobweb.

"Airport," he repeated.

"Which?"

"The nearest," Remo bit out. "Fast."

"You got it," the cabby promised. "Hope you don't lose your enthusiasm by the time I get you to her."

But Remo Williams wasn't listening. He was inhaling the sweet musky scent that to him meant pure sex, adoring the odor but hating himself with a deepening passion.

15

Kimberly Baynes woke up on her own hotel bed on the sixth floor of the Watergate Hotel with a stiff neck.

Her eyes tried to focus. The events of the day had come back to her. She had awoken late. The previous day's newspaper lay before Kali, as it always did. But instead of a ripped and ragged clipping, one hand clutched a brochure offering limo service to Dulles Airport that had previously rested on the writing desk.

Kimberly had gone to the airport, knowing that Kali would provide the victim. And the man in the black T-shirt had accosted her. And just in time, too. Her bra had been digging into her shoulders something fierce.

The last thing she could recall was that the man in the black T-shirt had been about to kill her. She knew intuitively that was his intent. The hand took her. And a silver light exploded within her frightened brain.

She remembered nothing after that. A warm breeze was coming in through the window, disturbing the maroon drapery. That was wrong. She never left the window open.

Kimberly sat up. First she noticed that all four hands were free. She remembered struggling to unleash the hidden pair with their tightly knotted yellow rumal when the silver light exploded.

So how had they gotten loose? And how had she gotten here?

"Kali will know," she whispered, turning to the nearby bureau.

But where her mistress had squatted, there was only emptiness. Only a moist spot on the polished dresser top and a single white elbow. Disconnected.

Kimberly jumped from the bed, her four arms reaching

out. She stepped on an already mashed hand, recoiling with a flutter of many hands.

"Oh, no! Mistress Kali! No."

All over the floor, the vessel of Kali lay in segments—maimed, dismembered. conquered.

Had she been conquered too?

No.

The voice came from deep inside her head.

"Hello?" Kimberly said aloud. "Is that you?"

Yes. I live.

"But your vessel—"

My temporary vessel. You are my vessel, Kimberly Baynes, my intended vessel. I have been preparing you just as you have nurtured the clay that housed my spirit. I gave you the body of a woman years before your rightful time, and so you are a woman in fact. You are my avatar. I am your soul.

Kimberly sank to her knees on the rug. Four yellow-nailed hands assumed prayful shapes. Her eyes closed, her face tilted toward the white plaster sky of the ceiling.

"I know, I've known it ever since—"

Ever since your breasts grew and the nub of Kali's nether limbs sprouted from your sides. Clay is only clay. It served its purpose. I blessed you with two of my many arms, the better for you to work my will. You and I are destined to be one.

Kimberly frowned. "Where are you, anyway?"

"Inside you. A seed. I am but a seed which germinates in the dark loam of your soul. In time, I will sprout. We will grow together, you and I, Kimberly Baynes. And at the foretold time, we shall flower as one. You must obey me until then."

"What do I do, my mistress?" Kimberly asked.

You must go to the Caldron of Blood.

"Where is that?"

The Caldron of Blood is not a place. It is a hell you and I will create together, in a land far from here. And when it begins to bubble, He shall come.

"He?"

Our enemy, my mate, your murderer and lover in one.

Kimberly's eyes went wide.

"I'm not a virgin anymore!"

He lusts for us both now. He will seek us out. And He will find us—but only after we have stirred the blood in the Caldron and the world careens toward the Red Abyss.

Kimberly Baynes fought back tears of shame. "I obey."

An insistent knocking came from outside the hotel door.

Kimberly climbed to her feet.

"Who is it?" she called, folding two pairs of hands over her exposed breasts.

"Hotel security. Are you all right in there?"

"Yes. Why?"

"Because there's some kinda clay head down on the sidewalk with pieces of your window in it. I'm going to have to come in."

"One minute," Kimberly said. "Let me get my scarf . . . I mean, my robe."

The door opened only long enough for the hotel security man to catch a good look at a pair of naked breasts, and more hands that he expected pulled him into the room and wrapped something tight around his throat.

"She loves it!" Kimberly cried exultantly. "Don't you?"

I love it. Don't forget his wallet.

16

Mrs. Eileen Mikulka had been executive secretary to Dr. Harold W. Smith for a nearly a decade.

She had seen a great many unusual sights in that time. One had to expect the unusual when one worked in a private hospital that included warehousing the deranged. She had gotten used to the occasional escapee, the padded rooms, and the straitjacketed patients who sometimes howled their madness in voices so frightful they carried over to the administration wing of Folcroft Sanitarium.

There was nothing unusual about the man who abruptly appeared before her desk asking to see Dr. Smith in an urgent tone.

She looked up, one hand going to her modest décolletage.

"Oh! You surprised me, Mr. . . ."

"Call me Remo. Tell Smith I'm here."

"Please take a seat," Mrs. Mikulka said crisply, lifting her chain-hung glasses off her chest and placing them on her nose.

"I'll stand."

"Fine," Mrs. Mikulka said as she reached for the intercom. "But you needn't stand so close to the desk." She recognized the man now. He had once worked for Dr. Smith in some menial capacity. He was an infrequent visitor. Mrs. Mikulka was under the impression he had once been a patient. It would explain the urgent look on his face and the unnerving way he stood right up to the edge of the desk. He leaned over, both hands resting on her blotter.

Those eyes made Mrs. Mikulka shiver. They were the deadest, coldest eyes she had ever seen. Even if they did look a little haunted.

"Yes, Mrs. Mikulka?" came the crisp, reassuring voice of Dr. Smith through the tinny out-of-date intercom.

"I have a . . . gentleman named Remo here. He has no appointment."

"Send him in," Dr. Smith said instantly.

Mrs. Mikulka looked up. "You may go in now."

"Thanks," the man said, edging around the desk to scuttle toward the door.

What on earth is that man's problem? she asked herself as he abruptly spun and sidled through the door with his back to her.

She shrugged, returned her glasses to her chest, and resumed her inventory work. It seemed the commissary was dangerously low on prune-whip yogurt, Dr. Smith's favorite. She would have to order more.

Dr. Smith watched Remo enter the office with owlish interest. The door snapped open. Remo slipped in quickly, dropping to the long leather divan that sat next to the door in a fluid, unbroken motion. He crossed his legs quickly. His face was crimson.

Smith adjusted his rimless glasses curiously. "Remo?"

"Who else?" Remo said, pushing the door closed with his hand from his seated position.

"Is something wrong?"

"We gotta find her!"

"Who?"

"Kimberly."

Smith blinked. "I thought she was . . ."

"She's not. And she got away."

"What happened?"

"I just told you!" Remo said hotly. "I went back. She wasn't dead. She got away from me. End of story. Now we gotta find her. And don't just sit there looking befuddled. Get those computers of yours going. This is an emergency."

"One moment," Smith said firmly, coming from behind his desk. He crossed the Spartan, slightly shabby office in less than a dozen long-legged strides.

Standing over Remo, Smith saw his flushed features, his harried expression, and the way he hugged his folded leg into his lap. The body language was wrong. This was not Remo's body language, he thought. Remo was casual, if not cocky.

"Remo, what you have just told me makes no sense whatsoever," Smith said in a level no-nonsense voice.

"It's what happened," Remo said tightly. "Now, are you going to do your job so I can do mine, or do I have to plant you back in that seat and hold your hands through the early steps?"

Remo's dark eyes locked on Smith's. Dr. Smith's gray orbs met them unflinchingly.

"You told me she was dead," Smith persisted.

"My mistake."

"Everyone makes mistakes," Smith said in a reasonable tone. "So you went back, found her alive, and she eluded you? Is that it?"

"That's as much as you need to know," Remo growled, averting his eyes.

"I need to know her identity. You were going back for her ID. Did you find it?"

"No," Remo said flatly. He adjusted his folded leg. Smith recalled that Remo usually folded his with one ankle resting on the opposite knee, his bent leg forming a triangle with the thigh in repose. An open-legged cross.

Today, however, Remo crossed his right leg over his left one. A more defensive cross. Not Remo's style. Not even in the early days before he had learned Sinanju.

"Remo," he began evenly, "for as long as I have known you, you've never struck a fatal blow that did not turn out to be fatal. As long as I have known you, you have never mistaken a live body for a dead one. What have you to say to that?"

Remo shrugged. "Hey. I was having a bad night, okay?"

"You are a professional," Smith went on with unrelenting logic. "You are the heir to the House of Sinanju. You do not make these kinds of mistakes. Now, tell me, what happened when you went back to Kimberly's hotel room?"

Remo's hard eyes held Smith's as a play of emotions raced across Remo's face—anxiety, anger, impatience, and hovering behind them all, something else. Something Smith had never seen on Remo's face.

When Remo looked down to the floor, Harold Smith realized what it was. Embarrassment.

"We had sex," Remo admitted in a dull voice. "After she . . . died."

Smith swallowed. It was not the answer he had expected. He adjusted his tie.

"Yes?" he prompted.

"Maybe I should back up." Remo sighed. "I went back. She wasn't dead. I know I did her, but she wasn't dead. Not anymore. She attacked me."

"And?"

"She was too much for me."

"Are you serious? A call girl?"

"She wasn't a call girl anymore. She wasn't Kimberly anymore."

"What was she, then?" Smith asked.

"Kali. Or a puppet of Kali's. I know the spirit of Kali had been in the clay statue. I smelled her scent before I destroyed it. Then I smelled it from that . . . thing."

"Thing? What thing?"

"Kimberly," Remo said, still looking at the floor.

"Why do you call her that?"

"She had four . . . arms, Smitty."

"Kimberly?" Smith's voice was thin with uncertainty.

"Just like the statue. Except Kimberly's arms were alive. They tried to strangle me. I fought. Thought I beat her. But she jumped me. Then that smell came again. Just like the last time. I could fight her, but I couldn't fight the smell, Smitty." Remo looked up. His eyes were hurt. "It touched something deep in me. Something that Chiun had always warned me about."

"The Shiva delusion?"

"I don't know what you'd call it," Remo admitted. "But she called me Shiva too. If Kimberly wasn't Kali, how would she know to call me that? And if she was Kali, what does that make me?"

"Kali is a mythical being, as is Shiva. They have no basis in reality, no connection with you."

"Explain the four arms," Remo retorted. "The statue. I heard its voice, saw it move. Explain the best sex I ever had."

"Sex?"

"She had four arms. She was incredible. I never experienced anything like it. You know the curse of Sinanju—mechanical, boring connect-the-dots sex. It was different with Kimberly. I couldn't get enough."

"Remo, there is only one explanation for all this," Smith said flatly.

"Yeah?"

"A hallucinogenic drug."

"I know what I know," Remo growled.

Smith put his hands in his trouser pockets.

"Hallucinogens induced in gas form could account for everything you have just described," he went on. "If fact, it is the only possible explanation, which you will see, once you calm down."

"Do hallucinogens cause permanent hard-ons?"

"Excuse me?"

"You heard me."

"I rather doubt it," Smith said dryly.

"Then why can't I uncross my legs in mixed company?" Remo snapped.

Smith swallowed again. This time he nervously adjusted his rimless glasses instead of his tie. He retreated to his desk. Pressing the concealed stud, he brought his computer terminal up to view, where it offered its keyboard like an unfolding tray of white chocolates.

Smith attacked the keyboard.

"What are you doing?"

"I am beginning a trace of this woman Kimberly. That is what you want, is it not?"

"Yeah," Remo said thickly. He did not sound enthusiastic.

Smith looked up. "Are you prepared to execute my orders, Remo?"

"I guess so."

"Are you prepared to terminate this woman if the order is given?"

"No," Remo admitted.

"Why not?"

"Because I think I'm in love with her," Remo said miserably, slowly withdrawing a long length of yellow silk from his pocket. He brought it up to his nose and began to sniff it, his eyes growing avid and sick all at once.

17

The customs inspector zipped open the shoulder bag with a fierce rip of his arm.

"Any contraband?" he demanded, not looking up.

"No," said Kimberly Baynes, holding her chin in one hand, as if in thought. It was the best way to keep her broken-necked head vertical.

"Alcohol? This is a Moslem country. No alcohol is allowed to enter."

"I'm not carrying any alcohol."

"Drugs?"

"No."

"Pornography?"

"Of course not."

The inspector pulled out a fistful of yellow silk scarves. He looked up, his dark sloe eyes questioning.

"So many. Why so many?" he demanded.

"It's an American custom."

"Explain."

"When we have hostages, it's customary to tie a yellow ribbon around a tree. These are my yellow ribbons."

The inspector considered this explanation. Wordlessly he stuffed the yellow tendrils of silk back into the bag and without zipping it closed returned it to Kimberly Baynes.

"Entry allowed," he said gruffly. "Three months. You must not work in that time and you cannot take more money from our country than you brought with you."

He stamped her passport with a pounding jerk of his rubber stamp, saying, "You are hereby permitted to enter Hamidi Arabia. Next!"

The bazaars in the Hamidi Arabian capital of Nehmad teemed with humanity. Arab men in flowing white *thobes* and headdresses tied with plaited ropelike *agals* moved like the lords of the desert. The women, mostly in black *abayuhs* that masked them from head to toe, gave silently before them, their eyes evasive and mysterious.

And joking and laughing U.S. servicemen and women moved through the spectral Arabs in twos and threes for protection, buying fruit from the stalls and sipping soft drinks to fend off dehydration.

Still carrying her bag, Kimberly returned their smiles and winks as they passed. Suggestions that she join them for a Coke were politely declined.

She wanted nothing from any of them. The person she needed to fill the Caldron with blood would show herself. Kali had promised her this. And Kali never lied.

Specialist Carla Shaner still couldn't believe she was in Hamidi Arabia.

Only a few weeks ago she had been a paralegal in Hingham, Massachusetts. Her Army Reserve status was good for nearly five thousand dollars per year in supplemental income—this in return for the weekend training sessions and a month each summer at Fort Devens.

When the call-up came, she had been scared. But her unit was not a combat unit. Their job was military justice, and the very fact that she had suddenly found herself stationed in Hamidi Arabia told her that the United States government had expected to be running war-crimes tribunals.

And since the U.S. Army didn't try war criminals until there had been a war, she had existed in a state of low-level apprehension, certain hostilities were about to break out.

Today her concern was the terrorist threat. U.S. service personnel had been warned that every time they entered the capital they were at risk to pro-Iraiti terrorist attack.

She walked through the bazaar with her eyes open. Despite the brutal heat, her sleeves were rolled down and her regulation blouse was buttoned up to the top button in deference to the sensitive Hamidi mores. She had been told to watch out for the Mutawain—the Hamidi religious police, who could insist upon her deportation for offenses ranging from holding hands with a man in public to brazenly displaying her seductive ankles.

Carla thought it was all a bunch of crap, but at least she

didn't have to wear one of those medieval *abayahs*. They looked hot.

Few U.S. civilians prowled the bazaars these days, so Carla was surprised to see a blond woman in a flowing yellow chiffon dress walking through the dirty street like a Fifth Avenue mirage.

Carla walked up to her, smiling. An American woman to talk to. This was better than a letter from home.

The blond was quick to smile. Carla liked her smile. Of course she was from America, the blond said.

"Oh, where?" Carla asked, barely containing her glee.

"Denver."

"I'm from Massachusetts!" Carla burbled, thinking: Any port in a sandstorm.

They found a Pizza Sheikh whose English sign was repeated in Arabic, and swapped stories while the ice-choked Cokes kept coming and the blazing Arabian sun descended to the superheated desert sand.

Carla learned that Kimberly was twenty-two, a reporter with the *Denver Post*, and had a "crick" in her neck from sitting too close to the air conditioner on the flight over. Carla thought the way her head kept lolling to the left was more than a crick, but let it pass.

Kimberly asked a lot of boring questions about Carla's job, her unit, the distance to the neutral zone, and other reporter-type questions. When she could get a word in edgewise, Carla asked about home—now broadly defined as the continental U.S.—and hung on every answer.

Strange how fascinating it all was, after so many months stuck in the sand.

Finally Carla stood up, saying, "Listen, this has been great, but I gotta get on the bus back to the base."

"Is that where you're stationed?" Kimberly Baynes asked.

"Yeah, and it's a three mile-ride. If I miss my bus, I gotta walk. No, thank you," she laughed.

"I'll escort you to the bus," Kimberly offered.

"Fine by me."

They walked through the cooling dusk. Sand blew in the air. Sand always blew in the Hamidi Arabian air. The sun was sinking, a breathtaking ball of smoldering fire.

And somewhere between the Pizza Sheikh and the dusty street corner where a khaki bus waited, Kimberly offered Carla Shaner her yellow silk scarf.

"Oh, no. I couldn't take that," Carla protested, laughing.

But Kimberly refused to take no for an answer. She even insisted on tying it around Carla's neck for her.

"Over here," Kimberly said, gently pulling her into an alley. "There's more light over here."

Actually, Carla found, there was less light in the alley. That was where it got cloudy. Then fuzzy. Then dark. Very dark.

When Carla Shaner's uniform left the alley, she was no longer wearing it. She lay in the dark alley with her moist purplish tongue collecting windblown sand the way an ice cream cone collects jimmies.

The yellow scarf encircled her throat, tied in an intricate knot that the Royal Hamidi Police were later forced to cut with a knife in frustration.

Kimberly Baynes caught the last bus to the base. More than one serviceman's eyes bugged out at the sight of her generous, button-straining bust. She sat with her arms modestly folded over her chest. One hand covered her name tag.

The Star in the Center of the Flower of the East Military Base lay three miles north of the Hamidi Arabian capital city of Nehmad. For nearly a year it had been under a joint Hamidi Arabian/U.S. command. For all that time it had remained in a state of high alert.

In theory, this was a symbol of U.S./Arabian cooperation. In practice, it meant no one was in charge.

So every twelve hours, the command structure was rotated. The U.S. general would grumblingly vacate his office and Prince General Sulyman Bazzaz of the Royal Hamidi Armed Forces and his aides would take up residence. The official language of the base became Arabic and the guards were changed at the main gate.

Which, at sundown, meant that a quartet of Hamidi Arabian sergeants huddled in the guardshack playing backgammon and chewing sweet dates.

When they heard the approaching bus from the capital, one poked his blue-bereted head out and saw that it was the American bus. He waved it through without checking. He was not afraid of infiltrators or terrorists. Not with the mighty American Army there to protect him, praise Allah.

Thus did Kimberly Baynes penetrate the Star in the Center of the Flower of the East Military Base.

Hours later, she left in a wide Humvee—the jeep's wide-bodied descendent—which she had commandeered from a swaggering Hamidi corporal by putting her ample chest under his nose and strangling him with a length of yellow silk used as a ligature as he contemplated her bursting buttons.

Kimberly was stopped at the gate as she drove up to it.

"What is your business?" the sergeant in charge of the gate asked her in his native tongue.

"I don't speak Arabic," Kimberly said patiently, bathing the sergeant in the sweet radiance of her American smile.

And while the sergeant went into the guardshack to get the Sergeant in Charge of Speaking English, Kimberly gunned the Humvee and sent it running along the undulating dips and rises of the benighted Hamidi Arabian desert. No one followed.

She drove north. Toward the border and occupied Kuran.

And in the back of her racing mind, a small hollow voice said: *Well done, my chosen vessel. Well done.*

"Thank you."

But next time, remember to kill your victims more slowly. For it is not the dead that I truly love, but the dying.

18

Maddas Hinsein, President of the Republic of Irait, field marshal of the Iraiti Armed Forces, and self-styled Scimitar of the Arabs, entered the simple conference room dressed in an olive-green general's uniform and black beret like a sullen bull moose walking upright.

His Revolting Command Council jumped to their feet, their arms stiffening at their sides, their eyes identical dark pools of fear.

"Sit," said President Hinsein, and his Revolting Command Council slammed their rumps into the hard wooden chairs with coccyx-threatening force.

Under his bristly mustache, President Hinsein smiled.

Under their identically brushy mustaches, his Revolutionary Command Council smiled, showing flashing white teeth and bringing fear wrinkles to their eyes.

After ascertaining there were no poisoned tacks on his chair, the President sat, saying, "Give me your status reports."

"The Americans are too afraid to attack, Precious Leader," said the defense minister, praying that the Americans would not bomb until after the meeting was over. He did not mind being bombed. He just did not want to be in the same room with Maddas Hinsein when the B-52's roared overhead. There were worse things than bombs.

"And the cowardly Hamidi Arabians?" he asked of his information minister. His voice was subdued. Grave without being worried.

The information minister smiled a sick little smile as he spoke.

"Cowering behind the trembling American defensive line," said the information minister, who knew full well that elite Hamidi Arabian forces were dug in at forward positions less than a mile below the Kuran–Hamidi Arabian neutral zone, along with units of French, British, Spanish, Greek, and Tahitian troops. It was rumored the Italians had taken a wrong turn in Egypt but would be on station no later than the turn of the century.

He dared not tell the President that this was no longer a case of the U.S. supporting the soft, weak Hamidis, but virtually the entire world now encircling their beleaguered country.

"Excellent," said the President. "It is time to gather intelligence for the day."

And each man felt his heart leap into his throat like a frisky salmon as the President of Irait reached for the dreaded black device and aimed around the table, clicking the button.

Even though it was only a TV remote-control unit, such was their fear of the Scimitar of the Arabs that they each flinched by turns. Maddas Hinsein smiled appreciatively at each flinch. He had been the palace torturer to the previous President, whom he tortured into abdicating.

When the remote unit triggered the big-screen TV at the far end of the room, under the twelfth-century fresco of the Arab hero Nebuchadnezzar riding a chariot, they turned their heads as one to behold the soul-freezing CNN logo, their only source of hard intelligence—and the one thing that could get them all hanged as traitors should the President choose to believe the wrong reports.

More than one hand stole under the table to manually choke off an imminent liquid accident.

A woman newscaster appeared on the screen. Though her words were in English, Arabic subtitles reflected her report.

"The United Nations joint command today reported that the array of forces now numbering units from virtually every standing army of the world, less Italy, are only three months away from hammering out a workable command structure."

"Lies," President Hinsein smiled. "Flimsy propaganda."

"Lies. Yes, lies. Transparent fabrications." The murmurs of agreement rippled around the long table. Laughter came easily.

"In Washington, Reverend Juniper Jackman, perennial presidential candidate and shadow senator to the District of Columbia, announced that he would go to Abominadad and attempt to win the release of BCN news anchor Don Cooder, now in his fourth day of captivity."

"Tender the Reverend Jackman an invitation to visit Abominadad," the President told his information minister.

"Yes, Precious Leader. Shall I have him detained?"

"No," muttered President Hinsein. "He is an ass-kisser. I do not arrest those who understand where to place their lips."

"Of course."

And every man in the room made a mental note of their President's pronouncement. If there was one good thing about Maddas Hinsein, it was that he spoke his mind exactly.

The report continued.

"In other news today, the citizens of La Plomo, Missouri, today held a rally in support of U.S. hostages in Irait and occupied Kuran, tying yellow ribbons around every tree in the tiny farm community, struggling to return to normalcy after last spring's catastrophic poison-gas-storage accident."

His chin cupped in his strong hands, his elbows on the table, Maddas Hinsein narrowed his liquid brown eyes at the words.

This warning signal went unnoticed because all eyes were on the TV screen and the flickering images of U.S. farmers busily tying yellow ribbons around a huge oak tree.

They were shouting at the top of their lungs.

"Mad Ass Mad Ass Mad Ass."

"See?" Maddas Hinsein crowed. "Even the American farmers support me. They despise their criminal government for denying them the right to sell their grain to the proud but hungry Iraiti people. It is just like Vietnam was. A bottomless pit of sand."

No one dared contradict the President. They knew, whereas their leader did not, that Americans had learned a bitter lesson in Vietnam and would go to any length to avoid repeating the experience. Including pulverizing storied Abominadad.

Then the camera panned to an obvious caricature of Maddas Hinsein hanging from a noose. A boy in a green-and-brown-checkered shirt brushed the straw-stuffed effigy with a lighted torch. Licking flames crawled up its legs. In moments the effigy was blazing.

The cry "Mad Ass Mad Ass Mad Ass" swelled.

And every sweaty face along both sides of the conference table jerked back to take in their President's reaction.

Maddas Hinsein leapt to his feet, hands gripping the table

edge, ready for anything. A few more attempted to choke off bladder releases by crossing their legs.

"Why do they call my name so strangely?" Hinsein demanded. "Do they not know how to pronounce my name, which is revered by all Islam and feared by the infidels who dwell beyond Dar al-Harb?"

No one answered at first. Then, seeing the growing darkening of their leader's face, everyone attempted to answer at once.

Maddas Hinsein brought order to the room by whipping out his sidearm and waving the muzzle at every face. Hands that had been under the table surfaced. The trickle of running water came. No one wanted to be mistaken for an assassin with a concealed pistol—the chief reason that the Revolting Command Council met around a large square table with almost no top other than a thin border around the edge.

Silence clamped down like an aural eclipse. The weapon stopped pointing at the information minister, who wore a military-style uniform and about a gallon of sweat where his face should be.

"You. Tell me."

"They are making fun of your name, Scimitar of Islam," he said in a shaking voice.

"Maddas *is* my name."

"In English, 'mad' means something else."

Maddas Hinsein's meaty face gathered in puzzlement.

"What?"

"It means 'angry.' "

"And the other word?" Maddas asked slowly.

"This word, O Precious Leader, has the same sound as the backside of a man."

Maddas Hinsein blinked his deadly emotionless eyes.

"Angry Ass?" he said in English.

The information minister swallowed. "Yes," he admitted.

"Me?" he said, pointing at his chest with his own gun. Everyone silently beseeched Allah for the gun to discharge and preserve Irait from this madman. It did not.

"Yes," the information minister repeated.

Maddas Hinsein threw his head to one side, thinking. His eyes crinkled. His mouth gave a meaty little pucker.

"I have heard this English word," President Hinsein said slowly. "Somewhere. But it did not mean 'angry.' "

The gun whipped back toward the information minister. "It means 'crazy'!" he snarled.

The Revolting Command Council gasped as one.

"Both!" the information minister bleated. "It means both!"

"You lie! How can a word mean two things?"

"The American are like this! Two-faced! Is it not so?" the information minister asked of the room.

The Revolting Command Council was silent. No one knew the safe answer, so no one spoke.

And getting no response, the President turned his pistol toward a perspiring general. "Answer this. Does 'mad' mean 'angry' or 'crazy'?"

" 'Crazy,' " the general said quickly, hoping he would not be shot dead in the face.

He was not.

The President said, "Thank you." Then he shot the information minister in the face. The man's head snapped back with such force that it carried him and his hardwood chair backward.

The information minister's body jerked and quivered like a convict in an electric chair that had fallen over.

Calmly the President of Irait holstered his pistol, muttering solemnly "I will not accept lies to my face." He sat down. "So," he added, "the Americans think I am a crazy ass, no?"

"Allah will punish them," said the defense minister, not looking at the quivering body.

President Hinsein patted down the luxurious mustache that was repeated on every male face over the age of fifteen throughout the land. His solemn eyes grew reflective.

"Crazy Ass," he muttered.

"They insult all Arabs with such talk," spat the defense minister bitterly.

"Crazy Ass," repeated the President thoughtfully.

"We will pass a law condemning to death any who repeat this slander," a general vowed.

"Crazy Ass," Maddas said again. And he began laughing. "Maddas Hinsein, Scourge of the Arabs," he cried. "Scimitar of Arabia. Uniter of the Arab Nation. That is me. I am one crazy-assed Arab, am I not?"

"Yes, President," the assembled Revolting Command

Council said in well-rehearsed unison, "you are one crazy-assed Arab."

He threw his head back and gave vent to an uproarious peal of mirth. Tears squeezed from the corners of his amused eyes.

The others joined in. Some tittered. Others guffawed. But no one refused to join in, though their laughter was not reflected in their eyes. Their eyes, instead, were sick with fear.

With a final burst of laughter, Maddas Hinsein settled down. He brushed his mustache. His strong chin found his folded hands once more as his elbows took their usual positon on the table edge. A serious, intent expression settled over his dark, troubled features.

"I will show them what a crazy ass I am," he said darkly. "Issue the following proclamation through our Propaganda Ministry."

No one moved. When Maddas Hinsein saw that no hand picked up pen to transcribe his all-important words, he said, "Where is the minister of information?"

"Dead," he was told.

"You have shot him."

Maddas Hinsein peered past the man who last spoke. He saw the twitching knee in the air.

"He is not dead. He still moves," Maddas pointed out.

"He is dying."

"Until he is dead, he is not excused from his patriotic duty. Give him pen and paper."

The defense minister hastily obeyed, crushing the information minister's oblivious fingers around a pen and slipping a sheet of paper in the other hand. As his leader began to drone on in a monotone, he did not worry about the lack of animation on the dying man's part.

There was no ink in the pen. Irait had run out of ink in the fifth month of the international blockade, when it had been discovered that ink made an acceptable salad dressing.

Previously, they had pissed on their salads.

19

Harold Smith paused at the door and cleared his throat before knocking briskly.

"Come in," Remo Williams said. Smith entered.

He found Remo seated cross-legged on a tatami mat in the middle of the bare floor, a half-eaten bowl of rice at one knee. Across the room, a TV set flickered and a world-famous face filled the screen. The rugged face was showing signs of strain, especially under the eyes. The dark pouches hung almost to his chin.

"This is Don Cooder, BCN anchor reporting live from Abominadad, Irait, reminding you that BCN was first to report from Abominadad, first with an exclusive interview with President Hinsein, and now we're proud to be the first to have an anchor taken hostage. BCN. We're here so you don't have to be."

"I hate that guy," Remo muttered, lowering the sound with a wave of his remote.

"He is not very popular," Smith said dryly.

"He was the jerk who helped that dipshit girl with the neutron bomb—Purple Haze or whatever her name was—get a working core just so he could boost his ratings," Remo said bitterly. "Chiun might still be here if he hadn't stuck his oar in. I hope he rots in Abominadad."

"Are you feeling any . . . um . . . better?" Smith inquired.

"Step around and take a look," Remo said. "But I warn you, it's not a pretty sight."

Coloring, Smith declined the invitation.

"The FBI laboratory results on the silk scarf came in," he offered.

"Yeah?" Remo grunted, shifting the mat around to face Smith. He kept one hand draped strategically across his lap.

"Other than human perspiration odors and other common organic chemical traces, they report no unusual odors attached to the sample."

"No? Well, their machines must all have broken noses or something, because the thing reeks of her."

"I smelled nothing when I took the scarf from you," Smith said firmly.

"Yeah, well, take a whiff of this," Remo said, snapping another scarf from his pocket. He sniffed it once before tossing it to Smith. Smith caught it and distastefully brought it to his pinched face. He sniffed shortly and lowered the cloth.

"I smell nothing. Absolutely nothing."

"See a doctor about that cold," Remo said, yanking the scarf back with a sudden jerk. He held it close to his nose, Smith saw. Remo's eyes reminded him of his own daughter's, back in the terrible days before she kicked her heroin habit. He shuddered inwardly at the smothering memory.

Smith adjusted his tie.

"I have other news."

"You find her?"

"No. But I know who she is now."

"She's Kali."

"Her name is Kimberly Baynes. There has been a nationwide APB out for her for nearly a month. It is believed she was abducted by a sex maniac who slew her grandmother and a next-door neighbor."

"Tells us nothing," Remo said dismissively.

"On the contrary, Remo, Kimberly Baynes is the only surviving offspring of the late president of Just Folks Airlines, A. H. Baynes III."

"Another dynasty falls," Remo said bitterly.

"I cannot pretend to understand it, but obviously the girl retains some memories of the Thuggee cult to which her family belonged."

"What's the big deal? If you had been forced to join a cult that strangled travelers for their wallets, it would leave an impression even on you."

"Kimberly," Smith said, "was only eight when she was liberated from the cult. That would make her thirteen now."

Remo snorted. "Thirteen? She was twenty if she was a day."

"Records do not lie. She is thirteen."

"She had the body of a twenty-year-old. She was twenty. Maybe nineteen. I'm not into kiddie humping, Smith."

"I am not suggesting you are. What I am trying to say is this. Kimberly did not have four arms. I have seen her school medical records. They are very clear on this point."

"I told you—"

Smith's hand shot up.

"Let me finish, please," he said. "I have checked with the Watergate Hotel. The woman they describe as Kimberly Baynes—she used that name when she registered —was clearly more than thirteen years old. That leads to only one conclusion. That this woman is impersonating the abducted girl for some unfathomable reason."

"It fits. So who is she?"

"I have no idea. An FBI forensics team has checked her room for fingerprints. They are not on record. But I do have something to show you."

"Yeah, what?"

"This," Smith said, holding out a sheet of fax paper. Remo took it.

"That's her," Remo said, looking at a charcoal sketch of the woman he knew as Kimberly. His dark eyes lingered on the image.

"You are certain?"

Remo nodded. "Where'd you get this?" he asked, returning the sheet.

"FBI artist's sketch," Smith said, folding the sheet and returning it to an inner pocket. "It was constructed after extensive interviews with the hotel staff."

"Oh," Remo said in a disappointed voice. "So that's it? You came here just to tell me you have zip?"

"No, I've come to suggest that in your current state, it might be better if you do not prowl the Folcroft corridors. The staff are becoming nervous and inquisitive. I would like to suggest you return home."

"No chance. He's just waiting for me."

"I cannot understand this belief of yours, Remo. The Master of Sinanju is deceased. The dead do not trouble the living."

"Tell that to Chiun."

"I wonder if this is not merely a manifestation of your extreme grief. Your relationship with Chiun was a combative one. Are you certain you are not projecting your grief onto an empty house?"

Remo stood up, his lower legs lifting his body with a scissors motion. Smith averted his eyes with embarrassment.

"Why are you asking me all these idiot questions instead of doing your job?"

"I *am* doing my job. The security of CURE depends on the inner circle of agents—you and I, as matters now stand—being effective."

"Don't sweat my end. Find Kimberly before she starts this Caldron of Blood she warned me about."

Smith's eyes flicked to the silent TV screen.

"Is that why you are monitoring the Iraiti situation?"

"Know any other global tinderboxes?" Remo growled.

"Yes. Cambodia. Russia. And China. Among others."

"None of which are steamed up about a missing ambassador. What's Washington planning, by the way?"

"I do not know." Smith turned to go. "I will inform you once my computers have traced this Kimberly Baynes impostor. In the meantime, I would ask that you remain in this room as much as possible."

"Count on it," Remo snapped, dropping back into his lotus position. He tapped the remote. The sound came up.

"Day Four," the voice of Don Cooder intoned. "As I greet this new day, possibly the first of many that might be as countless as the desert sands themselves, I ask myself this one question: What would Walter Cronkite do in a situation like this? . . ."

"He'd say 'Get a life,' " Remo told the unresponsive TV screen as the door silently closed after a troubled Harold Smith.

20

Kimberly Baynes drove as deep into occupied Kuran as the Humvee's gas tank would allow. When it coasted, grumbling and sputtering, to a stop, she shouldered her bag and began walking.

She came upon a detachment of uniformed Iraiti troops performing "security operations" in an outpost town.

Security operations in this case consisted of dismantling the smaller buildings and loading them onto trucks as the weeping women and children watched helplessly.

The larger buildings were being systematically dynamited. But only because they would not fit into the sand-painted military trucks. They jackhammered the street signs loose and tossed them in with the dismantled houses. Even the asphalt sidewalks were chewed into hot black chunks and thrown in.

Kimberly walked up to the nearest Iraiti soldier and said, "I surrender."

The Iraiti soldier turned, saw Kimberly's U.S. uniform, and shouted over to his commanding officer in incomprehensible Arabic.

"I surrender," Kimberly repeated. "Take me to Abominadad. I know the secret U.S. plan to retake Kuran."

The two men exchanged glances. Their guns came up. In Arabic they called for more men.

After virtually every Iraiti soldier had surrounded her—some five in all—Kimberly realized that none of them spoke or understood English.

One touched her pale cheek curiously. He pushed Kimberly's head upright. When he withdrew his dirty fingers, it tilted left again. They laughed uproariously.

"They don't speak English," Kimberly muttered nervously. "What do I do, O Kali?"

Go with them.

Worry quirking her lips and violet eyes, Kimberly Baynes allowed herself to be taken to one of the half-standing large buildings, even though she was certain they were only going to gang-rape her.

Her suspicions were confirmed when they stacked their rifles in a corner and started unbuckling their belts.

One of them had her bag. He pulled out a long yellow silk scarf.

"What do I do? What do I do?" Kimberly whispered.

Show them your tits.

"Here," Kimberly said, reaching for the scarf. "Let me show you how this works."

The soldier let her loop the harmless silk around his throat. The others laughed, anticipating a long afternoon with the unsuspecting blond American servicewoman.

"Ready?" Kimberly asked.

Without waiting for an answer, she pulled the ends of the scarf in opposite directions. The fabric made his throat muscles balloon around it. His face went scarlet. The Iraiti gurgled his horror. His tongue slid from his gagging, yawning mouth.

The Iraitis laughed, thinking their fellow soldier was having sport. The girl was very slim. She did not look strong at all. Besides, she was a female, and every Arab man knew how weak the other sex was.

When his face turned blue, they changed their minds. They converged on the woman, who oddly enough let their comrade fall into a swoon and began unbuttoning her blouse to expose her prodigious brassiere.

It was the type that fastened in the front. She unhooked it. The Iraiti eyes brightened in anticipation of the pale breasts that were about to be revealed.

Their anticipation turned to horror when two long crablike arms unfolded themselves, snapping a silken scarf between them with nervous, predatory tugs.

As one, they took a step back.

By then it was too late. The unclean heathen thing leapt for them, and they all fell to the floor in a gang throttle in which everyone participated, but only one person survived.

Kimberly Baynes emerged from the damaged building

modestly buttoning up her uniform blouse and commandeered one of the sand-colored trucks.

She drove due north.

Somewhere, there would be an Iraiti detachment that spoke English. And she would find it.

Not that Kali complained about the delay. She was enjoying the ride immensely.

"Did I do better that time?" Kimberly asked.

They writhed magnificently, Kali told her.

21

The house was dark.

Remo had walked all the way from Folcroft. He had not started out for the house. He had never expected to set foot in it. Ever again. Too many memories, as he had explained to Smith.

What had happened was that he had started to feel the call in his blood. The call of Kali. He had first dragged out a silken scarf to satisfy his craving. But it had only made him yearn for her more.

Jerking every scarf from his pockets, he threw them against the walls.

"You don't own me!" he cried. "You'll never own me."

The scarves slipped into little piles like limp discarded hand puppets—which was exactly how Remo felt inside his soul. Limp. Helpless. Cast off.

A cold shower had not helped, so he had stepped out into the hot night to walk, wearing underwear three sizes too small so his uncontrollable tumescence wouldn't be too obvious.

The heat only fired his blood. So he walked.

And in time he found himself on the tree-lined residential street that lay snug under the hills of the Folcroft Golf Course, where he had been living in a Tudor-style house. Remo had purchased it on recommendation from Chiun, only to learn later that he had been tricked into becoming Harold Smith's neighbor. For Smith owned an adjoining home. The Master of Sinanju had explained this away with a flowery platitude about the royal assassin needing to dwell close to the seat of power.

Remo's was a modest house. Nothing fancy. Not even the

white picket fence he had once dreamed he'd have. It wasn't a white-picket-fence kind of neighborhood.

As he passed through the zones of the pale yellow streetlight illumination—nightfall had come to Rye, New York—Remo's eyes went to the dark blank windows.

It looked empty, that house. As empty as Remo Williams felt.

He walked past it, his eyes glued to the windows, half-hoping, half-fearing to see a familiar wrinkled face in a window. He had lived there less than two years—an absurdly small segment of his total life, but such an overwhelming wave of nostalgia washed over him that Remo abruptly turned up the walk.

It was, he thought, as if he were drawn to the place.

At the door, Remo dug around in his pockets. Then he recalled that he had thrown the house key away in Tacoma—or was it Chicago?

The Yale lock cylinder resembled a brass medallion in the painted wood. Remo simply set his hard fingers around the edges. He twisted.

Slowly the lock turned like a flush dial. Wood and metal squealed, settling into a long low groan of protest. A panel split under the powerful force exerted by his inexorable fingers.

Wounded and beaten, the door fell open.

Remo stepped over the theshold, flicking a light switch that produced no light.

"Smith," Remo muttered. "Cut the electricity to save two cents." Remo grunted. At least Smith was consistent.

He went from room to room, his visual purple adjusted to the darkness. In the bare living room the big-screen TV lay idle, a video recorder and several stacks of tapes resting atop it. Chiun's British soaps. His latest passion.

No, Remo thought sadly, *last* passion.

Remo's bedroom was a simple room with a reed mat. Remo glanced over it without feeling or connection. It had only been a place to sleep. He skipped Chiun's bedroom and went to the kitchen with its simple dining table and long rows of cabinets. He opened them, touching the sacks and canisters of uncooked rice of all varieties.

It was here, Remo thought morosely, that he and Chiun had enjoyed their best times together. Cooking and eating.

And arguing. Always arguing. It had become a ritual with them. And now he missed it terribly.

Remo left the kitchen, going to the storage room.

And he knew then what had impelled him to return.

Chiun's steamer trunks. Fourteen oversize lacquered trunks in every ungodly color imaginable. Emblazoned with dragons, phoenixes, salamanders, and other exotic creatures. They had been a pain in the ass to truck around during their vagabond days. But Remo would carry them to the moon and back for another combative afternoon with Chiun, listening to his carping and eating steaming bowlfuls of pure Javonica rice.

Dropping to his knees, he threw open a lid at random. Remo was not surprised to see that it contained an assortment of junk—restaurant giveaway toothpicks in colored cellophane, swizzle sticks, coasters, towels emblazoned with the crests of scores of hotels from around the world. Remo closed it, feeling sad. All this stuff carefully collected. And for what?

The next trunk contained rolls of delicately packed parchment scrolls, each tied closed with a different-colored ribbon. Here was the history of Chiun's days in America. These were what had called Remo to the house. He would have to return them to the village of Sinanju, where they would join the histories of past Masters.

Remo reached down to pluck one up. It looked to be the freshest.

He held it in his hand for a long time, fingers poised over the emerald ribbon.

Finally he simply replaced it unread. It was too soon. He could not bear to reexperience their days as seen through Chiun's jaundiced eyes. Remo closed the trunk.

The next one opened up on a sea of silks and fine brocades. Chiun's ceremonial kimonos. Remo lifted one—a black silk kimono with two orange-and-black tigers stitched delicately onto the chest, rising on their hind legs, their forepaws frozen in eternal combat.

A faint light made the tigers jump out from the shimmery ebon background.

"What?"

Remo turned, the kimono dropping from his surprised fingers.

Feeling his mouth go dry, he gasped.

"Little Father?"

For there, less than six feet away, stood the Master of Sinanju, shining with a faint radiance. He wore the royal purple kimono that he had last worn in life. His hands were concealed in the joined sleeves. His eyes were closed, the sweet wrinkles of his face in repose, his head tilted back slightly.

Remo swallowed. Except for a bluish cast, Chiun looked as he had in life. There was no corny opalescent glow like in a Hollywood ghost. No saintlike nimbus. None of that ghostly stuff.

Still, Remo could see, dimly, the shadowy bulk of the big-screen TV behind the Master of Sinanju's lifelike image.

"Little Father?" Remo repeated. "Chiun?"

The bald head lowered, and dim hazel eyes eased open as if coming out of a long sleep. They grew harsh when they came into contact with Remo's own.

The sleeves parted, revealing birdlike claws tipped with impossibly long curved nails.

One trembling hand pointed to Remo.

"What are you saying?" Remo asked. "If it's about my going through your trunks—"

Then it pointed down, to the Master of Sinanju's sandaled feet.

"You did this last time," Remo said. "And the time before that. You're telling me that I walk in your sandals now, right?"

The eyes flashed anew. The hand pointed down, the elbow working back and forth emphatically, driving the point home again and again.

"I'm going back. Really. I have something to clear up first."

The elbow jerked.

"I was on my way but Kali came back. I don't know what to do."

With the other hand the spirit of Chiun indicated the floor.

"You can't hear me, can you?"

Remo put his hands in his pockets. He shook his head negatively.

The Master of Sinanju dropped silently to both knees. He rested tiny futile fists against the hardwood floor and began pounding. His hands went through the floor each time. But their violence was emphatic.

"Look," Remo protested, "I don't know what you're trying to tell me. And you're starting to drive me crazy with all this pantomime stuff. Can't you just leave a note or something?"

Chiun sat up. He formed strange shapes with his hands and fingers.

Remo blinked. He peered through the half-light.

"What is this?" he muttered. "Charades?"

Chiun's crooked fingers twisted this way and that, forming Remo knew not what. He thought he recognized the letter G formed of a circled thumb and forefinger bisected by another index finger, but the rest was a meaningless jumble of pantomine.

"Look, I'm not following this," Remo shouted in exasperation. "Why are you doing this to me? You're dead, for Christ's sake. Why can't you just leave me alone!"

And with that, the Master of Sinanju came to his feet like ascending purple incense.

He approached, his hands lifting to Remo's face.

Remo shrank back. But the hands plunged too quickly to evade.

"Noooo!" Remo cried as the whirl of images overtook his mind. He smelled coldness, visualized blackness, and tasted brackish water—all in one overwhelming concussion of sensory attack. His lungs caught in mid-breath—from fear or what, he didn't know. It felt like the oxygen had been sucked from them.

He sank to his feet, eyes pinched shut, breathing in jerky gasps.

"Okay, okay, you win!" he panted. "I'll go! I'll go to Sinanju. I promise. Just stop haunting me, okay?"

The images swallowed themselves like water swirling down a drain.

"What?"

Remo opened his eyes. The faint radiance was gone. In the half-light he thought he caught a momentary retinal impression of Chiun's dwindling afterimage. The Master of Sinanju had thrown his face to the heavens. Remo could almost hear his wail of despair.

Now Remo knew. The Master of Sinanju had gone to the Void—the cold place on the other side of the universe where, according to Sinanju belief, those who had dropped their mortal shells were ultimately cast.

It was true! There was a Void. And Chiun was there.

Remo swallowed his fear several times before he found his feet. Now he understood. No wonder Chiun kept coming back. The Void was a terrible place. And it was the place Remo would one day go too. Remo shivered at the thought.

Perhaps he was better off a slave of Kali. He did not know. Remo reached into the open trunk and took up a shimmery bolt of fabric.

Then he left, sealing the front door by compressing the protesting hinges with the heel of his hand. They would have to be unscrewed before the door would ever open again.

Remo did not expect to see that done. Ever.

22

President Maddas Hinsein, Scimitar of the Arabs, left the presidential palace in his staff car. He was feeling very Arabian today, so he wore a blue-and-white burnoose whose headdress was held in place by a coiling black *agal*.

It was also excellent protection against the scourge of the Arab leader—the would-be assassin. For no one knew what Father Maddas, as his worshipful countrymen called him with childlike affection, would wear on a given day. A paramilitary jumpsuit, a Western-style business suit, or traditional bedouin garb. It was one of the many survival tricks he had learned in a lifetime of surviving the snakepit that was modern Irait.

The decree that all males of puberty age and above wear Maddas Hinsein mustaches was another. If all Iraiti men looked alike, Maddas reasoned, an assassin would have to consider well before shooting, lest he fire upon a relative. In that fractional hesitation sometimes lay the difference between glorious victory and ignominious death.

The staff car whirled him through the broad multilane highways and the sparse traffic, through Renaissance Square, where two huge forearms—cast from life molds of Maddas' own and expanded to the girth of a genie's arm—clutched curved scimitars to form an arch. On every building, on the traffic islands, and in the centers of rotaries, magnificent portraits of Maddas alternately smiled and glowered in testimony to the sweeping depth of his magnificent wardrobe. How could a man who so inspired his people, Maddas thought with deep pride, fail to unite the Arabs?

Presently the car brought him to Maddas International Airport, where a Tupolev-16 bomber sat on the tarmac.

Under armed escort, Maddas Hinsein entered the airport.

His defense minister, General Razzik Azziz, rushed forward to meet him.

General Azziz did not look well. Maddas preferred his generals to look unwell. If there was fear in their bellies, he was a safer president.

They exchanged salutes.

"*Salaam aleikim,* Precious Leader," said General Azziz. "The plane has just arrived."

Maddas nodded. "And this United States deserter, where is she?"

"For security purposes, we have not allowed anyone to deplane. The crew awaits you."

"Take me."

Members of his elite blue-bereted Renaissance Guard formed a protective circle around Maddas Hinsein as he strode in his familiar rolling gait onto the tarmac. A wheeled staircase was brought up to the aircraft, which had flown in from occupied Kuran carrying the deserter. She had presented herself to an astonished patrol.

Two airport security guards climbed the aluminum stairs and knocked on the hatch. They waited. Nothing happened. They pounded this time, shouting insults and curses in voluble Arabic.

This produced no result. They hastily clambered down the staircase and moved it in front of the cockpit. They climbed up and looked in the window.

Their manner became excited. They shouted. Other soldiers came running. From the top of the stairs they opened up on the occupied windows with AK-47's. Glass flew. Blood splashed, spattering them all.

Finally the shooting died down.

Reaching in, they hauled out the dead pilot and copilot. Their inert bodies slid and slithered down the wheeled staircase.

Maddas Hinsein saw the tight yellow knots around their throats. They contrasted sharply with the purplish-blue of their congested faces.

He frowned, his face a thundercloud of annoyance.

"What is this?" Maddas demanded of his defense minister.

"I have no idea," the general gulped.

Maddas drew his sidearm, a pearl-handed revolver. He placed the immaculate muzzle to General Azziz's sweating temple.

"If this is a trap," he uttered venomously, "you will soon have no brain."

General Razzik Azziz stood very, very still. He hoped that this was not a trap too.

The security men crawled into the cockpit. Soon the hatch popped open.

When a new staircase rolled into position, Maddas Hinsein ordered his Renaissance Guard to storm the plane. No shots were fired. Only when they called back that it was safe to board did Maddas Hinsein mount the stairs personally.

Just to be certain, he marched his defense minister into the plane at gunpoint.

When the man was not gunned down, Maddas Hinsein stepped in, towering over his men.

The crew sat in their seats, tongues out like those of parched dogs, their faces horrible purple and blue hues. Their stink was not that of corruption, but of bowels that had released in death.

Maddas Hinsein had no eyes for the dead. He wanted the American servicewoman who had promised his patrol the secret American order of battle.

But a two-hour search produced no American servicewoman, even though General Azziz repeatedly assured him that she had been aboard."

"She must have escaped," General Azziz swore. "Before I arrived here," he added.

"Have the responsible parties stood before a firing squad," Maddas Hinsein told his defense minister.

"But, Precious Leader, they are already dead. You see them about you. All of them."

Maddas Hinsein fixed General Azziz with his deadly gaze.

"Shoot them anyway. As a lesson to others. Not even the dead are safe from the firing squad."

"It will be done as you say, Precious Leader," General Azziz promised eagerly.

"And have the CIA spy—for that is obviously what she is—captured alive if possible. I will accept dead. No doubt, she is an assassin."

"As you command, Precious Leader."

As he was whisked from the airport, Maddas Hinsein was thinking of the yellow silk scarves and how much they resembled the yellow ribbons that American farmers had tied around their coarse western trees.

And he wondered what fate had truly befallen his ambassador to the United States.

The Americans were sending him a message, he decided. Perhaps their patience was not inexhaustible, after all.

23

The Reverend Juniper Jackman took great pride in his blackness.

It was his blackness that enabled him—despite a complete lack of credentials—to run for the office of the presidency and convince the media and a sizable but electorally insignificant portion of the American voters that he might actually win.

It was such a convincing con that on his last foray into national politics, Reverend Jackman himself actually caught the fever and fell under the sway of his own hypnotic speechmaking.

He came to believe he had a chance to become the nation's first black President.

He had no chance, but he clung to the whiff of victory straight through the primaries. The aftermath of his party's convention, where he wowed America with an arresting speech about catching the best bus, was a bitter comedown.

There was talk of Reverend Jackman running for mayor of Washington, D.C. Many of his constituents practically demanded it. But the Reverend Jackman declined the offer, saying he saw himself as a player in a larger area—global politics.

The truth was, he understood better than anyone else that if he won the mayor's race, he was sunk. What did he know about running a city? And he didn't want to end up like the last disgraced mayor of Washington. As the Reverend Jackman saw it, his only chance was to grab that presidential brass ring and hold on for dear life. They wouldn't dare impeach him. Not him. His blackness would get him in the door and his mouth would keep him in the Oval Office—even after the nation realized it had been scammed.

But the calls for the Reverend Jackman to run for some elected office were too strong for even him to ignore. Especially when, in the wake of the last election, the pundits began calling him irrelevant. So he had allowed himself to be drafted into the meaningless role of shadow senator.

It was perfect. No responsibilities. No downside. He could phone his work in. Often did.

Which, after he had launched his TV talk show—the reverend's latest scheme to acquire a national platform—was exactly what he needed.

Now, with an actual political office on his résumé, they stopped calling him irrelevant.

He was once again branded by the press as a shameless opportunist. The Reverend Jackman hated that tag, but it was better than being irrelevant. A shameless opportunist was at least a player. And if there was anything the Reverend Jackman needed to be, it was a player.

So it was that he sat in the plush cabin of his former campaign jet, the *Rainbow Soundbite*, winging his way over the Middle East to a rendezvous with destiny.

"I'll show 'em," the Reverend Jackman said, sipping a tumbler of pepper vodka.

"Yeah," his chief adviser slurred, hefting a tall rum and Coke, "those jerks in Washington are gonna sit up and take notice of you now."

"I don't mean them," Reverend Jackman snapped. "I mean those glory hounds at BCN. I ain't forgotten how they scooped me on Maddas. I had the first interview with that date-muncher all sewed up. And they sent in Don Cooder to beat me to the punch."

"We should never have broadcast our intentions. Secret diplomacy. That's what we gotta learn. Secret diplomacy."

"Damn Cooder is scoop-crazed. I hate people like that," Reverend Jackman said with a surly twist of his upper lip. His mustache contorted like a worm on a pin.

"Well, the Arabs got him now, and if this works, Juni, you gonna make that guy look as dumb as the time he promised to put a live neutron bomb on TV and ended up showing a twenty-year-old rerun about saving the humpback whale."

"I'll talk ol' Maddas into letting him go in my custody, and that ass-kisser Cooder will be kissing my ass all the way home. You seen him on TV? Man's scared. Never seen a man so scared. Probably has to change his underwear three times a day."

The two men laughed. Reverend Jackman looked out the porthole. Endless sand rolled beneath the starboard wing.

"What do you think, Earl? Maybe when I step off, I'll announce that I've come to trade places with Cooder. Think that'll work?"

"It might. But what if they take you up on it?"

"They wouldn't dare. I ran for President twice. Which is more than you can say for JFK, LBJ, and Ford. And Ford got in without even runnin'."

"Maybe you're right. We are brothers, us and the Arabs."

" 'Cept we got more sense than to dress up in our bed linen." Reverend Jackman sneered. "Then that's what I'll do. I'll offer myself in trade. We'd better work up a speech."

"What kind you want?"

"One that doesn't say anything but sounds good."

"I know that, but what do you want to be sayin', Juni?"

"As little as possible. That's how people like it. Just make sure it rhymes. I'm gonna hit the head. All this sand is making me thirsty and all this vodka is making me leakier than the State Department."

The *Rainbow Soundbite* touched down at Maddas International Airport after being cleared by Iraiti air-traffic control. It taxied up to Terminal B, where a wheeled ramp was pushed into place.

A cordon of Iraiti security officers in khaki and black berets kept the multinational press at bay. The press cheered the opening of the hatch door. They cheered the appearance of the Reverend Juniper Jackman as he stepped onto the top step.

They cheered because when they weren't reporting on events in Abominadad, they resided in the Abaddon Air Base, known to be a primary U.S. target in the event of hostilities.

Reverend Juniper Jackman lifted his hand to acknowledge the cheers. His pop eyes cast down to the reception committee and his youthful features broke into a frown.

"What is this crap!" he demanded. "I'm not going down there. I don't recognize anybody. They sent some flunkies!"

His chief adviser looked out. "Yeah, you right, Juni. I don't see hide nor hair of the foreign minister. I don't even see the information minister. Maybe that's him—the one with the brushy mustache."

"They all got brushy mustaches," Juniper Jackman growled. "You get on the phone. Call everybody you gotta. I ain't steppin' off this plane until they send somebody important to shake my hand in front of all this media."

"Gotcha, Juni."

The Reverend Jackman put on his famous smile and waved with his other hand. Cheers went up from the press. Juniper Jackman beamed. What the hell? This wasn't so hard to take. Some of the same jerks who'd bad-mouthed him on the air were now cheering to beat the band. He hoped they'd remember this moment the next time he ran for President instead of claiming it was like making a fry cook chairman of the board of McDonald's without having to work his way up.

Reverend Juniper Jackman switched hands until they got tired. The press cheered until they were hoarse.

"What's keeping you?" Jackman hissed through his wilting smile.

"I'm being stonewalled," his aide called back. "I don't like this."

"Maybe you ain't dialed the right number yet."

Then a quartet of soldiers came up the stairs, trailed by the mustached man in the blue business suit.

They took Reverend Jackman by the hands. Smiling, he attempted to shake hands with every one of them.

But shaking hands was not what the Iraiti soldiers had in mind. They took Reverend Jackman by the upper arms and forcibly marched him down the steps.

Trying to put the best face on it because of all the cameras, the Reverend Jackman lifted his arms to wave. His arms were held down.

"What the F is goin' on?" Reverend Jackman undertoned in panic.

The Iraiti in the blue business suit spoke up.

"Reverend Jackman, so happy to see you. I am Mustafa Shagdoof, deputy information minister. On behalf of our benevolent leader, President Maddas Hinsein, I welcome you as a guest to our peace-loving country."

"Thanks, but I . . ." Reverend Jackman's eyes started suddenly. "Wait a minute! What do you mean by guest?"

"What we say," the deputy information minister said,

displaying an officious smile. "You are entitled to our hospitality."

"You ain't by any chance plannin' on duressing me?"

"Do you feel duressed?"

"As a matter of fact . . ." Reverend Jackman nearly stumbled. He looked up.

They reached the bottom of the stairs.

The deputy information minister addressed the gathering TV cameramen. "On behalf of the Republic of Irait, I formally welcome Reverend Jackman as a guest of the state. He will remain our guest until our own ambassador is accounted for."

If anything, Reverend Jackman's staring eyes protruded further. They resembled hard-boiled eggs with sick black spots at one end.

Thinking "Might as well go for broke," Reverend Jackman sucked in a deep breath.

"I came to trade myself for Don Cooder," he shouted. "You hear me? I'm not afraid to take his place." The sweat crawled down the reverend's face like transparent worms.

From the back of the TV crew a familiar Texas drawl was raised in excitement.

"That's me! That's me! Let me on that damned plane!"

And hearing that familiar voice, Reverend Juniper Jackman turned to the Iraiti deputy information minister.

"Just between you and me, I don't suppose you'd take my assistant instead of me? I'll throw in the plane. You can keep Cooder too."

"You should be very happy here in Abominadad," the deputy information minister said.

"What makes you say that?"

"You already wear the politically correct mustache."

Word of the detention of the Reverend Juniper Jackman was satellited from Abominadad to Washington through the Cable News Network.

The President received the report in writing during a cabinet meeting. He didn't know whether to laugh or cry. No love was lost between him and the reverend, but the man was a political figure of some standing. When word of this hit the streets, there would be enormous pressure that he take action. Especially from the black community.

"Excuse me," the President told his cabinet. "Gotta make a call."

The President walked the lonely halls of power to the Lincoln Bedroom. Perching on the side of the antique bed, he opened the nightstand drawer, revealing a dialless red telephone.

He picked it up, triggering an automatic connection.

Hundreds of miles north, at the other end of the dedicated line, an identical telephone rang on the desk of Harold W. Smith.

"Yes, Mr. President?"

"The Iraitis have taken Reverend Jackman hostage."

There was silence on the line as both men considered whether that was truly as bad as it sounded.

"They're threatening to give up Dan Cooder," the President added.

"Unfortunate," Smith said at last.

"They want their ambassador back. What do I do? If I ship them a corpse, they'll do the same. I don't want to go to war to avenge that glory-hound minister."

"I believe I can help you on this one," Smith said at last. "Leave the rest to me."

Harold Smith hung up the phone. An hour ago, he would have had to inform the chief executive of the United States that he couldn't send his special person to the Middle East. His special person refused to go anywhere unless it was into the arms—the four arms, according to his delusion—of a woman he believed was the reincarnation of the Hindu goddess Kali.

But in the last hour, Harold Smith had made a breakthrough. Unable to trace Kimberly Baynes—or the woman who used that name—through the usual computer taps, he had reprogrammed the search to trap any Baynes with a feminine first name.

An airline reservation in the name of Calley Baynes had bubbled to the surface of the vast active memory. He might not have paid it much attention, but the flight's destination was Tripoli, Libya.

And as he wondered what this Calley Baynes would be doing in Tripoli, it sank in that his computers had provided a way to convince Remo to accept this assignment.

Provided Harold Smith was prepared to lie now and blame his computers later.

He shut down his terminal and sent it retreating into its hidden desk recess.

Remo, he felt confident, would be more than happy to go to the Middle East. But Smith would not send him to Libya. He would send him to Irait.

He just hoped that in his present state Remo Williams was up to the task.

24

"I have found . . . ah, your Miss Baynes," Harold Smith told Remo.

"Where?" Remo's voice was calm—calmer than Smith had expected.

It was dark in the room. Only the bluish TV etched Remo's head and shoulders in the blackness. The sound was off. Remo had not turned his head once in the darkness.

"Hamidi Arabia."

"I've been there. It's all sand. She'll be hard to track down."

"I am working on that," Smith said. "In the meantime, the President has asked that we intervene in the Juniper Jackman situation. He has been designated a guest under duress."

Remo grunted. "Another breakthrough for jive diplomacy. Maybe Maddas will draft him as his vice-president."

"That is not funny."

"So how do we fix the problem?" Remo wondered.

"By liberating the reverend from Abominadad."

Remo perked up. "Do I get to nail Maddas?"

"No. That is not on the menu. Get Jackman to Hamidi Arabia. By the time you conclude this matter, I should have Miss Baynes's exact whereabouts and you can deal with that loose end."

"Then I was right," Remo said slowly. "The Middle East is where the Caldron of Blood will start to boil."

"Are you all right?" Smith asked.

Remo paused. "I went to the house. He was there, Smitty."

"Chiun's ghost?" Smith said dryly.

"I don't know what you'd call it. But I saw him. And I made him a promise."

"Yes?"

"I promised I would return to Sinanju."

"And what did Chiun . . . er . . . say?"

"Nothing. He looked at me like a drowning man. I don't understand, but I made the promise. I'm going to Sinanju. I'm going to do my duty."

"What about the assignment? And Kimberly Baynes—or whoever she really is?"

"I'll handle both of them. I'll have to. Then my responsibility will be to fulfill my duty to the House."

"As you wish. I will make the arrangements to get you to Hamidi Arabia. The entire country is in a high state of nervousness. I thought I'd send you on a military flight. It would be better in your . . . um . . . condition as well. I'll arrange for someone to liase with you."

"No need," Remo said.

"Oh?"

"Just get word to Sheik Abdul Hamid Fareem."

Smith started. "The ruler of Hamidi Arabia? And what shall I say?"

Remo stood up in the darkness and Smith saw the play of bluish TV light on the folds of his black silk garment.

Remo turned, shadows crawling across his face. They settled into the hollows of his eyes so they became like the empty orbits of a skull in which diamond-hard lights gleamed faintly. He tucked his hands into the wide sleeves of his long ebony kimono, on which facing tigers reared in frozen anger.

"Tell him the Master of Sinanju is coming to Hamidi Arabia," Remo Williams said quietly.

25

Everything Maddas Hinsein knew about global politics, he had learned in the coffee shops of Cairo.

Young Maddas had spent several years in Egypt in the aftermath of a failed attempt to assassinate the Iraiti leader of that time. There he had argued about Arab unity with students from the nearby Cairo University.

They were smooth-faced man-boys, their heads filled with citified dreams. He could never understand their appetite for loud talk. They argued forever—never learning the great truth of Maddas Hinsein's life.

It was far, far quicker to shoot those whose views were unacceptable than to argue back.

Although no older than the university students, Maddas was already a hardened veteran of internecine political warfare. After the failed assassination attempt, although wounded in the leg, he had narrowly escaped capture by the Iraiti secret police. Limping through the flat opulence of Abominadad, he had ducked into an alley as the ululations of their sirens drew nearer, ever nearer.

He happened to encounter an old woman in the alley. She wore the traditional black *abayuh*, which covered her like a shroud, black eyes peeping through her veil.

Maddas had approached her in the same direct way he had pursued his career as an Arab revolutionary.

"*Sabah al-Heir*," he had said. "May your morning be bright."

"*Abah al-Nour*," she murmured in reply. "May your morning be bright also."

As he knew she would, the woman modestly averted her eyes. And Maddas Hinsein reached down with one hand for the hem of her costume and lifted it straight up.

With the other, he yanked out his pistol and shot her once in the chest.

Stripping the body of the undamaged garment, Maddas Hinsein had pulled it over his head, hating himself for having to stoop so low. Wearing female garb was repugnant to him. Killing the woman was one thing—in revolution one recognized certain necessities—but being forced to wear soft garments was entirely different.

Besides, the woman was old, he saw as he pulled the veil from her face. She had had her life. And Maddas Hinsein was a man of destiny.

In the flowing black *abayuh*, Maddas Hinsein had traveled across the punishing desert, the traditional Arab respect for women saving him from search and inevitable capture. The longer he traveled, the safer he felt. He began to feel almost invincible when wrapped in this ebony shroud, his face masked, his life secure from harm. And as the miles melted behind him, Maddas Hinsein discovered a wondrous truth. He grew to enjoy the feel of the *abayuh* swathing his bulky, muscular body.

Upon reaching the Egyptian frontier, Maddas Hinsein had reluctantly folded the precious garment and carried it under his arm, telling the authorities it had belonged to his poor deceased mother.

"It is all I have to remember her by," he had told the curious border guards. He brushed a soulful eye with a spit-moistened finger, producing a convincing tear.

The sight of such a bear of an Arab moved to tears convinced the Egyptian border guard. They let him pass.

During the years in the Cairo coffee shops, Arab unity was on every lip. It was the Grand Dream, the Great Hope, and Paradise on Earth all in one. The reason was profoundly simple. No one could remember a time when there had been such a thing as Arab unity. So everyone was secure in the belief it would be wondrous. And in that atmosphere, Maddas had learned the lessons he had carried with him into his leadership days.

Truth one: the Arabs were disunited because imperialists kept them this way.

Truth two: the Arabs were meant to be united and only awaited a strongman like a modern Nebuchadnezzar, the Babylonian king who had captured Jerusalem in 597 B.C.

Truth three: for as long as the United States vied with

Russia for world domination, Irait would be protected by the USSR from U.S. adventurism.

Truth four: Maddas Hinsein was destined to be the man who would unite the Arab nation under the Iraiti banner. This was Maddas' sole contribution to the discussions. Doubters were shot in the back at his earliest opportunity. Soon the Four Great Truths were discussed without dissent.

Had Maddas Hinsein learned his history from books and not idle conversation, he would have learned that the Arabs had enjoyed unity but once in their long history. And that had been under the prophet Mohammed, over a thousand years ago. Then Mohammed had died. United Araby was quickly dismembered under the ravenous talons of Mohammed's heirs.

Had he read newspapers, Maddas would have learned that the cold war had become a thing of the past and that Irait lay naked and exposed, no longer important in the global new world order that had shifted from ideology to the ultimate reality of international politics—economics.

So when after nearly a decade of unending war with his neighbor, Irug, Maddas Hinsein found his treasury bankrupt, he turned on his nearest oil-rich neighbor and swallowed tiny defenseless Kuran—hide, hoof, warp, and woof.

The unexpected appearance of a multinational force on his new southern border, when reported to him in the middle of the night by his defense minister, prompted him to conclude one thing: his adviser was drunk. And since alchohol was forbidden to Moslems, he had had the man shot before a firing squad. Then he had downed a stiff belt of cognac.

When the reports from the field told him that such a force not only existed but also was growing daily, President Hinsein had had the adviser exhumed and returned to his place of honor at the Revolting Command Council as a gesture of contrition.

"Let no man say again that Maddas Hinsein is not a man who readily admits his mistakes," he pronounced, as his advisers sat around the big table holding their noses against the stench of corruption.

Only when the corpse had begun to fall apart was he returned to his shallow grave. With full military honors.

It was in those early days of the U.S. buildup that Maddas, who had kept the nameless old woman's *abayuh* in a sealed trunk, exhumed it for the first time since his Cairo days.

The fine fabric reassured him as it had in the days he crouched under donkey carts as the secret police—his secret police now—blew past.

He knew it would protect him until the Soviets came to succor him.

When word came that the Soviets had joined the global embargo, Maddas Hinsein had taken to carrying the *abayuh* in a briefcase, and toting the briefcase wherever he went.

And at night, when he slept, he slept swathed in its protective folds. He told himself that this was to facilitate his escape in case of a coup, or worse. But the truth was far different.

The truth was that Maddas Hinsein loved to wear the *abayuh*.

He had first begun to suspect these tendencies in Egypt. Once he had assumed the presidential office—by doing away with the previous President, his mentor—President Hinsein had buried the *abayuh* in a trunk, where it would not tempt him. And most of all, where his wife, Numibasra, would never find it. The woman was a witch. And her brothers, Maddas knew, secretly plotted against him. Only because he would never have heard the end of it from his wife did Maddas refrain from having them beheaded.

One day, he told himself. One day.

But today Maddas Hinsein's thoughts were not of his wife and her cutthroat brothers, but of the reports he was receiving from his general staff.

Maddas paced his office. The aides would come to the door, knocking their timid, sycophantic knocks.

"I am receiving no one," Maddas barked. "Give me your report and go."

"They have found more dead soldiers," the aides called. "The yellow cords around their throats."

"Soldiers exist to die," Maddas spat back. "They are martyrs now and better off."

"The defense minister wants to know if you plan a military response to these outrages?"

Maddas Hinsein stopped pacing. The black *abayuh* skirt rustled against his shiny black paratroop boots.

This was the question he feared. He had brought the wrath of the world down on his head through his own ignorance, but he dared not admit it. So he had hunkered down, giving pronouncements, calling on rival Arab nations to join him in a jihad. And he had been ignored. Nothing that he had done worked. No threat. No bluster.

And now his own high command, the cowardly toadies, were demanding to know what response he would make to this CIA assassin who was terrorizing Abominadad.

"Tell him," Maddas said at last, "I will make a response to the world once this infidel strangler is brought to my door. And if he is not, then I will demand the defense minister's head instead."

The aide rushed away. Beneath the black cloth covering his face, Maddas Hinsein smiled suavely.

That would keep them occupied. Maddas Hinsein would not be stampeded into war by one mere CIA assassin-spy.

Lifting his hands over his head, he snapped his fingers in an ancient syncopation and performed the dance of the seven veils in the privacy of his office, throwing his hips out with each snap and humming under his breath.

"Mad Ass Mad Ass Mad Ass," he crooned. "I am one crazy-assed Arab, and the whole world knows it."

But as the hours passed, the aides kept coming.

"More dead, Precious Leader. Strangled."

"We have searched everywhere, Precious Leader. The she-wolf is not to be found."

"The minister of the interior, Precious Leader, has been found in his quarters. Assassinated with a yellow cord."

"Do you not see what the Americans are trying to do?" Maddas thundered back. "They are trying to trick us into war. I will not have war on their terms, but on mine."

That had held them another hour while Maddas luxuriated in the feel of the fine *abayuh*, bumping and grinding merrily.

Then came a knock unlike any other. More tentative, more faint of heart. The knock of a fear-struck coward.

"Precious Leader," the quavering voice began.

"What is it?" Maddas barked.

"I am very sorry to report this to you, but the Renaissance Guard surrounding your home has been decimated."

"They were the flower of Iraiti manhood, how can this be?"

"They were strangled, Precious Leader. Yellow silk knots about their strong Arab necks."

"And my family? Of course they have escaped while their

noble defenders held their ground, spilling their very red martyrs' blood."

The silence brought Maddas Hinsein up from his couch. He yanked the *abayuh* hood from his face. Striding over to the door, he roared through it.

"I have asked a question!"

"I am sorry, Precious Leader. Your family is . . . dead."

Maddas' soulful eyes went round.

"My wife too?"

"I am so sorry," the aide sobbed through the wood.

"And her brothers, my brothers-in-law?"

"Gone," he choked. "All gone. It is a day of mourning. But fear not, the Americans will pay. We will scorch the earth under their heathen feet. The blood of your martyred family will sear their lungs. You have only to give the word and we will repay the aggressors in blood."

But Maddas Hinsein wasn't listening to his aide's grief-twisted voice.

He was feeling a coldness settle into his stomach and lungs.

"They want war," he said huskily. "The crazy Americans are trying to force me to attack. They must be insane."

26

The Military Airlift Command C-5 Galaxy that carried Remo Williams from McGuire Air Force Base also carried a single cabled-down M-IA1 Abrams tank, the Army's latest. It was one of the last to be shipped in support of Operation Sand Blast.

The bulky vehicle left little room for Remo in back. But he insisted on riding in the cavernous cargo bay, sitting on a tatami mat so he wouldn't get engine oil on his fine silk kimono, which he had had altered to fit him by a dumb-struck tailor.

Remo sat in a lotus position, the drumming of the Galaxy's turboprop engines making everything in the cargo bay vibrate with soul-deadening monotony.

Early in the flight, Remo had found the vibration and absorbed it until his body no longer vibrated in sympathy with the great propellers. Only the neat edges of his mat did.

The flight was long and boring. Remo sat comfortably, the kimono fabric stretched tight over his lap. It hid his persistent erection.

Even though he had left most of the yellow scarves that had belonged to Kimberly Baynes—or whoever she was—behind at Folcroft, Remo couldn't get her out of his mind.

What would happen when they met again? He wanted her more than he had ever wanted a woman, but not in a good way. He lusted for her. Yet he hated her, with her many arms and twisted neck. And most of all he hated the thing that animated her. For Remo understood that Kimberly had died. Like a ghoulish puppet, Kali made her live again. And Remo would have to finish the job. If he could.

In the noisy back of the C-5, he closed his eyes and

concentrated on his breathing. It helped push out the memories—of her burning-hot, sensual hands, her eager red mouth, her insatiable sexual appetite. Remo had feasted on sex while in her arms, and he knew as long as they both lived he could never rest until he returned to that feast—or destroyed the table.

But it made him wonder. Would he lose Remo Williams at the feast? And would the spark deep within him that was Shiva the Destroyer consume all that was his identity?

Remo shuddered. He had never felt so alone.

Closing his eyes, he slept sitting up.

And in sleep, he dreamed.

Remo dreamed of feminine hands with canary-yellow nails. The hands surrounded him. First they caressed. Then they pinched at his soft tissues between caresses. Remo lay on a bed, his eyes closed. The pinching grew spiteful. The caresses dwindled. But Remo had already succumbed to the latter.

As he lay helpless, the biting fingers began plucking the meat off his bones. Remo opened his eyes in his dream and saw that below the waist he was a skeletonized collection of gleaming red bones. He screamed.

And Kimberly Baynes, her face painted black, snapped one of his bloody femurs in two and fell to sucking out the sweet yellowish marrow.

The changing pitch of the C-5's engines saved Remo from his nightmare. He awoke drenched in sweat under the unfamiliar feel of silk.

The plane was descending in a long gliding approach. The whine of the dropping landing gear pierced his drowsy ears.

Remo remained in his lotus position until he felt the sudden bark and bump of the fat tires hit, as they bounced and then touched down. Momentum dying, the plane rolled to a slow stop.

Remo stood up. He faced the rear gate. The hydraulics began to toil, dropping the gate and admitting a hot blast of desert air.

When the gate had settled into a kind of ramp, Remo stepped out into the blazing sun.

A cluster of people stood awaiting him. Spit-and-polish Arabian soldiers who looked dressed for a parade and civilians in flowing white *thobes*.

And standing in front of them, his knotted brown hands clasped before the familiar red-and-brown robes of his clan, stood Sheik Abdul Hamid Fareem, ruler of Hamidi Arabia. Upon recognizing Remo, his long dour face broke into a pleased smile, his tufted chin dropping.

Remo stepped forward with the assured pride of a Master of Sinanju. This was his first encounter with a head of state as Reigning Master and he wanted to make a good impression. He tried to remember the proper Arabic words of greeting. It had been so many years since he and Chiun had first met the sheik. Now, what was the word for "hello"? Oh, yeah.

Remo stopped only a foot in front of the sheik. Giving a short bow, he said, *"Shalom."*

The sheik started. All around, Arabic voices muttered darkly. A few surreptitious hands pointed down to the impolite bulge at the white infidel's midsection.

The sheik forced his frozen smile to stay fixed on his weathered old face.

"*Ahlan Wusahlan*," he said. "This means 'welcome.' "

"I knew that," Remo lied. "*Inshallah* to you too." He remembered Arabs were always salting their sentences with *inshallah*. You couldn't go wrong with *inshallah*.

"Perhaps it would be better to speak English," Sheik Fareem ventured.

"Good idea," Remo said, wondering if he had gotten "hello" right.

"Am I to understand that you carry on the affairs of the House of Sinanju now that the Master of Sinanju known as Chiun no longer walks the earth?"

"I have that honor," Remo said gravely. He decided to keep his answers short so he sounded more like a Master of Sinanju. Inside, he was itching to cut through the B.S. But he was Master now.

"The bond that binds the House of Hamidi to the House of Sinanju is too strong to be broken by death," the sheik intoned. "Come, let us walk together."

Just in time, Remo remembered that it was Hamidi custom for men to hold hands when conversing.

The sheik reached out for Remo's hand. Remo quickly stuffed his hands into his sleeves. They walked. The sheik's entourage trailed silently.

Sheik Fareem led him to a nearby striped tent beside which two sleek Arabian horses stood tethered, walking very close. That was another thing about Arabs Remo didn't like. They did all their talking practically nose to nose.

Remo only wished his breath didn't smell like liver and garlic mixed with Turkish tobacco.

They entered the tent, the others remaining respectfully outside. Taking places on a Persian rug, they faced one another. Remo declined an offered plate of sheep's eyes, as well as a bubble pipe. The sheik indulged in the latter quietly for some moments before he resumed speaking.

"You still serve America?" he inquired.

"Yes."

"We would pay more," he suggested, fingering his beard.

Remo was no more interested in working for Hamidi Arabia than he wanted to eat sand, but Chiun had always cautioned him never to alienate a potential client. Remo might have the luxury of declining the sheik's offer, but one of Remo's successors might not be so fortunate.

In his mind he said, *You old slave trader. Sinanju is for hire, not for sale.*

Aloud he said, "This is possible. My term of contract with America will end soon."

"We would pay much for the head of the Arab traitor Maddas Hinsein," the sheik suggested. "He who dares call himself the Scimitar of the Arabs." Fareem spat noisily in the sand. "We call him *Ayb al-Arab*—the Shame of the Arabs—a renegade who hides behind women and children rather than face the consequences of his foul overreaching appetites."

"If I come into possession," Remo said with a slight smile, "I might just make you a present of it."

The sheik took a quick hit on his pipe, the corners of his withered lips twitching. Remo realized he was trying to mask a grin of amusement.

"You have come here at the behest of the U.S. government," Fareem resumed, "an emissary of which told me to expect you. How may I repay the debt between Hamidi and Sinanju?"

"I need to get into Kuran. And from there into Irait."

"Death awaits any American who ventures into either place."

"I bring death," Remo told him. "I do not accept it from others."

The sheik nodded. "Well spoken. You are a true son of your teacher. The House is in good hands."

"Thank you," Remo said simply, feeling his heart swell with pride just as his stomach knotted in a sharp pang of grief. If only Chiun were here to hear the sheik's words.

"I will personally ride with you to the frontier and deliver you into the hands of the Kurani resistance. Would this serve your needs?"

Remo nodded. "It would."

"Then let us depart," the sheik said, laying aside his pipe. "Two horses await."

They stood up.

"Have you learned to ride a horse since you sojourned here last?" the sheik inquired.

"Yes."

A twinkle of pleasure came into the old sheik's wizened eyes.

"Good. A man who cannot ride is not much of a man."

"That's what they told me in Outer Mongolia, where I learned horsemanship."

Sheik Abdul Hamid Fareem frowned in the shadow of his ceremonial headdress. "They do not possess sound horseflesh in Outer Mongolia," he spat. "Only runt ponies."

"A horse is a horse," Remo said, adding under his breath, "Of course, of course."

The sheik gave the tent flap an impatient jerk, stooping as he stepped out. Remo followed.

"You will ride one of these beauties," the sheik said with pride, patting the flank of one white horse, who flared his pink nostrils in recognition. "They are the finest steeds in all Araby—which of course means the world. Are you man enough?"

Instead of answering, Remo mounted with a smooth, continuous motion that brought a slight nod of the Arab chief's *ghurta*.

The sheik took to his own saddle. He turned his steed around and slapped it with his reins. The horse plunged away.

Remo followed suit. They rode off into the desert, two warriors carrying on their shoulders the weight of thousands of years of tradition and glory.

27

Maddas Hinsein refused to come out of his office.

All day long, the nervous aides kept coming.

"Precious Leader, the UN have announced a new resolution."

"I do not care. They make resolutions because they are afraid to fight."

"This resolution has condemned the entire Irait command structure to be hanged for war crimes."

"Let them declare war if they wish to hang me."

"Precious Leader, there is no word from our ambassador in Washington. It is the third day."

"Have the defector's family hanged as collaborators."

"Precious Leader, the UN have decreed more sanctions against Irait unless Kuran is immediately relinquished and Reverend Jackman is allowed his freedom."

This required thought. Maddas Hinsein pulled his *abayuh* around himself tightly. It always helped him to think.

"We can defeat their tricks easily," he said at last. "I hereby decree that Irait and Kuran have merged into a single entity. We are henceforth to be known as Iran, and these cowardly resolutions no longer apply to us."

"But, Precious Leader," he was told, "there already exists an Iran."

"Who are our mortal enemies," Maddas spat. "Let them eat the UN sanctions."

The aide had no answer to that. He went away. Maddas grinned, pleased with himself. Throughout his career, he had always found a way around the laws of the civilized world. Why hadn't he thought of this before? Yes, if there were two Irans, they could not level sanctions against one without leveling them at the other. It was a diplomatic masterstroke, almost as brilliant as the mustache decree. The world could no more denigrate him as an ignorant, untraveled Arab again.

Then came the news that even Maddas Hinsein could not ignore.

"Precious Leader."

"What!"

"Word has just come from the villa of your mistress, Yasmini. It was attacked. The guards lie strangled, the contents of their bowels heavy in their pants. It is horrible."

"They died defending their leader's mistress," Maddas returned stiffly. "Greater love has no Moslem than this."

"There is good news, Precious Leader."

"What?"

"Your mistress, she is safe."

Maddas stopped his heavy pacing. "Safe?"

"Yes, the Renaissance Guard must have beaten off the attack with their dying breaths. For when the change of guard entered the villa, they found your mistress still living. Unstrangled. Is this not a glorious day?"

Maddas Hinsein blinked his moist brown eyes several times, his brutal mouth going slack in the privacy of his veil.

"Where is she now?" he demanded hoarsely.

"We have brought her here to the palace, where she is safe, of course. She awaits your pleasure."

"One moment," Maddas Hinsein said, climbing out of his *abayuh*. He hastily stuffed it into his briefcase and carried it out of the office. He emerged, his other hand on the pearl-handled pistol dangling in a hip holster.

"Take me to my beloved Yasmini," he ordered.

The aide hastened to obey. Two Renaissance Guards fell in behind, at a respectful distance. Respectful, because they knew that President Hinsein was in the habit of shooting on the spot guards who inadvertently stepped on the backs of his boots.

The aide brought them all to a black door on a lower floor. It opened on one of the fifty-five bedrooms he used in rotation.

"In here," he said, grinning with pride.

"How do you know that the woman inside is truly my beloved Yasmini?" Maddas Hinsein asked slowly.

The aide's grin collapsed. Obviously the possibility was a new one to him.

"I . . . she . . . that is . . ." The guard steadied his nerve with a deep breath. "When the guard entered the house, she sat quietly, as if awaiting rescue."

"What has she said?"

"Nothing. It is obvious she is in shock from her ordeal."

"One last question," Maddas Hinsein asked, taking out his revolver and jamming it into the aide's Adam's apple. The heavy barrel fixed the man's larynx in place. "What color is her hair?"

Since his jammed larynx couldn't move, the aide simply shrugged. He hoped it was the correct response. Knowing the color of the President of Irait's mistress's hair was probably one of the punishable-by-death offenses. Like shaving or cultivating a mustache larger than the President's.

"You did not remove her *abayuh*?" Maddas asked.

The head shook in the negative. That was definitely the proper response, he knew.

The gun discharged and the aide shook all the way to the floor and after.

"That was your mistake, fool," Maddas Hinsein told the crumpled body.

Gesturing with his pistol, Maddas turned on his two guards. "You and you. Enter and secure the prisoner."

The guards entered with alacrity. Maddas stepped away. If this was an assassination ploy, they would not emerge, and Maddas would run. If they did, he would have his answer to this puzzling turn of events. For one of Maddas Hinsein's deepest secrets was that he did not have a mistress. The *abayuh*-clad woman who sometimes sojourned in the suburban villa and sometimes in his own palace was none other than Maddas Hinsein himself.

Many were the tricks of survival, he thought grimly.

The guards emerged. One said, "She is handcuffed, Precious Leader."

"Did she resist?"

"No."

"Stay here," said Maddas Hinsein, stepping in with his pistol leveled, just in case they were co-plotters. It paid to be careful. Every leader of Irait in the last sixty years had died in office, and none had died in bed.

Maddas closed the door behind him.

The woman wore a black *abayuh* and veil that covered her face except for a swatch around the eyes. She sat demurely on a great bed, her long lashes lowered, her arms tied before her with heavy rope. Her head was oddly tilted to one side, as if listening.

Maddas paused to admire the cut of her *abayuh*. It was very fine. Perhaps he would add it to his collection.

"You are not my mistress Yasmini," he said, advancing.

The eyes looked up. They were violet.

"I know this because I have no mistress named Yasmini."

"I know," the woman said in perfect Arabic. Her voice was strange, somehow dark with portent.

"Before I shoot you dead, tell me how you know this."

"I know this," the woman said, "in the same way I know what fate befell your missing ambassador."

"What of the defector?"

"He did not defect. He was murdered. By an American agent. The same one who has been strangling your family and your advisers all over Abominadad."

"You have arranged to come here just to tell me this?" Maddas asked slowly.

"No. I have come to stir the Caldron of Blood. And you are my ladle."

And as Maddas Hinsein pondered those words, the prisoner stood up.

Maddas cocked his revolver. "I warn you."

The woman's *abayuh* began to lift and spread like wings, impelled by what, Maddas Hinsein knew not, but it was done with such eerie deliberateness that he held his fire out of stupefied curiosity.

The woman seemed to fill the room with her great black *abayuh* wings, and her shadow, palpable as smoke, fell upon him.

"Who are you?" Maddas demanded.

"I am your mistress."

"I have no mistress," Maddas barked.

"You do now," the woman said in American-accepted English. And both hands yanked off her veil, exposing tangled blond hair.

Maddas fired. Too late. A kicking foot knocked the pistol upward. The Scimitar of the Arabs never saw the foot strike. His eyes were on the two yellow-nailed hands that had emerged from hidden slits in the *abayuh* to untie the rope around her bound wrists.

The hemp fell away.

The revolver struck the floor and skittered into a corner.

But Maddas Hinsein's eyes were not on the weapon. He watched the eerie hands floating before the *abayuh* like pale spiders. They began clapping. The upper hands first, the lower ones joining in.

"What do you want of me?" Maddas croaked, mesmerized by those clapping hands. He licked his lips nervously. The sound in his ears stirred half-forgotten desires.

"It is not what I want of you, but what I can offer you," the strange four-handed woman whispered breathily as she drew close. The clapping hands switched off.

"What?" Maddas was sweating. But not with fear.

"I have come to spank you."

Maddas Hinsein's thick eyebrows quirked upward in time with his suddenly wet mustache like jumping caterpillars.

"I am yours, mistress," the Scourge of the Arabs intoned.

Then many hands were all over Maddas Hinsein, plucking his belt away, tearing at his pants, his underwear, and finally exposing naked skin.

They were busy, nimble hands. He felt helpless in their sure grip. Feeling helpless was a new sensation for Maddas Hinsein.

He wondered, as he was pushed onto the sumptuous bed, how this American woman knew his deepest, most secret desire. For Maddas Hinsein had not been properly spanked since he had become the Scimitar of the Arabs, and he missed it sorely.

The guards outside the room grinned at the slapping sounds emanating from within. It sounded as if their mighty leader were literally beating his mistress to death. The slapping went on forever. It was well known that Maddas Hinsein knew how to keep his women in line.

After a long time the ugly sounds of violence ceased.

A voice rose in protest.

"Please, do not stop," it implored.

One guard turned to the other.

"Do you hear?" he asked laughing. "She is begging for the corrective mercy of our Precious Leader."

The other did not join in.

"I think that *is* our Precious Leader," he muttered.

They listened. It was, indeed, the rumbling voice of Maddas Hinsein. He sounded unhappy.

A low woman's voice answered him. It was firm and unyielding.

Presently the door opened. A red-faced Maddas Hinsein stuck out his head. His eyes were shiny and wide. Sweat beaded his mustache.

"One of you take word to General Azziz," Maddas barked. "I want a tank column to attack the U.S. front lines. They will pay for the crimes committed against Abominadad."

A low murmur of sound drew him back in. The door shut. When it reopened, Maddas Hinsein had a change of orders.

"Use gas instead," he said. His eyes flicked back to the room. In a hushed tone, as if in fear of being overheard, he added, "Do it quietly. A quick strike and then retreat. Try not to bring the Americans down on our heads. I do not want trouble."

The door closed again. Through the heavy wood they could hear their Precious Leader's voice.

"I did as you bade, glorious one," he whimpered. "Now let the mighty rain of your discipline fall upon my penitent cheeks."

Relentless slapping sounds resumed.

The guards exchanged peculiar glances. They flipped a coin to see who would bear the strange message to the defense minister. They decided not to mention any of this.

28

Remo Williams shifted in the saddle, trying for a comfortable position. Normally, this was not a problem. Remo was trained to endure pain.

But enduring mere pain was one thing. Riding long hours in the saddle, a hard leather pommel rubbing into his tender crotch, was another. He had hoped leaving all but one of Kimberly's scarves would lessen his predicament. No such luck.

The one scarf he had brought was stuffed deep up one kimono sleeve. So far, he had resisted digging it out. But he thought about it constantly.

"You appear unhappy of cast," Sheik Fareem muttered, inclining his predatory face in Remo's direction.

"I still grieve for my Master," Remo said quietly.

"After so many years? In truth, you are a worthy son. Would that I had a son such as you."

Remo said nothing. He remembered back to the days when he and Chiun had first encountered the sheik. There had been a dispute between the sheik and Chiun on one side and Remo and the sheik's worthless son, Abdul, on the other. Remo's assignment had conflicted with an ancient understanding Sinanju had with the Hamid family.

During the confrontation, Remo and Chiun had been forced into mortal combat with one another. Chiun had pretended to be killed, sparing Remo. Since that day, the sheik had believed Chiun dead. Such was his sense of honor that he worshiped the Master of Sinanju's memory and honored Remo's continued existence.

"Whatever happened to Prince Abdul?" Remo asked after a while.

"He cleans stables in a pitiful border town called Zar,"

the sheik spat. "Allah is just. But I have taken into my heart a nephew, the son of my wife's sister, to be my son in spirit. He is called Prince General Bazzaz. He has brought the House of Hamid both joy and pride, for he commands my army."

Remo nodded. "I've seen him on TV." He neglected to mention that the prince general looked like an operatic buffoon strutting around before the cameras and claiming that the U.S. forces were in Hamidi Arabia merely to "support" the frontline Arab units.

"If Allah is good to us," Sheik Fareem murmured, "we will meet him on the frontier. For he is now engaged in installing the best defenses money can buy along the front lines."

"Look forward to it," Remo said without enthusiasm, his eyes on a trio of camels that had darted across the path. They galloped like ungainly antelopes, speedy but awkward, spitting and snorting as they passed from sight.

His eyes noting the awkward bulge at Remo's crotch, the sheik wondered if all Americans were so lusty in their grief. It was truly a riddle.

They were stopped by a column of Arab soldiers a few miles south of the Hamidi–Kuran neutral zone.

Upon recognizing the sheik, the Arabs fell to their knees. Instead of bowing to the sheik, who sat astride his Arabian steed, they faced a different direction entirely and touched the sand with their palms and foreheads, muttered words escaping their lips.

"I thought Arabs were used to the desert heat," Remo said, watching the peculiar display.

To Remo's surprise, the sheik dismounted. Unfurling a small Persian rug, he likewise faced the same way, joining in the muttered praying. For that was what it was, Remo realized. They were facing Mecca.

Their oblations done, Fareem climbed to his feet. The others got up, then knelt again. This time at the sheik's feet.

Remo sat impatiently in his saddle. The soldiers addressed their king. The king replied formally. All of it went in one ear and out the other where Remo was concerned.

When they were done, the soldiers found their feet and formed an escort. The sheik remounted and they got under way once more.

"What was that all about?" Remo asked.

"They were concerned for my safety, alone in the desert," Sheik Fareem supplied.

"You weren't alone," Remo pointed out.

The sheik smiled. "That is what I told them. And that I had all the protection a man could need in the honored one who rode at my side."

Remo nodded, his eyes on the undulating landscape ahead.

He squinted. On the near horizon, a line of strange shapes appeared in the shimmering, quaking heat.

"What the hell?" he muttered.

During their journey from the base, they had skirted several military positions, including a line of American Bradley Fighting Vehicles draped in sand-colored netting arrayed in battalion formation. The American line had been the innermost bulwark. Oddly, it was also the largest.

Beyond that had been an Egyptian platoon, a Syrian squad, and other pockets, including a group of extremely morose Kuranis. Remo had asked the sheik why the strongest force had not been on the front line.

"Because it is the privilege of our fellow Arabs to defend and preserve Arab soil from the godless aggressor," the sheik had said proudly.

"You picked the right troops," Remo had replied politely, recognizing cannon fodder when he saw it.

The Hamidi defensive line was the smallest of these, Remo saw. Barely a squad of overdressed soldiers in braided powder-blue uniforms, clustered around traditional desert tents and an assortment of military vehicles, mostly APCis. There wasn't a single tank on the line, as Remo had expected, considering the estimated fifty thousand Soviet-made Iraiti tanks that lurked somewhere beyond the undulating horizon.

The Hamidi Arabian first line of defense was a string of sand-camouflaged trucks with open beds. They faced away from the neutral zone, as if poised for an immediate retreat.

Mounted on the flatbeds, their giant blades facing enemy territory, were the largest fans Remo had ever seen in his life.

They stood over twenty feet tall, gleaming blades protected by steel cages. Except for the size of the devices, they might have come off a Woolworth shelf.

"I don't believe it," Remo blurted out.

The sheik grinned his pleasure at the compliment.

"Awesome, are they not?" the sheik gloated. "Only a week ago, we had fans but half that size. My nephew, the prince general, conducted an inspection tour and saw the paltry blades and pronounced them inadequate to repel the Iraiti challenge. We have factories going twenty-four hours a day producing more. By autumn, the entire border—hundreds of miles long—will be so equipped."

"What good are fans against tanks?" Remo blurted out.

The sheik spat. "No damn good, by Allah. We do not fear Iraiti tanks. If the Iraitis send tanks, the Americans will bomb the hell out of them. It is their nerve gases that make even the most fearless of bedouins shiver in the hot sun. If they dare use their gases, we will blow them back into their cowardly faces. *Inshallah!*"

At the sound of that barked exclamation, a young man in an outrageous white uniform festooned with gold braid emerged from an air-conditioned tent.

"Uncle!" he cried, his dusky face lighting up.

"My nephew! Come, I have a great warrior you must meet."

As Remo and the sheik dismounted, Prince General Sulyman Bazzaz approached. He carried a bejeweled swagger stick and his radiant grin seemed like a hologram floating before his face. Even from a hundred yards away Remo could smell his after-shave. And he wasn't even trying.

"O long-lived one!" the prince general said, ignoring Remo. "You have come to see my handiwork."

"It is good, but it must wait. I must present an old friend of the Hamid family, the Master of Sinanju." The sheik indicated Remo with a flourish of his camel-hair *thobe*.

"Call me Remo," Remo said, putting out his hand. It was ignored. Remo tried to stuff both hands into his pants pockets, but the pocketless kimono resisted the gesture.

What a pain, Remo thought. *I'm never going to get the hang of this diplomatic stuff.*

"Who is this man?" the prince general asked in Arabic, eyeing Remo's hands with distaste. They were powdered by blowing sand.

"Look, let's cut to the chase," Remo said, abandoning decorum. "I need a lift into Kuran."

This brought a response from the prince general. "For what purpose?"

"He is on a secret mission for America," the sheik confided, drawing his nephew close to him with an insistent tugging on the prince general's braided sleeve. The two men huddled.

Remo folded his arms, but the swathlike kimono sleeves made it as impossible as pocketing them. He tucked them into his sleeves instead, feeling foolish as the wind kicked up, blowing powdery sand up his kimono skirt.

As the two Arabs talked, a whirlwind meandered by, seemingly coming from nowhere, a wavering column of whirling sand so dense it was impossible to see into its core.

No one paid it any special heed, although headdresses were pulled close to keep out the windblown grit. Interested, Remo watched the whirlwind blow past the position, dip into a shallow wadi, and carry airborne sand over the horizon.

When the two Arabs broke their huddle, the prince general stepped up to Remo and shook his hand with a loose-fingered grip.

"I am delighted to meet an old friend of my uncle's. Ask and I shall grant your wish."

"How deep can you get me into Kuran?"

"As deep as you wish," Bazzaz said, surreptitiously wiping his right hand on the side of his immaculate thigh. "It is barren sand for hundreds of miles."

"Then let's go. I'm in a big rush."

Prince General Bazzaz led Remo and the sheik to a low-slung APC-type vehicle. It bristled with electronic sensors and spidery antennae. It might have been a NASA-surplus moon-rover.

"This is the perfect chariot for you," he said with toothy pride. "It is completely gasproof. It is German-made."

"Is that supposed to impress me?" Remo asked.

"Possibly. For you must understand that the Iraiti nerve gases are also made by Germans."

"The Black Forest must be hopping these days," Remo said.

"Not as much as Kuran is today. But we shall soon change that," Prince General Bazzaz promised, winking at his proud uncle, hovering nearby.

"Now you're talking," Remo said.

"Yes. Of course I am talking." The prince general looked puzzled.

"Skip it," Remo said wearily. "American slang."

The prince general and the sheik exchanged glances. They returned to muttering in Arabic. Remo wondered what they were saying, but decided it wasn't important enough to worry about.

"Is he CIA?" Prince General Bazzaz wondered, eyeing Remo. "I have heard they are not normal."

"No. You must forgive him. He is in mourning."

"He is a very lusty mourner," Prince General Bazzaz commented, noting the odd hang of the American's robe below the waist.

"I do not understand that either," the sheik admitted. "He has been that way for some four hours."

Bazzaz's eyes widened. "Truly? Perhaps he has Arab blood."

"Only Allah knows. Now, quickly, do as he bids. I do not relish being on the front lines."

The radiant smile returned to the prince general's well-tanned visage as he returned to Remo's side.

"All has been arranged. I will have my personal driver conduct you. Where do you wish to go? Exactly?"

"Abominadad," Remo said casually.

"Abominadad? You go to kill Maddas?"

"I wish."

"You wish what?"

Remo sighed. "Never mind. Let's get this caravan on the road."

"Truly." The prince general lifted his voice in Arabic. *"Isma!"*

A corpsman approached, looking more like a hotel doorman than a soldier. He listened to the prince general's rapid instructions with bright black eyes.

The prince general turned to Remo.

"It has been settled. You will be driven to the town of Fahad. We have resistance contacts there. You will find them on Afreet Street. Ask for Omar. He will get you into Irait."

"Great. Let's go."

The driver opened the side door of the APC for Remo.

He was surprised to find that the front seat was covered in white mink. The dashboard looked like Spanish leather.

"Let me guess," Remo asked the prince general. "This is your personal chariot?"

"Yes. How did you guess?"

"It's wearing the same perfume you are," Remo said, climbing in.

"It is Old Spice. I bathe in it daily."

The sheik drew up to the open door. He took Remo's hand in both of his. Before Remo could stop him, the old sheik kissed him twice. Once on each cheek. Remo let this pass.

"*Salaam aleikim*, Master of Sinanju," he said.

"Yeah, *shalom* to you too," Remo said.

Then a warbling siren jumped to life. It came from the prince general's tent. Every light on the APC's high-tech dashboard blinked and blazed like a Christmas tree.

"What the hell is going on?" Remo shouted.

"*La!*" Prince General Bazzaz shouted in a horrified voice. The sheik paled so fast his beard seemed to darken.

All over the camp, Arab soldiers jumped into rubberized chemical-warfare garb. Others, more brave, leapt for the trucks. Some manned the great fans. Others climbed into the cabs, where they shut themselves in, hitting dashboard buttons that engaged the great northward-pointing fans.

They roared into life, kicking up billows of obscuring sand and confirming for Remo what he had only begun to suspect.

It was a gas attack. And Remo was caught in the middle of it.

29

In the darkness, there was nothing. No sound. No taste. No light. No heat. Cold was a mere recollection, not a palpable sensation. Only the memory of coldness and wetness and a bitter, bitter metallic taste.

Yet it was cold in the darkness. There was wetness. Water. It, too, was cold. But it did not feel cold because there was no feeling.

Somewhere in the darkness a spirit spark flickered. Awareness returned. Was this the Void? The question was unspoken. The answer nonexistent. Awareness faded. This was not the correct time. Perhaps the next time, he would try. Again. If there was a next time. If an eternity had not already crawled by since the last period of awareness.

As consciousness dimmed, a voice, female and discordantly musical, like a bell of basest metal, cut through the soundlessness of the abyss.

You cannot save him now. He is lost to you. He is mine. You are dead. Finish your dying, stubborn one.

The voice descended into low, diabolical laughter that followed his sinking mind into the blackest of pits that should have felt cold, but didn't.

Yet it was.

30

Remo shut the APC door against the blowing sand. The dashboard was going crazy—gas-warning instruments, he decided. Either that or Old Spice had leaked into the electronics.

All around him, Arab soldiers flew into action. He was surprised at their discipline. Soon, every fan was roaring. The noise was like a million airplanes preparing for takeoff.

Prince General Bazzaz raced for a nearby helicopter. Its rotor roar blended with the rest. In a swirl of sand it took off, the sheik on board. Instead of retreating, however, the helicopter flew toward the north. Both members of the royal family were wearing gas masks. Remo was surprised at their apparent bravery.

Everyone had gotten into a gas suit by this time, including Remo's driver. Remo searched the cockpit for a mask of his own. He found one clipped under the dashboard. He pulled it over his head. It was a filter mask, with no attached oxygen tank. When he inhaled, the air smelled of charcoal, but it was breathable.

For several minutes the Arabs tended their fans, manually rotating them so their airstreams overlapped.

"Modern warfare," Remo grumbled. "Maybe next year they'll have automatic turning gears. Like K-Mart."

The helicopter quickly returned, blowing up more sand and adding to the confusion. Remo decided to wait for the sand to settle down before driving off. If anything, it got worse. Oddly, the sand seemed to be blowing back from the front lines, despite the fans' furious output. The blades were completely enveloped in dusty clouds.

Through the triple-paned windshield Remo could hear panicky exclamations in Arabic, none of which he understood.

Prince General Bazzaz fought his way through the gathering grit. He pounded on the door.

Remo opened it. "What's wrong?" he shouted over the din.

"We must retreat." His voice was muffled by his mask.

"Why? The fans are doing fine."

"The Iraiti are advancing. It is war."

"With tanks?"

"No, they have outsmarted us. They have fans too. And theirs are bigger than ours."

"You're joking," Remo exclaimed.

"I am not. This vehicle is needed for the retreat. I am sorry. You are on your own."

"Thanks a bunch," Remo said dryly.

"You are welcome a bunch. Now, please, step out."

"Not a chance," Remo snarled, gunning the engine.

The prince general jumped back. He wasn't accustomed to disobedience. While he was getting used to it, Remo slammed the door.

Turning, the prince general gave out a cry. The trucks started up. They advanced. That is, they went south, driving toward Remo, their fans blowing to beat the band, but doing nothing more to dispel the sandstorm.

Carrying Bazzaz, the helicopter lifted off in the swirl, turning its tail and flying low to the ground. And the truck line roared past Remo.

The dashboard gas sensors raised their screeching to a new level. Remo reached up under the leather and found a nest of wiring. He pulled them loose. The screeching stopped, although a few angry lights still winked.

"That's better," Remo muttered, sliding behind the wheel. He started the APC lumbering forward.

"Abominadad, here I come," he said.

Remo sent the APC bouncing over the dunes and wadis. Visibility soon dropped to zero. The color of the sandstorm slowly changed. It went from dun to a mustard yellow, until it resembled airborne diarrhea.

Holding the wheel steady, Remo relied on his natural sense of direction. He knew, somehow, that he was driving true north, and that was all that concerned him.

He didn't see the oncoming truck until its sand-colored grille emerged from the swirl like a shark with bad teeth.

It was a light truck, Remo realized. It was barreling

straight at him, a goggle-eyed driver behind the wheel and canisters spewing the diarrhea-yellow gas mounted atop the cab.

"Screw him," Remo said, holding his course.

The heavy APC slammed into the truck without stopping. The grille caved in, its front tires lifting high. It tried to climb the APC roof, but its rear wheels lost all traction.

It bounced away, upsetting its twenty-foot rear-mounted fan. The cage crumpled when it struck sand. The blades chewed themselves to pieces against the mangled framework.

Remo wrestled the wheel around to get a better look at the truck. It lay on its side, wheels spinning. The fan lay several feet away. From the overturned cab, hissing yellowish billows of vapor spewed angrily. Remo glimpsed a battery of spilled gas cylinders, now no longer bolted to the dented cab roof.

The cab had been split open and a driver sprawled in the sand, holding his throat and gulping like a beached flounder.

His gas mask lay at his elbow, but he was too busy dying to look for it.

"Remind me not to crank down the windows anytime soon," Remo muttered, grateful for the sealed gas-proof vehicle.

In the distance, a line of similar trucks barreled south, as if impelled by their great fans. But the fans were pointed in the direction they traveled, pushing churning billows of gas ahead. Wind resistance pushed it back. The gas went everywhere except where it was supposed to.

"What the hell," Remo said to himself. "Juniper can cool his heels in Mad Ass's dungeon a little longer."

He sent the APC rolling after them.

Remo drew up alongside one, and pulling the wheel to the right, inexorably crowded the truck into the next one in line.

The drivers' peripheral vision was impaired by their gas-mask goggles, so the first time they realized they were in trouble was when their spinning wheels rubbed one another.

At the speed they were traveling, that meant instant disaster.

Remo watched the first two trucks collide and spin away, tumbling, throwing off whirling fan blades and rags of gas.

They landed wrapped together in an impossible contortion of metal.

From that point on, it was just a matter of sideswiping each underweight truck with the armored APC until it tipped over or lost control.

After the last truck ate sand, Remo wrestled the APC north once more and played with the steering until his body told him he was attuned to magnetic north. The approximate direction of Abominadad.

He settled down for the ride, one thought uppermost in his mind.

How had Chiun done it all those years? The damn kimono was hotter than hell.

31

Major Nasur Hamdoon was tired of shooting Kuranis.

He had been glad to shoot Kuranis during the early heady days of the reclamation of Kuran. Especially when the ungrateful Kuranis resisted being returned to the Iraiti motherland with their puny small arms, stones, and Molotov cocktails. Who did they think they were—Palestinians?

Did they not understand that all Arabs were brothers, and destined to be united? It was very strange. Nasur had expected to be welcomed as a liberator.

So when the liberated Arabs of Kuran turned on him with their pitiful weapons, Nasur indignantly shot them dead in the streets. The surviving Kuranis went underground. They planted bombs. They sniped from rooftops.

And the Iraiti troops under Major Hamdoon's command simply rounded up civilians at random and had them executed by various methods. Sometimes they were simply bled in the streets, their blood collected in glass beakers to be stored as plasma in the unlikely eventuality the Americans summoned up enough courage to attack.

This had been the good old days, Major Hamdoon thought unhappily as evening came to the Kurani desert. There had been many Kuranis to shoot and many excuses to do it.

Not now. Now he lived in his lone T-72 tank—practically the only safe haven in the entire country. In fact, it was virtually the only habitation in Maddas Province, as occupied Kuran was now called.

Perched high in the turret, Major Hamdoon trained his field glasses down the lonely Irait–Kuran Friendship Road. It stopped dead only twenty kilometers south of here—the Hamidi Arabs having impolitely declined to pay for extension in the good old days when Irait battled Irug in another war of President Hinsein's creation. But for their stinginess, Major Hamdoon thought morosely, they would have been liberated as well. Major Hamdoon looked forward to their ultimate liberation. As he was based in the inhospitable marshy southern region of Kuran—now Irait's thirteenth province—he had had no opportunity to share in the redistribution of wealth imposed on fat, too-rich Kuran.

For there was nothing worth stealing in southern Kuran.

So Major Hamdoon bided his time and hoped the Americans would finally attack. That would provide the excuse to assimilate the corrupt and lazy Hamidi Arabs. And he would have plenty of U.S. Marines to shoot. Major Hamdoon had grown sick at heart from shooting fellow Arabs—even ones who had the indecency to make themselves prosperous while other Arabs went without.

A throaty engine roar pricked up his ears. It came from the south. He raised his field glasses. An unfamiliar squarish vehicle was coming up the Friendship Road—which was very interesting, since, technically, it went nowhere.

Major Hamdoon squinted through the field glasses, cursing the infernal dark. When the Americans made their inglorious but inevitable tactical mistake, he expected to plunder their night-vision goggles from their dead bodies. He had heard that they cost four thousand dollars each. That was five figures in Iraiti *dinars*.

Moonlight caught and silvered a fast-traveling vehicle coming up the road. Major Hamdoon's heart quickened with anticipation. The vehicle was traveling without lights. It must be the Americans!

Reaching down into the hatch, he touched the turret-turning lever, sending the smoothbore cannon grinding toward the road. His tank lay athwart the road. The vehicle, whatever it was, could not pass.

His hand leapt to the cannon trigger. But on reflection, he held his fire. A 125-millimeter shell would no doubt ruin his expensive night goggles. He would intimidate the Americans into surrendering, instead. But he would not bleed them. Their blood was not good enough to sustain Arab lives.

The vehicle was low and wide and armored, Major Hamdoon saw when he turned on the gimbal-mounted spotlight.

"Halt!" he cried in thick, accented English.

To his pleased surprise, the vehicle obediently coasted to a stop. A door clicked open and a man stepped out. He was tall and lean, walking with an easy confident grace. He wore a long black garment like a Hamidi *thobe* or a Kurani *dishdash.*

He was no American, Major Hamdoon thought disappointedly. And he wore no night-seeing goggles.

The man drew near.

"What do you do here, *effendi?*" Major Hamdoon asked in Arabic.

To his surprise, the man answered in English.

"Help me out, pal. I'm looking for the town of Fahad. Know it?"

"Who are you?" Major Hamdoon asked slowly, puzzled because the man did not act like an aggressor.

"Just a nameless traveler trying to get to Fahad."

"I would know your name."

"Remo. Now, point me to Fahad, and while you're at it, get that tank out of my way." The man rotated his hands absently.

"You sound like an American," Hamdoon suggested in an unsteady voice.

"And you sound like an Arab with half a brain."

"Is that an insult?"

"Is Maddas Hinsein full of shit?"

"I asked my question first."

The American's thin mouth quirked into a smile. He did not flinch from the thousand-candlepower searchlight. His eyes simply squeezed down to nearly Oriental slits. They gleamed blackly, menacingly. Unafraid.

Major Hamdoon tapped the cannon control, dropping the smoothbore until it was pointing directly at the approaching figure's black chest.

"Are you prepared to die, unbeliever?"

"Not till you point me to Fahad."

"I will never do that."

Suddenly the American executed a kind of circus flip. He tumbled into the air, to land, perfectly balanced, on the cannon's long bore.

This was an eventuality that Major Hamdoon had not been prepared for at the Iraiti Military Academy. If he fired, he would miss completely.

So Major Hamdoon did the next best thing. He threw the turret-turning lever back and forth wildly.

The turret jerked right, then left, then right again.

The American walked up the barrel to the turret with breezy assurance. He didn't bother lifting his arms to balance.

Major Hamdoon hastily tilted the searchlight into his eyes.

The man simply ducked under the cone of light. Casually he plucked Hamdoon from his perch. He did this with one hand, without even disturbing his balance. This impressed Major Hamdoon, who had understood that Americans were inept in all things—except making movies.

"Hi!" he said. "Want me to repeat my question?"

"It will do you no good," Major Hamdoon said stiffly. "I am a Moslem. We do not fear death."

The man's hand jumped out. Two fingers struck the searchlight glass. It was very thick. Still, it shattered into fine glassy gravel. Sparks flew. Something sputtered and burned.

"Please do repeat," Major Hamdoon said in his most polite English.

"Point me the way to Fahad."

The major pointed north up the Friendship Road. "It is back that way."

"How far?"

"Less than seventy kilometers."

To Hamdoon's horror, the American frowned. "How many miles is that?" he asked.

"As many as you want," the major said, not understanding the question.

"I love a cooperative Iraiti," the American said pleasantly. "Now, get this pile of junk out of my way."

"Gladly. In return for a favor of equal value."

A slow smile crept into the American's face. In the failing light, his eyes floated like evilly glowing stars in the skull-like hollows of his eyes.

"Sure," he said laconically. "Why not?"

"I will trade you this information in return for your best pair of night-seeing goggles," Major Hamdoon said boldly.

"Why do you want them?"

"So I can see the Americans when they come."

"I got news for you, pal. They're here."

The Iraiti looked momentarily confused. "But there is but one of you."

"One's all that's needed. Now, move that tank."

"I refuse until you give me something for my eyes that will turn night into day."

"You mean day into night," the American said.

"Yes, I mean that," Major Hamdoon said, wondering how he had gotten the American words for "day" and "night" confused for so long.

Then the American lifted two fingers of one hand and drove them into the major's eyes so fast there was no pain. Only sudden blackness.

And as the major fell into the sand, wondering what had happened, the American's cheerful voice rang through the night that would last to the end of Nasur Hamdoon's days, saying, "Don't sweat it. I'll move the tank myself. You just enjoy the view."

The town of Fahad was virtually a ghost town when Remo rolled into it hours later. Dawn had come by this time. He had encountered minimal resistance along the road. Just the occasional two-man patrol in Land Rovers.

After ascertaining from the first two of these patrols that he was indeed on the correct road to Fahad—and by the way, he could consider himself a prisoner of the Iraiti Army—Remo didn't bother to leave the APC to break any Iraiti necks. He just ran them down where they stood.

The more he did this, the more impressed he was by German engineering. The APC barely gave a bump as it passed over the bodies. And either they were slow to scream or the soundproofing was excellent too.

As he lumbered through the town, Remo made a mental note to look into a German model if he ever had personal need of an armored personnel carrier.

Fahad had been virtually picked clean, he saw with disgust. Some buildings still stood. None had glass in them. Only a few windows had actually been broken by violence. They had simply been removed, sashes and all.

Remo looked for street signs. There were none.

"Damn. They even took the frigging street signs. How the hell do I find Afreet Street?"

A woman in an ebony *abayuh* ran for cover when he lumbered around a corner. A child threw a rock that bounced harmlessly off his sandwich-glass windshield.

He saw no uniformed troops. But then, he saw hardly anything of human life of any persuasion.

In the center of town was a disturbed patch of dirt that had once been some kind of park. Remo could see the fresh stumps of date trees, evidently carried away to Iraiti lumberyards. The dirt was freshly turned.

"Don't tell me they took the grass too?" Remo wondered aloud.

In the middle of the park, a derrick reared up. Remo was surprised that it too had not been driven back to Irait. But as he made a circle of the park, he saw why.

A man in a white Arab costume hung from the derrick cable by the neck. It obviously served as the local gallows.

Remo braked and got out.

Cupping his hands to his mouth, he called out in English, "Anyone home? I'm an American. Friend or foe, come get me."

A moment passed. A bird squawked somewhere. It sounded hungry.

Then out of the hovels of Fahad, men, women, and children poured. The men were old, the women frantic, and the children, like children everywhere, excited by the commotion.

"Americans!" they shouted. "The Americans have come. It is the Americans."

"There's just one of me," Remo told the approaching stampede. This cooled them off faster than a water hose.

"There is only you?" an old woman asked, creeping from a doorway.

"Sorry. Look, I need to find Omar. Sheik Fareem sent me."

The woman pushed through the crowd. "Omar the freedom fighter?"

"Sounds about right."

"He is behind you, American who has come too late."

Remo turned. The only person behind him hung from a derrick, where a falcon alighted to begin pecking at his eyes. After a few pecks, the bird flew away. He was obviously not the early bird. That bird had taken Omar's eyes long days ago.

Remo addressed the crowd.

"How easy is it to get to Abominadad from here?"

A toothless old man said, "Can you read Arabic?"

"No."

"Then you cannot get to Abominadad from this Allah-forsaken place. What few street signs survive are in Arabic, and the way is long and winding and full of Iraiti dogs." He spat in the dirt.

"I gotta get to Abominadad," Remo said.

"If a man is desperate enough, anything is possible."

"Is that a hint of encouragement?"

"If one is willing to surrender himself to the Iraiti invader," Remo was told, "one might get to Abominadad from here. But only if one is valuable to the Iraitis. Otherwise they will carve your belly with their bayonets."

"Why would they do that?"

"Because they are bored, and they already know the color of Kurani entrails."

"Gotcha. Where can I find the nearest detachment of Iraitis? I need guys who speak English."

"There are Iraitis in the next town. Hamas. It was to Hamas that our young women fled, fearing rape. The Iraitis tortured some of the old women to learn where they went. Now they are dead and the flower of our womanhood are being defiled by these so-called Arab brothers."

"Tell you what, point me to Hamas and I'll see if I can't break a few Iraiti skulls for you."

"Done. But tell us, American, when will the Marines land?"

"They would have landed ten years ago if you'd let them. But now, I don't know. Maybe tomorrow. Maybe never. But if I can get to Abominadad, maybe the Marines won't be needed."

Hearing that, the old woman turned to the others. "By the command of Allah, help this righteous American to find his way to Hamas."

The Iraiti checkpoint leading to Hamas consisted of a beige T-72 tank with a thrown track on one side of the road and a jeep up on blocks on the other. A reclining corporal snored on the tank's fender and another sat behind the jeep's tripod-mounted machine gun, smoking a Turkish cigarette that Remo could smell from three miles away. He was running with the air vents open.

Remo pulled up. The two Iraiti soldiers blinked in stupefied surprise as Remo emerged from the APC, clapping his hands to get their attention.

"This Hamas?" he asked. "Where all the women went?"

Their eyes noticed the bulge below Remo's waist, and the two Iraitis jumped to an instant conclusion.

"You are an American deserter?" one asked. The corporal on the tank. He looked sleepy.

"Maybe."

"You come to trade that fine vehicle for Arab women?"

"That's it." Remo said. "You got it exactly. Take me to the Arab women and it's yours. The pink slip's in the glove compartment."

The Iraiti in the jeep threw the charging lever on his .35-caliber. He sneered.

"You are too late."

"I am?"

"The women wore out three weeks ago. But if you are so eager to have sex with Arabs, we have a few men who can accommodate you."

Remo frowned. "How about we just skip that part and I just surrender?"

"You are not in control here."

"I have all of the secrets of the American offensive plans in my head. Just take me to someone in charge and I'll spill my guts to him."

"You will spill your guts to me or I will spill your guts into the sand."

"I'll pass," Remo said, moving on the jeep low and fast.

The startled gunner jumped into action. The perforated barrel burped, spitting fire in all directions.

Remo felt the shock waves of passing bullets fly over the back of his head. None struck him.

He came up under the startled gunner's nose and took hold of the wooden barrel-changing handle, gave it a twist, and the barrel fell into the front seat, where it set the upholstery smoldering.

"Did someone say something about guts?" Remo asked.

"I am not afraid of you," the gunner spat. "I am a Moslem. Moslems welcome death."

Remo gave the man the flat of his hand and something to thank Allah for at the same time.

"I hope you're happy now," he said after the gunner

collapsed, his nose inverted and his brain full of worm tracks made by driven bone chips.

Remo went over to the tank. The tank soldier's legs were disappearing down the turret. Remo jumped up and caught them.

"I suppose you're a Moslem too," he called down.

A hollow voice echoed up from the tank's innards.

"Yes, but I am a death-fearing Moslem."

"Then you're not going to like what I'll do to you if I can't find someone in authority to surrender to."

"See Colonel Abdulla. He will accept your surrender. Gladly."

"Colonel Abdulla speak English?" Remo asked.

"As good as me."

"How many Arab women you wear out?"

"Too many to count. I am sorry I have left none for you, lusty one."

"Don't give it another thought," Remo said casually, pulling the soldier's legs in opposite directions. The splintering of his pelvic bone was louder than the soldier's anguished screams. It lasted longer too.

Colonel Jassim Abdulla was reluctant to accept Remo's unconditional surrender. He was in the middle of fornicating with a goat and was at a critical stage. To withdraw, or not to withdraw. It was a question that haunted Iraitis in peace as well as in war.

Remo, who had never seen anyone hump a goat before, had a question.

"Why are you doing that?"

"Because there are no more living Kurani men, and if I do this to my men, it would be bad for morale." The colonel's face was reddening with exertion.

By that, Remo took it to mean that Colonel Abdulla was one of the sexually misdirected Iraitis the late gunner had offered him.

The goat bleated in fear. Feeling sorry for it, Remo grasped one quivering horn and tugged. The goat slipped from the colonel's tight embrace with a slurpy *pop*! of a sound, leaving the colonel to pump his seed over the barren Kuran sand.

His eyes were closed, so he didn't notice that he was humping dead air.

When he was done, Colonel Abdulla came out of his crouch and noticed Remo's problem. His thick Maddas Hinsein mustache lifted with his grin.

"Why did you not mention your problem?" he said, pulling up his pants. "The goat could have waited. Goats make excellent—how do you say it?—sloppy seconds."

"Pass," Remo said. "You don't seem surprised to find yourself face-to-face with an American," he added.

"The Americans are overdue. I know this. Why do you think I am busy making time with a goat? After the Marines hit the beach, there will be no more goats for Colonel Abdulla, alas."

"Spoken like an Iraiti with goatshit on his pecker. How about surrending—"

"Where are the rest of your Americans?" the colonel asked.

"Sorry to disappoint you, but there's only me."

The colonel's face fell. "You must be mad. I cannot surrender myself to one lone American. My Arab pride would suffer."

"You got it backward, Achmed. I've come to surrender to you."

"Why?"

"Don't ask me that question and I promise not to tell Maddas Hinsein when I see him in Abominadad that you like to bang goats."

The colonel gave this proposition serious thought.

"Deal," he said. He offered a hand that smelled of goat. "Shake?"

"No. How soon can you get me to Abominadad?"

His dark eyes going wistfully to Remo's bulge, the colonel sighed. "Long after your magnificent instrument has tired."

"Don't bet the war on it," Remo said glumly.

32

Maddas Hinsein didn't hear the ringing telephone through the satisfyingly meaty smacking sounds. Then they stopped.

"Why do you deny me, my sweet?" he asked, lifting his face off the fluffy pillow, unhappiness writ large in his deep soulful eyes. They were in a torture chamber deep in the Palace of Sorrows, lying on a medieval iron bed. The spikes had been replaced by a mattress.

Poised above his naked beet-red behind, four hot-pink palms hovered. One disappeared from view. It returned, clutching a telephone receiver. The hand—its nails as yellow as banana peel—brought the mouthpiece to Maddas' unhappy lips.

"Attend to business first, and I will finish you after."

"Yes, O all-adept one," the Scourge of the Arabs said meekly.

Maddas' voice lost its submissive coloring. "Have I not told you I was not to be disturbed?" he barked into the phone.

"A thousand pardons, O Precious Leader," his defense minister replied in a shaky voice. "Our offensive has collapsed."

Maddas blinked. Of course. The gas attack. He had been having such a good time, he had forgotten he ordered it. In truth, he half-expected to die at any moment from U.S. blockbuster bombs, so he had left the operational details to his generals.

"What happened?" he wanted to know.

"The trucks fell over. Should we send more trucks?"

"No. Obviously they have larger fans than even our spies in Hamidi Arabia reported. Have all our spies recalled and executed."

"But that will give us no spies in enemy territory."

"No spies are preferable to wrong spies. Do this, or I will have your children hanged in front of your eyes."

"But I have no children. You are perhaps thinking of the previous defense minister's children, whom you had chopped up and served to his wife. Cold."

"Then I will have the previous defense minister's wife beheaded before your eyes," Maddas Hinsein bellowed. "Do this!"

"At once," the defense minister said crisply. He hesitated. "There . . . there is further intelligence, Precious Leader."

"Speak."

"Our brave forces have captured an American spy. He has promised to reveal all of America's attack plans."

"I have heard this before . . ." Maddas growled. "Man or woman?"

"Man. Definitely. He is one horny infidel, too."

"Is this man tall with dark hair and eyes, with wrists mightier than any Arab's?"

Thinking it was a trick question, the defense minister hesitated.

"Answer!" Maddas roared, unhappy that the delicious stinging sensation was deserting his overstimulated backside.

"Yes, Precious Leader. But how did you know?"

Maddas pushed the receiver aside with his chin.

"You spoke truly. He has come."

"Never doubt me," Kimberly Baynes said sweetly. "All you desire will come to pass if you never doubt me."

He turned his mouth to the receiver again. "Have him brought to me."

"At once, Precious Leader."

Kimberly Baynes replaced the receiver on its cradle. She adjusted the black cords that kept Maddas Hinsein, absolute master of Irait and Kuran, spread-eagled and helpless on the four-poster bed. He lay on his stomach.

Maddas buried his face in the big pillow. "You may finish me," he said with a muffled sigh.

"The man who comes is an American agent."

"I know. Please, continue your patriotic duty."

"He is the one who tied the yellow scarves around the necks of your family and all the others now cooling their flesh in the Maddas Morgue."

"He will pay for this with his life," Maddas vowed. "No doubt he pretended to be a woman the first time because he is a cross-dresser. There is nothing lower. Except a Jew."

"No. There is a better fate in store for him."

Maddas lifted his head. "The best fate for a would-be assassin is to die as an example to other assassins who dream of taking my place."

"He is the finest assassin in the world. He could serve you."

"I have all the assassins I require. Now, please, my red-lipped pomegranate. Continue."

"This one could strike at any enemy you name, fearless, without compunction, without any chance of failure."

Kimberly Baynes's words made Maddas Hinsein forget his stinging backside.

"How can I control such a person?" he asked, interested.

"You need not. I will do that for you. For he is fated to be my soul slave forever."

"Just as long as you preserve your artful hands for the corporeal buttocks of Maddas Hinsein and none other."

"Of course."

A firm hand pushed his face into the scented pillow and the hands began their delicious rippling tattoo.

Maddas sighed contentedly. This was the good life. How could a man who felt this good not end up lording it over all Arabia?

Remo Williams was feeling good.

After he had convinced Colonel Abdulla to accept his surrender, there had been no delays. A helicopter had ferried him to a desert airstrip where a Sukhoi-7 airplane awaited him, its engines kicking up clouds of stinging sand.

Remo was escorted to a seat just behind the pilot's compartment and as an honored deserter was asked if there was anything he would like.

"Rice."

He said it more as a wish than expectation. But to his astonishment, a tin tray of cold rice was brought before him. He ate it greedily, using his hands.

He was feeling good. The hard part was over. Soon he would be in Abominadad. He had it pretty well worked out in his mind what he would do once he was there. They would take him to Maddas. He wouldn't take no for an answer. He would tell Maddas that he would give up his secrets only in the presence of Reverend Juniper Jackman and Don Cooder—so they would be witnesses that he was betraying his country freely and without torture.

Once they were all in the same room, Remo would take total control of the situation. Maddas would be his lever. They would all be flown to safety or Maddas would get it.

Maybe, Remo thought, handing his tray back to the uniformed orderly, Maddas would get it anyway. After what he had seen in Kuran, Maddas Hinsein deserved to be flayed alive and dunked in carbolic acid for a thousand years. Smith might not like it, but accidents did happen. Besides, he reminded himself, after this outing, he might not have to deal with Smith ever again.

After he caught up with Kimberly Baynes in Hamidi Arabia, that is. He shoved that problem from his mind.

The plane came in low over Abominadad. From the air it looked like any one of a number of third-world cities. Most of it consisted of the cheap, poured-concrete high-rises Russia had put up all over the third world. The green domes of mosques and minaret spires added an Eastern seasoning. Here and there gas fires blazed over idling refineries. Irait controlled a quarter of the oil produced in the world, but UN sanctions had deprived them of chemicals needed to refine the crude.

Thus, Remo thought with pleasure, U.S. cars ran freely while in Irait no traffic flowed at all.

Remo's gaze was arrested by the crossed scimitars of Arab Renaissance Square, held aloft by Brobdingnagian replicas of Maddas Hinsein's thick forearms. He recalled a recent television report that claimed the hands were identical to Maddas' own—right down to the fingerprint whorls.

Noticing Remo's interest, an orderly boasted, "Those scimitars were forged by a famous German swordmaker and cost many millions."

"The Germans were certainly getting their share of Maddas' party," Remo muttered.

There was a military honor guard waiting to escort Remo to an armored car. Every one of them looked like a clone of Maddas Hinsein. There were fat Maddas Hinseins, skinny Maddas Hinseins, as well as the tall and short varieties.

Altogether, Remo decided, the quicker he got the job done and got himself out of Abominadad, the better.

A uniformed official stepped forward. He looked like Maddas Hinsein's third cousin. "Welcome to Irait," he said stiffly. "I am the defense minister, General Razzik Azziz." He did not offer Remo his hand.

"Glad you could take me out of tourist season," Remo said dryly.

The man's eyes pinched tighter. He smiled officiously. But deep in his eyes Remo could read contempt for his offer to betray his own country.

Fine, Remo thought. Let him think that. At least until I pull this off.

The car whisked them from Maddas International Airport and under the same upraised scimitars he had seen from the air.

"I wouldn't want to be under those babies if there's an earthquake," Remo remarked as they passed under the shadow of the gleaming blades.

"They are as sharp as the finest blades in all the world," General Azziz said proudly. "They are the swords that will slice through world opposition, leaving all the universe disemboweled before Iraiti power."

"Catchy," Remo remarked. "You ought to have cards printed up saying that."

The defense minister went silent. Remo had expected to be pumped in advance of the meeting with whomever they were taking him to first.

"Where are we going?" Remo asked, remembering his plan. "I got a lot to say and I don't intend to waste it on flunkies."

"Our Precious Leader, Maddas Hinsein himself, has requested your presence in the Palace of Sorrows."

"Suits me," Remo said, frowning. This was easier than he had thought. He wasn't sure he liked that. Still, maybe it was the will of Allah or something.

The armored car slid down a ramp and into the bowels of the palace, a baroque stack of limestone and iron that seemed to hunker down as if expecting an imminent aerial attack.

In the basement, Remo allowed himself to be frisked. They had done this before he got on the plane, and again before he had gotten off. He hoped this would be the last time. No telling what these guys did with their hands. He had not been impressed by Arab hygiene.

This time, the soldiers discovered the yellow scarf of Kali he had tucked deep into one sleeve of his black silk kimono.

For some reason, this excited them. They began chattering in Arabic, waving the scarf under one another's noses.

"We must confiscate this," the defense minister said sternly. "For the protection of our Precious Leader."

"Fine by me," Remo said, eyeing the scarf. "But I'll want it back after the interview. It's a good-luck charm."

The look the Iraiti soldiers gave him told Remo that they expected there to be no "after the interview"—at least not for him.

Fine, Remo thought. Let them think that too.

They went up in an elevator, where black-bereted guards wielding AK-47's met them. Remo was surrounded and marched down a long corridor. At the end of it was a double-valved door of some dark, expensive wood.

Remo assumed this was the President's office. He figured this would all be over in an an hour or two. Three, tops.

Two guards stepped forward and threw open the doors.

Remo entered.

Two more guards stood at attention on either side of a wide bare desk, spines straight, chins up, their heads cocked back. Matched Iraiti flags framed the figure seated behind the desk.

Remo had to look closely to be sure, but the seated figure differed from the identically mustached guards in his bull-like physique. The other guys were too skinny. There was no doubt.

Remo was face-to-face with President Maddas Hinsein.

The self-styled Scimitar of the Arabs stood up, one hand going habitually to a pearl-handled revolver.

Remo suppressed a grin. A lot of good a six-shooter would do him when things got busy.

The doors closed behind him. Remo sensed the trailing guards deploying themselves in front of the door and at other strategic spots around the room. He waited until they were in position, noted each heartbeat for future reference, and stood with his hands hanging at his sides while the defense minister strode up to the President of Irait.

They whispered conspiratorially. Maddas Hinsein's face frowned like a chocolate bunny melting in the sun.

Defense Minister Azziz turned to Remo.

"You may speak to our beloved Maddas. I will interpret."

"Tell him I know everything about the U.S. attack plans," Remo said in a staccato voice. "I know the date and exact time the U.S. will strike. I know where they will cross the border and I know every air target on every Pentagon contingency plan."

Remo paused. The defense minister rattled off a few dozen words in Arabic. Maddas never took his intent eyes off Remo as he listened. He nodded once, shortly.

"I'm willing to give this up in return for two things," Remo added.

The words were translated.

"First," Remo went on, "I want safe haven in Irait. A nice home. A couple of women. No dogs. Good food. A car. A handsome salary. And a tax exemption. What I have to say is worth a lot to you people. I expect to be compensated."

Maddas absorbed the translation in silence. He brushed at his mustache thoughtfully. When it was over, he mumbled a curt statement.

"If you expect to reside in our country," the defense minister said, "our Precious Leader insists that you grow the proper mustache."

"I'm not through here," Remo broke in. "But the mustache is okay. What I have to say, I gotta say in front of Don Cooder and Reverend Juniper Jackman. Nobody else. They gotta take everything that happens here back to the U.S. with them."

The defense minister's eyes shot up. "Why do you demand this thing?"

"Simple," Remo said. "I didn't just up and decide to go over. I was with the CIA. Some bureaucrats in my government screwed me over. I want them to know what screwing me over costs. Maybe they'll be sacked when the shit hits the fan."

Maddas Hinsein's dark eyes flashed as he took in Remo's translated words. A faint grin tugged at his cruel mouth.

Remo smiled inwardly.

That's right, he thought. *Swallow it whole, you dumb hairbag. When I'm done with you, they'll be calling you Dead Ass.*

Remo let his smile come to the surface. "So what do you say? Do we have a deal or what?"

Muttering under his breath, Maddas Hinsein lifted both hands, palms upward. He sounded like a priest giving absolution, and not the brutal dictator that had brought the world to the brink of World War III.

The defense minister lifted his head from the huddle.

"Our Precious Leader agrees to all this. But he has one question to ask you."

Remo folded his arms. "Shoot."

"What is the significance of the yellow scarf you carried concealed on your person?"

That was the one question Remo hadn't anticipated. His brow furrowed.

"I got a wicked cold," he said at last, sniffing loudly. "It's sort of . . .an industrial-strength handkerchief. Yeah. that's it. A handkerchief."

And at that, Maddas Hinsein's belly shook with laughter. He threw his head back.

All around the room, the guards acquired quirked expressions. They did not know whether to join in or not. Maddas, hearing their silence, threw up his hands in encouragement.

The uproarious laughter traveled around the room.

Only Remo's lips were not touched by it. He didn't see what was so funny.

And then an inner door came open.

One guard was alert enough to catch the sudden movement. He went for his pistol.

But Maddas Hinsein beat him to the draw. A single shot split the guard's breastbone and splattered fragments of his heart muscle against the wall behind him.

That killed the laughter. To say nothing of the guard.

Remo was barely aware of this. For in his ears was a dull roaring. And in the doorway stood a woman in black, her familiar violet eyes radiant and mocking in the ragged eyeholes of her *abayuh*. Her two visible hands were clasped before her, fingernails yellow and vicious.

And from her seductive but unclean body emanated an odor that found his nostrils like invisible tentacles.

"Oh, no!" Remo coughed, feelings his legs go weak as water.

He slammed to his knees, fighting the scented tentacles of Kali with frantic hands. But it was too late.

"Prostrate yourself before me, O Master of Sinanju," Kimberly Baynes said triumphantly.

And Remo touched his forehead to the Persian rug, squeezing hot tears from his eyes.

It had been a trap. And he had fallen for it. Sinanju was finished.

"I'm sorry, Chiun," he sobbed. "I blew it. I meant to fulfill my promise. I really did. Now I'll never see Sinanju again."

33

The President of the United States paced the War Room of the White House like a caged tiger.

He had been there ever since the first report of a nerve-gas attack on the Kuran–Hamidi Arabian neutral zone.

"We have to strike now," the chairman of the Joint Chiefs of Staff was saying. He was nervous. The Washington *Post* had run a page-one feature that said his career hung in the balance over the outcome of Operation Sand Blast. Since everyone from Capitol Hill to Foggy Bottom believed the *Post*, he knew it would become a self-fulfilling prophecy if it wasn't already true.

"I need more facts," the President bit out. "If this thing spills across borders, we have a real mess. The whole Middle East could go up. There's no telling how Israel will respond. No telling."

"We have the men, the might, and the machines," the chairman rattled off. "All we need is the word."

The secretary of defense piped up, as the President knew he would. The rivalry between the JCS and the DOD was legendary.

"I want to advise caution, Mr. President. The Iraiti forces are dug in deep, in secure defendable earthen berm positions."

"Exactly why we should bomb Abominadad," the chairman put in. "We don't even have to move our troops. A quick decapitation and it's all over. No more Mad Arab."

"Not with a million Iraiti under arms, poised to move south, Mr. President." the secretary countered. "I agree with the chairman of the JCS. We can take out Maddas and his command structure overnight. Destroy his forward tank units and dismember his logistical tail inside of a week. But I'm thinking past that. We're dug in with Syrian, Egyptian,

Kurani, Hamidi, and other Arab forces. If we bomb, who's to say that it won't be every man for himself out in that desert? The Syrians would turn on us in a flat second if they saw this as the U.S. bombing Arabs."

"Nonsense. The Hamidis have been egging us on to launch a preemptive strike since this thing began. The exiled Emir of Kuran has given us carte blanche to conduct offensive operations on his own soil. Nerve gas, neutron bombs, anything."

"And everybody knows the Emir has written off his own country," the secretary shot back. "He's gone north, trying to buy up Canada. He doesn't care. And other Arabian forces are with us only because the Hamidis have paid for them in hard cash. They're virtual mercenaries. And stabbing allies in the back is practically an Arabian tradition. Look at their history."

The President cut in on the brewing argument.

"What are the casualties?" he asked testily. "I want to see casualty figures."

Both men got busy. They worked the phones. When they came back, their faces were surprised.

"No casualties on our side," the chairman reported.

"That's my understanding as well," the secretary added.

"After a nerve-gas attack?" the President asked.

"Reports from the field indicate that when the gas blew out of the neutral zone, the Hamidi first line of defense advanced."

"The Hamidis stopped the attack?"

"No, their advance was tactical. It was actually some sort of a reverse retreat."

"Reverse—"

"They cut and run," the secretary of defense said flatly. "Away from the gas. It was Sarin. Bad stuff. A nerve agent. Fatal in seconds."

"So what took out the Iraiti forces?" the President wanted to know.

"No one knows," the chairman admitted. "They just collapsed."

The President frowned. He was thinking about his one wild-card asset on the ground over there. The CURE card. He wondered if Smith's special person had had anything to do with this.

"Any further action?" he asked.

"No," the chairman said. "It's been four hours now. It appears they simply made a halfhearted probe of the Hamidi line and pulled back."

"I think they're cranking up the pressure over their damned ambassador," the secretary of defense offered.

The President shook his head. "And all we have to offer them is a corpse. It's as if they've guessed the truth and are retaliating."

"Maddas is just the type to react like that," the chairman said tightly. "I say we pound him flat."

The President frowned. "It makes no sense. He knew that this would be the start of war. Why did he make a half-assed move like this one? What could possibly be gained?"

"Maybe he had no choice," the secretary said.

"Say again?"

"Maddas knows he's outgunned. Maybe he was responding to pressure from his inner council. There have been some pretty strange reports coming out of Abominadad. Rumors of attacks on the Hinsein household. One has it that his entire family got it. They've always been conspiring against him. Maybe they made their move and he struck back. Maybe it was internal opposition. Whatever, he's a strongman. He's got to show his strength or he gets toppled. There's a lot of pressure on him."

"Possibly," the President thought. "What's CNN been saying?"

The secretary of defense went to a nearby TV and turned it on.

In sober silence they watched the procession of reports and rumors coming out of the Middle East, as presented by a sober anchorman whose jet hair resembled a licorice sculpture.

"In a statement issued by the newly renamed Iranian Foreign Ministry today—that's the Arab Iran, not the Persian one—the Iraitis have assured the relatives of Reverend Juniper Jackman that he is well and is enjoying his new status as a guest of the state. Abominadad promises this will continue, but hinted that the reverend's fate is linked to that of the still-missing Ambassador Turqi Abaatira."

"What are the media saying about the Jackman thing?" the President muttered.

"They're unanimous," the secretary of defense returned.

"They think you should nuke Abominadad for daring to kidnap a former presidential candidate."

"If I do that, Jackman buys the farm. So does Cooder."

"A lot of reporters are hot to move into Cooder's chair," the secretary said flatly.

The President grunted. The chairman started to speak, but a graphic came on the screen just to the left of the anchorman's coiffed head. It showed a dead-eyed man with high cheekbones.

"A new mystery tonight is the identity of the American defector Abominadad has claimed went over to their side today. Although his name has not been released, a statement from the Information Ministry claimed it was a major defection, with grave repercussions for the U.S. effort to isolate Iran."

"Which Iran do they mean?" the chairman demanded.

"The bad one," the secretary replied, thin-lipped.

"I thought they were both bad."

The President shushed them angrily. He was very pale as he watched the screen.

The image switched to the familiar Maddas Hinsein clone who read all his prepared statements and speeches over the air—because Maddas was too assassin-conscious to enter a TV studio, it was rumored.

The spokesman read his prepared text in droning Arabic. Crude English subtitles flicked on and off the screen under him.

"The defector," it read, "is known to be the premier assassin in the direct employ of the President of the United States himself. But no more. President Maddas Hinsein announced today that this assassin has now seen the criminality of the U.S. stance and has agreed to perform necessary services for Irait—I mean, Iran. From this day forward, our Precious Leader has proclaimed, no head of state who has aligned himself with the un-Arab forces arrayed against us can sleep safely in his bed. For the—"

The President shut off the TV with a savage stab of his finger. His face was sheet-white.

"Maddas must be really desperate," the chairman said. "Imagine trying to convince the world that we have hired assassins on the White House payroll."

No one spoke.

"We don't, do we?" the chairman said.

Behind the President's back the secretary shook his head no. But the President was unaware of this.

"We remain on stand-down," he said hoarsely.

"Until when?" the disappointed chairman demanded.

"Until I say otherwise," he was informed.

The President left the room.

The secretary and the chairman stared at each other.

"That last report really got to him, didn't it?" the chairman undertoned.

"You know how that crazy Arab gets his goat. The guy's a barbarian."

"Well, if I had a crack at him, he'd be like Attila the Hun."

The secretary of defense looked at the chairman of the Joint Chiefs of Staff with a single eyebrow raised questioningly.

"History," the chairman said.

The President went to the Lincoln Bedroom and lifted the CURE line with trembling fingers.

Harold Smith picked up on the first ring.

"Smith, I have just seen your special person on television."

"You have?" For once, the usually unflappable Smith sounded perturbed. That did nothing to reassure the President.

"I did. On a news clip out of Abominadad. According to the report, he has gone over to their side."

"Ridiculous," Smith said instantly.

"Maddas is saying that every pro-Kuran world leader had better watch out. He's Irait's assassin now."

"Sir, I cannot believe—"

"Tell me this, Smith. If he has gone over to the enemy, am I safe?"

"Mr. President," Harold Smith said truthfully, "if Remo has become a tool of Maddas Hinsein, none of us are safe. He could remove you from office while you sleep and no one could stop him."

"I see. What do you recommend?"

"Go to an unknown location. Remain there. Do not tell me where it is. I have to assume I am at risk as well. And I could be made to talk if Remo was bent on extracting information from me."

"Good thinking. What else?"

"If I can verify this report, you have no choice but to

order the organization shut down. If Remo has gone over, all knowledge of CURE and our working relationship is at Maddas Hinsein's disposal. He could make it public. All evidence must be eradicated."

"Shut you down, Smith?" the President said, aghast. "You're my only hope of surviving this thing. You know this man. How he works. What his weak points are. How to reason with him."

"Let me look into this, Mr. President. Please stand by."

The line disconnected abruptly.

The next ten minutes were among the longest of the President's life. No post-midnight waiting for election returns had ever dragged by with such heart-stopping slowness. Presently the red telephone rang.

"Yes," the President croaked.

Smith's voice was grave, with the suggestion of a quaver in it. "Mr. President, I have seen a replay of the CNN report with my own eyes. It is my inescapable conclusion that this is no hoax or ploy. Remo has defected. I can only suspect the reasons. But for the sake of your own political survival, CURE must cease."

"My political survival be damned!" the President retorted. "It's my skin I have to worry about first. And the nation's survival. I want you ready to advise me. There must be some countermeasure to this guy."

"The only countermeasure I am aware of, Mr. President," Harold W. Smith said slowly, "died several weeks ago. I see no good options."

"Stay by the phone, Smith," the President ordered tightly. "I will be in touch."

34

"So," President Maddas Hinsein said, after the video crew withdrew from his office, "this is the assassin who has committed murder all over my fine nation."

"He does not understand Arabic," Kimberly Baynes said.

Both of them were looking at Remo Williams.

Remo was looking at Kimberly Baynes with a mixture of desire and fear in his deep eyes.

Kimberly wore the *abayuh*, her face was uncovered, her blond hair cascaded over her shoulders. As she hovered near him, her hidden arms fluttered and disturbed the long lines of the *abayuh* with spidery grace. She had kept them hidden while the crew filmed Remo on display, and only removed her veil after they had gone.

"His eyes," Maddas told Kimberly. "I do not like the way he looks at you."

"He desires me with his body, but despises me with his mind," Kimberly said laughingly.

"He is too dangerous. He must die." Maddas reached for his revolver.

"No," Kimberly said quickly, one yellow-nailed hand intercepting Maddas' gun hand. "We have a use for him."

"What value can one man possibly have? Soon the Americans will know their finest assassin is under my control. That is all that is neccesary."

"You do not understand, Scimitar of the Arabs, this man is more powerful than your greatest division. He is the incarnation of the Destroyer, and in this form he will do anything I tell him to. Including eradicating the Hamidi Arabian royal family."

Maddas blinked.

"Would that not be fitting, O Precious Leader?" Kimberly said mockingly. "This man destroyed your family."

"And did me a tremendous favor," Maddas said quickly. "They were beasts, especially my wife's brothers. I am better off without them. And with you."

Kimberly smiled her blond smile.

"What does that matter?" she pressed. "Your generals know you have lost face. You must restore it. Why not loose this man upon your enemies, the Hamidis?"

"Because of all the forces arrayed on my southern border," Maddas Hinsein said truthfully, "only the Kurani Emir and the thrice-damned Hamidi itch for my skin. The Americans need provocation. The rest of the world follows their lead. But the Hamidis know that I covet their wealth and oil refineries. They know American staying power is limited." He shook his fleshy head slowly. "No, if I strike the Hamidi royal family, they will attack in turn. All of them will attack."

"So, you are a coward, after all."

Maddas flinched. "No Iraiti could call me that name and not be chopped into shish kebab," he flared.

"No Iraiti understands Maddas Hinsein as I do," Kimberly said. "If I disappear, there is no one strong enough to attend to your special . . . needs."

Maddas' dark features tightened in concentration.

And one hidden hand slipped from a slit in the black *abayuh* and roughly pinched Maddas Hinsein on the backside. He gave a little jump.

"Do not do that in front of the prisoner," he hissed, rubbing himself.

"Think of him as a tool. Just as I think the same of you."

Maddas Hinsein cocked a thumb at his broad chest. "I am the destined uniter of the Arabs."

Kimberly smiled. "And I am the only one who makes you purr. Your gas attack has failed. There has been no counterstrike. You are safe to strike again. This time in secret. Send this assassin to kill the one most dear to the sheik. It is a humilation he deserves."

"Agreed. But it will bring war down on my head. Is that what you want?"

"Yes," Kimberly Baynes said, drawing close to Maddas Hinsein like a black raven with a sunflower head. "War is *exactly* what I want."

Maddas looked aghast. "You want my ruin?"

"No, I want to see you lord of the Middle East, and if you obey me in every way, that is exactly what you shall be."

Maddas Hinsein furrowed his dark brow. His eyes went to those of the American assassin who was called Remo.

The man obviously worshiped Kimberly. He had obeyed her in every respect so far.

"How do we know that once he is free, he will carry out your will?" he asked at last.

"Very simply, Precious Leader. Because I will go with him."

"Why?"

"Because we are destined to dance the Tandava together."

"I do not understand. Is that an American word?"

"No. It is more ancient than even Arabic. And in time you will understand all."

"Very well. But do not spank him. You are my mistress now. Your ministrations are reserved for Maddas Hinsein alone."

"Of course. I only have hands for you."

Kimberly drew near Remo. Remo gritted his teeth. Sweat broke out over his face. Her nearness was unbearable. The way she swayed when she walked, the knowing, mocking light in her violet eyes. Hadn't they been blue before? He must have been mistaken. He wanted to run from her. He also wanted to push her down on the dirty floor and rut like animals.

But Remo did neither. He had been commanded to stand at attention, and so he stood, arms at his sides, his manhood at half-mast under his black kimono.

"I told you that you would come to me," Kimberly said in English.

"I came," Remo said dully.

"We are going on a trip together. To Hamidi Arabia."

"Yes."

"You know Sheik Fareem?"

"Yes."

Kimberly laid spidery hands on his shoulders, saying, "Tell me truly. Who is his closet relative?"

"His son, Abdul."

Cupping Remo's jaw, Kimberly turned his head around

so their eyes met. "Then you will kill Abdul. Before my eyes. As a sacrifice to me. Do you understand?"

"Yes."

"Are you ready?"

Remo's mind screamed no, but he was helpless.

His mouth said, "Yes."

But his heart told him that even the cold Void would be better than this living hell.

35

Harold Smith tried to reason it through.

It made no sense, none of it. Why would Maddas Hinsein initiate a lame gas attack on the Hamidi Arabian front lines? It was as if he were trying to bait America into a war Hinsein could not possibly win.

His behavior was incomprehensible. He blustered and boasted and hurled desperate empty threats in a foolish attempt to forestall what the world thought was an inevitable all-out assault on Irait—now officially the Republic of Iran. That last decree, as nothing before it, told of the man's desperation.

Army intelligence dismissed the failed nerve-gas attack as the result of the usual confusion stress placed on a command structure when hostilities appear imminent. But Smith had run a thorough character analysis on Maddas Hinsein. He was fifty-four years old, nearly the top life expectancy of the average Iraiti male. A visionary, he would do anything to prolong his life and fulfill what he perceived as his destiny as the liberator of the Arabs.

He was not reckless, but ignorant. He had stumbled into this situation through miscalculation. It was not in his character to attack against such overwhelming odds.

And now he had Remo in his power. Somehow.

As the CURE terminal scrolled news digests emanating out of the Middle East, one report caught his eyes.

"My God," Smith croaked.

He read an AP digest of a rash of strangulations that had taken place in the Star in the Center of the Flower of the East base.

Two people had been throttled—an Arab motor-pool corporal and a U.S. servicewoman, Carla Shaner. They had both been strangled with yellow silk scarves. This fact was the cause of much speculation in the Arab press, inasmuch as yellow ribbons symbolized U.S. hostages. Infidel Moslem-hating elements in the U.S. armed forces were being blamed.

Smith ran an in-depth computer analysis of the incident. A picture emerged. A picture of a nameless non-Arab American woman who had strangled the U.S. servicewoman, stolen her uniform, and used it to gain entry to the base, where she subsequently strangled the Hamidi corporal and obtained a Humvee vehicle.

To what purpose? Smith wondered.

"To penetrate Irait," he said hoarsely in the shaky fluorescent light of his Folcroft office. "To incite the other side." And suddenly Smith understood why the Iraiti ambassdor had been strangled with a yellow scarf in Washington. That was simply phase one, designed to exacerbate U.S.-Irait tensions.

"Who is this woman?" Smith asked the walls. "What goal could she possibly have in doing this?"

He recalled with a brain-clarifying shock the pretext under which he had sent Remo into the Middle East. The Calley Baynes who had flown to Libya was also the woman pretending to be Kimberly Baynes. But who was she?

Smith shut off the news-digest program and went into the airline file. There, siphoned off the national network of travel-agency and airline reservation computers, lay the last six months' worth of passenger reservations.

Smith called up the Middle East runs and ran the name: "BAYNES, KIMBERLY."

After a moment the screen said: "BAYNES, KIMBERLY, NOT FOUND."

He keyed in: "BAYNES, CALLEY."

Up came: "BAYNES, CALLEY."

Under the rubric was a record of a flight from Tripoli to Nehmad, Hamidi Arabia.

With a tight grin of triumph, Harold Smith logged off that file and began a global search of the name Calley Baynes.

His smile quirked downward. The computer spat out another "NOT FOUND."

"Odd," he muttered. He stared at the screen. The name was an alias. Why had she chosen it?

Smith reached into his in basket, where the FBI artist's

reconstruction of the Washington strangler reposed. He stared at the face. It was a pretty face, almost innocent.

On a hunch, he keyed into the FBI nationwide alert for the true Kimberly Baynes—the thirteen-year-old girl who had been reported kidnapped from her grandmother's Denver house.

Up came a digitized photo of the missing poster. It showed a wide-eyed innocent young blond girl.

Smith placed the artist's sketch next to the screen. But for the more mature lines of the face, they might have been sisters. There was a definite familial similarity.

Smith executed a thorough check of social-security records, looking for any Baynes-family female cousins. He found none. There were none.

Smith called up the digitized photo once more. And this time he noticed that the missing poster noted a tiny scar visible on the chin of the real Kimberly Baynes.

A scar reflected on the FBI sketch too.

"How can that be?" Smith muttered. "There must be ten years' difference in their ages." As he stared, Smith noticed other too-close congruities. Too many to be coincidence.

Then it struck him. And cold horror filled his marrow. Suddenly everything that Remo Williams had said, the apparent nonsense about the Caldron of Blood and living Hindu gods, no longer seemed so preposterous.

These two—young girl and mature woman—were the same person.

And Harold Smith realized there was another way to spell Calley.

Kali.

"This cannot be," he said, even as he realized it was. He dug deep into his files, pulling up a long encyclopedia entry on the Hindu goddess Kali.

Harold Smith scanned the text. He learned that Kali was the terrible four-armed mother goddess of Hindu myth. Known as the Black One, she was a horrible personification of death and womanhood, who feasted on corpses and drank blood. She was, he read, the consort of Shiva the Destroyer, who was known as the Red One.

"Red One," Smith muttered. "Remo said Kimberly had called him that. And they would dance the Tandava in the Caldron of Blood."

Smith called up "TANDAVA."

"THE DANCE OF DESTRUCTION SHIVA DANCES IN CHIDAMBARAM, THE CENTER OF THE UNIVERSE," he read, "THUS CREATING AND RECREATING THE UNIVERSE OVER AND OVER."

He went to the Shiva file. Most of the information he knew. Shiva was one of the Hindu triad of gods, personification of the opposing forces of destruction and reintegration. His symbol was the lingam.

Smith input "LINGAM."

The definition was succinct: "PHALLUS."

And Smith remembered Remo's rather personal problem.

It was all, he decided, too much to be called coincidental.

Woodenly he logged off the encyclopedia file.

He leaned back in his chair, his gray eyes slipping out of focus.

"What if it's true?" he whispered, his voice awed. "What if it's really true?"

Stunned, he reached out for the red telephone. He hesitated, grimacing. What could he tell the President?

He turned in his big swiveling executive chair.

Out beyond the big picture window—his only window to the world during time of crisis—a bluish moon was rising over the liquid ebony waters of Long Island Sound. They were as black as an abyss.

Harold Smith was a practical man. The blood of his rock-ribbed New England ancestors flowed through his veins. Men who had come to a new world to carve out a new life. They had planted according to the almanac, worshiped in Spartan churches, and put aside family and farm when their country had called them to war and national service. Unsuperstitious men. Patriots.

But he knew in his heart that no ordinary power could sway Remo Williams to join the Iraiti side. He knew he had inadvertently sent Remo into the arms—the four arms, if his story could be believed—of an unclean thing that, whether or not she was Kali, possessed a supernatural power even a Master of Sinanju could not resist.

And he had lost Remo.

Now the world teetered on the edge of what Kimberly Baynes—if she truly was Kimberly Baynes anymore—called the Red Abyss.

No, Harold Smith realized, he could not tell the President. In truth, he could not do anything. He could only hope that some power greater than mortal man would intervene before the world was lost.

Harold Smith steepled his withered old fingers, as if in prayer. His dry lips parted as if to invoke salvation.

Smith hesitated. He no longer knew which gods he should invoke.

Finally he simply asked God the Father to preserve the world.

He was no sooner done than one of the desk phones shrilled in warning.

Smith turned in his seat. It was the multiline Folcroft phone. At this hour, it could be only one person.

"Yes, dear?" he said, picking up the phone.

"Harold," Maude Smith said. "How did you know it was me?"

"Only the director's wife would call at this hour."

Mrs. Smith hesitated. "Harold, are . . . are you coming home?"

"Yes. Soon."

"I'm a bit nervous tonight, Harold."

"Is something wrong?"

"I don't know. I'm uneasy. I can't explain it."

"I understand," Smith said in a comfortless voice. He was not good at this. He always had problems being warm. Even with his wife. "All this war talk."

"It's not that, Harold. I saw the strangest thing tonight."

"What is that?"

"Well, you remember those strange neighbors who lived next door. The ones who moved?"

"Of course I do."

"I thought I saw one of them not an hour ago."

Smith blinked, his heart racing. Remo! He had returned.

Smith took hold of his voice. "The young man?"

"No," Mrs. Smith said. "It was the other one."

"Impossible!" Smith blurted out.

"Why do you say that, Harold?"

"I . . . understood he returned to his home. In Korea."

"You did tell me that, yes. I remember now." Mrs. Smith paused. "But I happened to look out the dining-room window, and I saw him in the house."

"What was he doing?" Smith asked in a strangely thin tone.

"He was . . ." Mrs. Smith's somewhat frumpy-sounding

voice trailed off. She gathered it again. "Harold, he was staring at me."

"He was?"

"I lifted my hand to wave to him, but he simply threw up his hands and the most ungodly expression came over him. I can't describe it. It was terrible."

"You are certain of this, dear?"

"I'm not finished, Harold. He threw up his hands and then he simply . . . went away."

"Went away?"

"He . . . vanished."

"Vanished?"

"Harold, he faded away," Mrs. Smith said resolutely. "Like a ghost. You know I don't put any stock in such things, Harold, but that is what I saw. Do you . . . you don't think that I could be coming down with that memory disease? Oh, what is it called?"

"Alzheimer's, and I do not think that at all. Please relax, dear. I am coming home."

"When?"

"Instantly," said Harold W. Smith, who did not believe in ghosts either, but who wondered if he had not beseeched the proper god after all.

36

Abdul Hamid Fareem had once been a prince of Hamidi Arabia. He was proud to bear the name Hamid.

But pride alone is not enough to make one worthy of standing in line to be the next sheik.

Abdul Fareem had been disinherited by his father, the sheik of the Hamid tribe. He had been forced to divorce his good wife, Zantos, whom he had not appreciated—doing this by pronouncing the words, "I divorce you, I divorce you, I divorce you," in the manner prescibed by Islam. Then he was forced to marry a Western woman of low morals, whom he did deserve.

The Western woman of low morals put up with him but three months as Abdul, exiled to Kuran, tried to scratch out a living as a moneylender. The white woman left when he had gone bankrupt. Lacking good judgment himself, he could hardly recognize a poor credit risk when he saw one.

When the Iraitis rolled over helpless Kuran, Abdul Fareem was the first to break for the border. And the first to find sanctuary.

He would have kept on going, straight for the emirates, but he had no money. Settling in the windblown border outpost of Zar, he earned a meager living as a camel groom. He let anyone who would listen know that he had once been a prince of Hamidi Arabia. And all had laughed. Not because they disbelieved his tale, but because they knew that fat Abdul Fareem had been of so base a character that even the right-thinking and kind sheik had disowned him.

Abdul Fareem had never sunk so low as these days. He had no money, no wife, no respect. Only the contempt of his fellow Arabs.

So it came as a tremendous surprise to him when soldiers

in desert camouflage utilities stole in and abducted him as he slept on a bed of straw and camel dung in an open-air stable.

They gagged his mouth. They bound his struggling hands and feet as his three-hundred-pound body squirmed helplessly. And they bore him off to a waiting Land Rover.

The Land Rover chewed up sand and barreled north. North—to occupied Kuran. Abdul Fareem's heart quailed at the fearsome realization.

They took him to a desert camp and flung him overboard like a sack of meal. It took all four of them.

Soldiers fell on him. Others, bearing video-camera equipment, trained their glassy lenses on his shame. Many brought lights that were trained on him. He felt like a bug. But then, he had always felt like a bug. A corpulent bug.

A woman stepped from between two lights. She was a black silhouette, her *abayuh* flowing, impelled by a warm desert breeze.

Bending over, she removed his gag. It flashed before his eyes, and he saw for the first time that it was of silk. Yellow. No wonder it had felt so fine in his mouth. It had reminded him of the silk sheets on which he had passed many nights with the good Arab woman who had been too good for him.

"If you have abducted me for ransom," he told the woman, "you have wasted your time."

The woman's violet eyes flashed. She turned to the others.

"Fools! This is a mere *fellahin*. He smells of dung. He is not the sheik's son."

"I am the sheik's son," former Prince Abdul insisted, gathering the ragged shreds of his pride around him.

Another figure stepped forward. He wore a black silk costume like a *thobe*, two tigers stitched on the chest. An American, from the look of him. His eyes were like gems of death.

"That is he," the man said in numb English. "That is Abdul Fareem."

"But he smells," the woman said, also in English. American English. She sounded like his wife. The loose one. He wondered why she wore the *abayuh*.

The man in the black tiger costume shrugged.

"He is an Arab," he said woodenly.

"My father will not ransom me," Abdul said in English.

"That is well," the woman said. "The money he will save can be put to your burial."

And at that, the video cameras began whirring.

The woman in the *abayuh* stood up. She faced the man in the silken regalia. "There is your first sacrifice to me. Lay his broken corpse at my feet."

And with tears coming into his cruel dark eyes, the vision in black silk strode forward. His strong hands lifted, the cables and thews of his thick wrists working and pulsing, as if fighting the task the hands were about to undertake.

Abdul Fareem felt implacable fingers take him by the neck. They lifted him, bringing pain to his strained neck vertebrae.

Inexorably his face was brought up to eye level of the man he understood Allah had ordained to be his executioner.

Fingers dug in. The pain came so quickly that Abdul Fareem's frightened brain seemed to explode in his very skull like a hand grenade.

The world went red. Then black. Then away.

Before his ears died, he heard the man's voice—twisted, as if he too were dying.

"I'm sorry," he choked. "I can't help myself."

And behind his pain, the American woman in the *abayuh* laughed and laughed and laughed like the drunken church bells of the infidels.

Sickened, Remo Williams dropped the limp corpse. It fell like a great bag of meat, shaking the sands.

He stepped back. The lights blazed in his tormented eyes. Kimberly Baynes drew near. She pushed the yellow silk scarf into one of his limp hands.

"You may have the honor of tying the rumal of Kali about his throat," she said. "For you are now my chief phansigar."

Remo knelt and did as he was bidden. He regained his feet. His stomach felt like an old kettle that had collected rusty rainwater. He wanted to vomit it up, but he could not. He had been instructed not to.

Kimberly Baynes stood looking down at the cooling corpse. Her violet eyes flared avidly. She saw a dab of blood at one corner of Abdul Fareem's slack mouth.

She fell on it eagerly and began licking like a dog.

It was then that Remo Williams lost control. He fell to his

knees and emptied out the contents of his stomach into the desert sand.

"Don't bother getting up, lover," her mocking voice called over. "You have hungered to mate with me since when we last met. This plump carrion we have together made shall be our nuptial bed. And he will be only the first as we dance the Tandava that will stir the Caldron of Blood and remake this planet into a Hell of Delight."

And despite his revulsion, Remo felt his manhood stiffen as if about to burst blood at the tip from desire. Like a whipped dog, he crawled toward her.

And he wept.

37

Harold Smith waited until Maude was asleep.

Slipping out of bed, he went to the hallway and padded in his ancient slippers to the end of the corridor, where he reached up for the pullcord that lowered the folding staircase to the attic.

The stairs creaked from disuse. Smith pulled them up after him, and only then turned on the light with a twist of a turn-of-the-century rheostat.

Since only Harold Smith ever ventured into his own attic, it was as tidy as the proverbial pin. A few old steamer trunks sat stacked neatly at the far end, covered with the fading labels of many half-forgotten trips. Nearby, his old army colonel's uniform—which still fitted—hung on a wooden coat hanger from the ceiling, protected by a dusty plastic dry-cleaning bag.

Smith ignored these artifacts. He went instead to a nest of electronic equipment, dominated by a modern videotape deck attached to a 1950's Philco TV set. Beside it, on the floor, sat an old-fashioned reel-to-reel tape recorder.

Smith knelt before the array. Although most of the equipment was antiquated, it still worked and was actuated by state-of-the-art sensors that he had secretly planted in the house next door—Remo's home.

Smith turned the tape recorder on, his face glowing cherry red from the tiny bubble monitor light. He jerked the lever that sent the tape wheeling back, stopped it with another twist, then hit the stainless-steel play button.

The quiet buzz of dead air came from the cloth speaker grille. Smith repeated the operation and got the same response.

Unlike the sound-actuated tape recorder, the video camera ran continuously. Smith checked it every day, and had even after Remo had vacated the house. The dwelling remained a security risk until it had been sold, owing more to Chiun's trunks than anything else. The Master of Sinanju had been in the habit of recording his assignments on his scrolls. No doubt sensitive, if distorted, information on CURE operations could be found in those scrolls.

Smith turned on the TV. A snowy black-and-white picture showed the dim outlines of a room. Smith stopped recording and rolled back the tape to approximately 8:45 that evening: the time his wife had pinpointed as when she had seen—or apparently seen—Chiun.

Smith watched a replay of the same dim room in silence. Minutes crawled past. Then a white light appeared.

Smith gasped.

The light devolved into the half-transparent image of a familiar kimono-clad figure.

The Master of Sinanju faced away from the camera. But the bald back of his head was unmistakable. It was Chiun. He stood immobile for perhaps three minutes. Then he simply faded away, leaving no trace.

Harold Smith turned off the recorder. Resetting everything, he padded back to the folding stair.

Dawn found him next door examining the darkened living room in his flannel bathrobe, purchased in 1973 at a yard sale and still serviceable.

The room was unremarkable, as was the floor where the apparition had appeared.

Smith stood on that spot, mentally summoning up every kernel of knowledge he possessed that related to paranormal phenomena. Smith did not believe in the paranormal, but over the years he had been exposed to enough imponderables that his once-razorlike skepticism had been dulled to a vaguely suspicious curiosity.

The room itself was unremarkable. No cold spot. He checked each window, knowing that lightning flashes had the ability to imprint the photographic image of a person who stood too close the glass. No angle of examination revealed a lightning-flash print, however. Not that he expected to find one. His video camera had absolutely picked up a three-dimensional phenomenon.

When he had exhausted every possibility, Harold Smith prepared to go.

He was walking to the kitchen when the light grew. It was lavender. Like a distant flare.

"What on earth?" Smith whirled. His gray eyes fluttered in disbelief.

The Master of Sinanju stood only inches away, looking stern and vaguely afraid.

"Master Chiun?" Smith asked. He felt no fear. Just a cool intellectual curiosity. He had never believed in ghosts. But having come to the conclusion that Hindu gods might have entered the affairs of men, he put his skepticism aside. Momentarily.

The apparition gave him a querulous look. It had animation. Smith reached forward. His hand passed through the image. His gray eyes skating about the room, he dismissed a holographic source for the image.

"Er, what can I do for you, Master Chiun?" Smith asked, at a loss for something more appropriate.

The Master of Sinanju pointed down at the floor.

"I fail to understand. Can you speak?"

Chiun pointed once more.

Smith tucked his white-stubbled chin in one hand. His pale eyebrows crept together in thought.

"Hmmm," he mused aloud. "Remo said something about this. Now, why would a spirit point to the floor? You cannot be pointing specifically at this floor, and therefore at the basement, because I understand you first appeared to Remo in the desert, where you . . . um . . . apparently died. Am I warm?"

Chiun's birdlike head bobbed in agreement.

"And you cannot be telling Remo that he now walks in your sandals because that would not be an appropriate message to give to me, correct?"

Chiun nodded again. His hazel eyes brightened with hope.

"Therefore, the meaning of your gesture is neither abstract nor symbolic. Hmmm."

Smith's fingers came away from his chin. He snapped them once.

"Yes, I understand now."

A look of relief washed over the wrinkled visage of the Master of Sinanju—then he was gone like a dwindling candle.

Harold Smith turned determinedly on his heel and left by the rear door, locking it with the same duplicate key that had given him secret access to install the monitoring equipment that might just have saved the Middle East from conflagration.

If he hurried.

38

For once, official Washington was not leaking.

Despite the Iraiti feint into forward positions of the Hamidi Arabian Defensive Fan—as the Pentagon called it with straight-faced soberness—the news media were unaware of the fact that for a few brief moments in the neutral zone there had been hostilities.

The blustering from Abominadad continued. And was ignored.

The story of the U.S. assassin-defector prompted only the most peremptory journalistic questions at the daily press briefing held at the Department of State.

"The U.S. government does not employ assassins," was the curt reply of the briefing officer, a serious-voiced spokeswoman who had been accused by the press of being dull as dirt. Which in journalese meant that she did her job and did not leak.

A reporter pressed the point.

"Is that a denial?" he asked blandly.

"Let me remind you of Executive Order Number 12333, which specifically forbids the use of assassination as a tool of foreign policy," she retorted. "And further, I can confirm to you that this individual, who has yet to be identified by name, is neither a current nor a past employee of the Central Intelligence Agency, the National Security Agency, or the Defense Intelligence Agency. We do not know him."

The briefing moved on to the real meat. Namely, the whereabouts of Reverend Juniper Jackman and news anchor Don Cooder.

"Our sources indicate that both men are sharing a suite at the Sheraton Shaitan in downtown Abominadad and are not—repeat, not—being used as human shields," the spokeswoman said.

"Are they getting along?" asked anchorwoman Cheeta Ching, who had lunged for Don Cooder's anchor desk like a hammerhead shark after a bluefin tuna.

A ripple of laughter floated through the press.

"I have no information on that," was the clipped, no-nonsense reply.

At the Sheraton Shaitan, Don Cooder was climbing the walls.

More accurately, he was trying to climb the door of the suite he shared with Reverend Juniper Jackman. The transom was too narrow to admit his brachycephalic head, never mind his body.

"I can't stand it anymore!" he howled in anguish. "That Korean witch has probably ruined my ratings by now!"

"Improved them, if you ask me," called Reverend Jackman from the bathroom. He had been sitting on the toilet, with the seat down, all during their captivity. He figured the tiled bathroom was the safest place to be in the event of a U.S. air strike.

"They won't strike while I'm a prisoner. I'm a national symbol," Don Cooder had said.

"You're a bleeping journalist," Reverend Jackman retorted hotly. "I'm a presidential candidate. They won't bomb 'cause of me, not you."

"Failed presidential candidate. You're irrelevant."

"Says who. Mr. Dead-Last-in-the-Ratings?"

"Me, for one. To ninety million people. Besides, you're a syndicated talk-show host now. That puts you on the same plane as Morton Downey Jr. There's an idea. Maybe he'll be your running mate next time."

They had argued thus for two days. The argument had grown particularly heated since Reverend Jackman had refused to give up the toilet seat to Don Cooder, fearing that, once lost, it could never be regained.

As a consequence, Don Cooder had been holding all bodily functions in abeyance for two days and was now approaching criticality. And he was not going to go on the rug. If they ever got out of this alive, his critics would be armed with another embarrassing personal anecdote for him to live down.

So, the closed transom looked like his best bet.

"If you're so important," Reverend Jackman taunted, "why are you trying to save your skin? I should be the one trying to escape. I'm a political bargaining chip."

"Trade?" Don Cooder asked hopefully, feeling his bowels move.

"No."

Cooder resumed his attempt to climb the door to the transom, impelled by visions of Cheeta Ching chaining herself to his anchor chair and refusing to give it up. She was a notorious glory hound.

And if there was anything Don Cooder despised, it was a glory hound.

Ultimately. it was not concern over the fate of either Don Cooder or Reverend Juniper Jackman that forced the President of the United States to cave in to the President of Irait's demands that Ambassador Abaatira be produced.

It was the American news media.

The ambassador's death was one of Washington's best-kept secrets. It had been easy enough to disclaim any knowledge of the ambassador's whereabouts when even his own consulate had no inkling of what might have befallen him.

But when CNN reports coming out of Abominadad replayed the accusation that Ambassador Abaatira had been murdered by U.S. agents, the President knew he had a problem.

"They're demanding answers," the President glumly told his cabinet.

"I say screw Abominadad," the secretary of defense said.

"I am not talking about Abominadad," the President said. "I'm talking about the media. They're sniffing around like bloodhounds after a possum. It's only a matter of time before they discover the truth."

As one, the President's cabinet looked up from their briefing papers. This was the first they knew that their President had direct knowledge of the Iraiti ambassador's fate.

This, more than anything else, explained why Washington was not leaking as it usually did.

It was the chairman of the Joint Chiefs of Staff, sitting in on a cabinet meeting because of the gravity of the situation, who broke the long hush with the question on all the world's lips.

"Do we know what happened to the ambassador?"

"He was murdered four days ago. We have the body on ice."

All around the room, eyes went round and fixed, like those of children listening to Halloween ghost stores around a wooded campfire.

No one said anything.

"Under the circumstances," the President said slowly, "it's only a matter of time before this thing breaks. We're going to have to get out in front of this thing. Pronto."

"If you mean what I think you mean . . ." the secretary of defense began.

"I do. I'm going to have the body released to the Iraiti consulate. No choice."

"There is no telling how Abominadad will react."

"Mr. President, let me suggest a first strike."

"Mr. President," the secretary of defense jumped in, "let me suggest that you ignore the chairman's suggestions, since this is a cabinet meeting and, strictly speaking, he is not a cabinet member."

"How about we adjourn to the War Room?" the chairman of the Joint Chiefs of Staff said hopefully.

The President held up a quieting hand.

"No first strike. I will have the body released. But we must be ready to react to the Iraiti response—no matter what it is."

Every man in the cabinet room understood what the President's words meant.

They were about to take a giant step closer to war.

39

In the lowermost dungeon of the Palace of Sorrows, Remo Williams awoke.

He tasted the dried blood on his lips.

And then he remembered the feverish bloody kisses Kimberly Baynes had showered on him as they lay on the corpulent body of Prince Abdul Fareem. The many yellow-tipped talons of Kali had taken him to an exquisite hell of sexual torment, after which he had collapsed on the sand, spent and unconscious.

Remo had awoken with the dawn.

The blazing sun had burned his skin to a lobsterlike hue. He was naked, but no longer erect. That pleasant relief had barely sunk in when Kimberly Baynes, also naked, stood up from her throne—the corpse on which a buzzard had already begun feasting—and lifted four arms to the sun.

"Stand up. Red One."

Remo had climbed to his feet.

"Now you are truly red, as befits Kali's mate."

Remo said nothing. Her parched lips were caked with rustlike dried blood. Her head lay on her shoulder, almost perpendicular to her broken neck. Behind her, the buzzard looked up, his ghoulish head tilted, in echo of Kimberly's own.

"Now what?" Remo asked dully.

Kimberly Baynes snapped a yellow silk scarf between two hands like a whip, her small breasts bouncing with each snap.

"We wait for the Caldron of Blood to churn. Then we will dance the Tandava together, O Triple World Ender."

But the Caldron of Blood did not begin churning. The sun

ascended and, hovering like a superheated brass ball, began its slow sink into desert and darkness.

Reluctantly Kimberly Baynes had donned her *abayuh* and ordered Remo back into his soiled kimono.

They had returned to Abominadad by plane and, after being whisked to the Palace of Sorrows, Remo had been cast into the dungeon, where he had immediately sunk into defeated, dreamless sleep.

Now, tasting blood on his lips, he stared into the unrelieved darkness with hollow, burning eyes.

If he was himself, he could have stood up and ripped through the thick iron-bound hardwood door to freedom.

But Remo was no longer himself. He was Kali's slave.

It would have been a fate worse than death, but Remo had had a taste of the Void—the cold merciless place where Chiun now suffered. Just as Remo suffered.

Alive or dead, on earth or in the Void, Remo no longer cared. He was beyond help, and beyond hope.

He would have preferred to die, but he knew what awaited him in death.

And so he waited in the dark.

40

It was a good thing that Turqi Abaatira was dead.

Had he been alive, the late Iraiti ambassador would have been in excruciating pain.

His dead body had spent four days in a refrigerated morgue under police guard while official Washington considered what to do with him.

When it was decided that the concern voiced in the press could not longer be ignored, a CIA "inert-assets" team came for the body. "Inert asset" is a CIA term for "inconvenient corpse."

The dead ambassador was taken to CIA headquarters in Langley, Virginia, where dirty Potomac river water was pumped into his lungs through a garden hose stuffed into his slack mouth. The inert-assets team leader in charge of the operation kept the water flowing until it backed up from the late ambassador's lungs and dribbled from his nostrils.

The body was then placed behind the wheel of a rented car, whose backdated papers would prove the ambassador had rented it the day he disappeared. The car was rammed into a soft barrier at sixty-two miles an hour—enough to put the ambassador's bloodless face through the windshield and create convincing scars.

The body was then extracted and cured in a water tank until the soft tissues turned puffy and gray from immersion. When the stomach became bloated from expanding intestinal gases to the equivalent of a third-trimester pregnancy, Ambassador Turqi Abaatira was pronounced "processed."

The car was then transported by car carrier to a sheltered section of Bolling Air Force Base and pushed into the river.

The CIA agent whose responsibility it was to "process" the ambassador's body watched the bubbles rising from the sinking car. When the last bubble blurped to the surface, he found a pay phone, where he made a call to the D.C. police.

The police, unaware that they had been set up to add credence to the story, dutifully investigated. Divers were sent in. A wrecker was called. And the body was extracted by paramedics who took one look at the puffy wormlike face and fingers and pronounced the body deceased.

The same medical examiner who had pronounced the ambassador dead of strangulation two days later went through the motions of a new autopsy. This time he certified the cause of death as drowning.

He didn't question the procedure. He understood the sensitivity that usually surrounded a diplomat's death, and had done this before.

More important, he had a son stationed in Hamidi Arabia whom he would like to see rotated back to the States alive when his tour was up.

Ambassador Abaatira's body, along with the falsified autopsy report, was released to a tearful Iraiti embassy staff. Word was cabled to Abominadad.

A long silence followed.

When instructions finally came back from the Iraiti Foreign Ministry, they were terse: "SEND BODY HOME."

Since the national airline of Irait was forbidden to overfly every country except Libya and Cuba, the body had to be flown to Havana, where an Air Irait civilian plane ferried Ambassador Turqi Abaatira on his last voyage.

At Langley, the CIA congratulated themselves on a cover-up well done.

At Maddas International Airport, Kimberly Baynes, wearing an all-concealing black *abayuh*, waited patiently for the body to arrive. She mingled with the tearful family of the ambassador, out of sight of President Maddas Hinsein and his escort, indistinguishable from the other women beneath her black veil. A national day of mourning had been announced. Flags drooped at half-mast all over the airport.

The plane touched down. The women threw back their heads and gave vent to mournful ululations of grief.

Unseen, Kimberly Baynes slipped from the passengers' waiting area to the cargo-receiving terminal.

In her black native costume, she lurked in the shadows as the polished mahogany coffin was hoisted onto a toiling conveyor belt and carried down to waiting baggage handlers.

The handlers lugged the coffin to a waiting baggage truck.

Five minutes passed while the driver of the truck finished a cup of bitter chicory coffee—the only kind available in sanction-strangled Irait.

In those five minutes, Kimberly Baynes slipped up to the coffin and unlatched the lid. Lifting it with both hands, she held it aloft while a second pair reached through slits in the *abayuh* to twist a long yellow silk rumal around the dead ambassador's puffy, discolored neck.

She pulled it tight.

No, tighter, a voice from deep within her urged. The same voice that had guided her through her days in Irait, imparting secrets and hidden knowledge and even teaching her Arabic in a way she could not understand.

"But he's dead. O mistress," Kimberly whispered.

His soul is not dead. Make it scream.

Kimberly threw herself into it. She pulled the rumal tighter and tighter with relish. The ambassdor's mouth actually fell open. With two fingers, she reached in and pulled out his long, discolored tongue. It looked like a short black tie hanging down his chin.

As a last gesture, she plucked his eyelids up. They had been sealed shut with spirit gum.

The Iraiti ambassador's fixed eyes held the same expression of horror that they had when Kimberly last saw him.

"It is done," Kimberly said, sealing the lid.

Excellent, my vessel. The tyrant Maddas cannot ignore this provocation.

"I am glad you approve, my lady."

I do. The tongue was a nice touch too.

41

The Army Corps of Engineers had already unloaded their earth-moving equipment when the army helicopter deposited Harold Smith in the fenced-off desert outside of Palm Springs, California.

A balding young lieutenant was running a Geiger counter around a crater that resembled a fused sinkhole of blackened glass, getting only a desultory clicking for his trouble.

"I am Colonel Smith," Harold Smith said, adjusting the collar of the old khaki uniform that had hung in his attic.

"Lieutenant Latham," the young man said, shutting off the machine and returning Smith's handshake. "Background radiation is normal, sir."

"I understood that. Are you ready to begin excavation?"

"We've been waiting for your arrival."

"MAC flights are hard to come by these days. Since Kuran."

"Tell me about it. Let me show you the size of the nut we have to crack."

They walked across the brittle glass. It gave under their feet with a crunching like a shattered but intact windshield of safety glass. Where the heavy equipment was, uniformed engineers clustered around a huge cap of concrete half-smothered by windblown sand. It resembled an ugly gray plug. Soldiers were sweeping the flat surface free of sand.

"I say we dynamite the sucker," Lieutenant Latham suggested. "Shaped demo charges should lift this stuff clean off."

"You will not use dynamite," Harold Smith said tightly.

The huddle of engineers turned at the sharp sound of Smith's voice.

"I'm the demolition expert," one said. "You must be Colonel Smith."

"I am, and you will use jackhammers."

"Begging your pardon, Colonel. But we're looking at a two-hundred-foot tube in which maybe ten tons of concete has been poured. It will take forever to jackhammer it all loose."

"We do not have forever, and you will extract the concrete with jackhammers."

The no-nonsense tone of the colonel's voice settled the matter. That, and his credentials. The army team thought Smith had been sent there by the Pentagon. The Pentagon thought he was on loan from the CIA. The CIA had been instructed by the White House to go along with the cover story.

"Okay," the lieutenant called out. "You heard the colonel. Let's unload those jackhammers."

They set to work. It was dawn. By evening, under Smith's expert guidance, they had made mounds of chunky concrete and opened a broken hole into the great well.

Smith approached. He was in his shirtsleeves, having aided in the lugging of concrete. His joints ached.

"What the hell is this thing anyway?" Lieutenant Latham wondered as he wiped smeared sweat off his face.

"The developer called it a Condome," Smith said, looking down an exposed flight of stairs.

"Excuse me, sir?"

"A Condome," Smith repeated. "A kind of underground condominium. It was intended to open up the desert to condominium development. In effect we are standing on a high-rise apartment building sunk into the sand."

"Sounds goofy to me."

"The accidental detonation of a neutron bomb ended the project," Smith said.

"That I read about." The lieutenant looked down. "Do you mean to say, Colonel, that these steps lead twenty-eight floors underground?"

Smith nodded. "I will go first," he said.

Accepting a flashlight, Smith went down. It was like walking into a cave with stairs. After descending two flights, it became no different than walking down the fire stairs of a skyscraper during a blackout. The undesertlike humidity was oppressive, but it was cool. Cool, Smith thought mordantly, as a tomb.

Spraying his flashlight beam in all directions, Lieutenant Latham piped up behind Smith.

"Is what we're looking for classified?" he asked.

"Specifically, yes. Generally, no."

Latham had to think about that a minute.

"Generally speaking, Colonel, will we know it when we see it? I mean, what should we be looking for?"

"A corpse."

"Oh." The lieutenant's tone implied: I don't like this.

Down and down they went, until the air was close and suffocating. The fire doors, when they had descended five floors, were impossible to open. The concrete had flooded deep. The air thickened with moisture content. Men began coughing. The echoes were comfortless.

Seven floors down, it was like breathing pond scum. Each floor below that was worse. They were able to work the doors open starting ten floors down. Then the search began in earnest through a manmade labyrinth of empty rooms and foul air.

Each successive floor gave up nothing larger than the occasional dead scorpion.

Finally, midway down the twentieth floor below ground, the cracked concrete stairs disappeared into tea-colored standing water.

"I guess this is as far as we go," Lieutenant Latham muttered. "Sorry, Colonel."

Harold Smith stood regarding the standing water, his flashlight darting this way and that.

"Divers," he whispered.

"What?"

Smith's white-haired head snapped around. His voice was charged with urgency. "I want a naval recovery team brought to this site."

"We can do that," Lieutenant Latham said. "Take some doing, but it's possible."

"*Now!*" Smith snapped.

"What's the rush? If your dead guy's down there, he's been dead a long time."

"Instantly," Smith repeated.

And to a man, the engineering team turned and marched

double-time back up the long flights of stairs to the breathable air of the surface.

Smith remained, staring into the water.

"Yes," he said slowly. "This is where he would have gone when the neutron bomb detonated. Water is a perfect shield against radiation. Yes."

Smith returned to the surface, where he dug his briefcase from the waiting helicopter. Sheltered from the others, who were working a mobile radio, he logged onto the CURE computers back at Folcroft.

The situation was deteriorating, he saw from the early reports.

The body of Ambassador Abaatira had arrived in Abominadad. Under the glare of TV cameras, President Maddas Hinsein had thrown open the casket. And had immediately thrown up at the sight of the bloated dead face with its blackened tongue and bright yellow ligature tied so tightly about the throat that the term "pencil-necked geek" fitted Ambassador Abaatira to a T.

The TV transmission had gone dead. Only silence, brooding and portentous, had come out of Abominadad ever since.

Meanwhile, a "peace offering" had been shipped to Nehmad, where the sheik himself had opened the long ornate box to find his only son, Abdul Fareem, strangled, his bloated body desecrated by a yellow silk scarf that seemed to have caused his liverlike tongue to disgorge in death.

Although the sheik had made a public pronouncement that his worthless son was better off dead, he was privately calling for a strike against Abominadad. Washington was resisting. War was near—nearer than it had been at any time.

And the master plan of Kali became clear to Dr. Harold W. Smith.

"She's trying to egg both sides into conflict," he said.

A cold lump of something indescribable settled into his sour stomach.

It was pure, unadulterated fear.

42

"You know what you must do." Kimberly Baynes said in a breathy voice.

"I do not know what more I can do." Maddas Hinsein insisted sullenly. "I have done all you asked me. I have attacked the front lines. There is no reply. The U.S. does not want war. I have sent the fat prince's body to his father, the sheik. He makes light of this provocation. The Hamidis do not want war. I do not want war. I have Kuran. I need only wait out the sanctions and I will have won. There."

Defiantly he folded his thick arms. His lips compressed until they were swallowed by his gathering mustache. They lay on a bed of nails in the private torture chamber of Maddas Hinsein, where no one would bother them. They had laid plywood over the nails.

"They dared return your beloved ambassador with the American symbol around his throat," Kimberly said. "You can't ignore that."

"There are other ambassadors," Maddas growled. "Ambassadors are more expendable than soldiers."

"You must answer this provocation."

"How?"

"I think you know what you must do."

"Yes, I know," he said, suddenly sitting up. "Let us have sex. True sex. We have not had sex together yet. Just spankings."

Kimberly turned away. "I am the bride of Shiva. I mate only with Shiva."

"Who is this Shiva?" Maddas Hinsein demanded roughly.

"A great being known as the Triple World Ender because he is ordained to dance heaven, hell, and earth into nothingness under his remorseless feet."

"I believe only in Maddas Hinsein and Allah. In that order. Sometimes in the Prophet Mohammed, when it suits me. Did I tell you he came to me in a dream?"

Interest lighted Kimberly's fair face. "What did he say?"

"He said I had screwed up. His exact words. That is why I do not always believe in the Prophet. The true Mohammed would never speak such words to the Scimitar of the Arabs."

"What do I do with you?" Kimberly Baynes asked, running her multiple hands through Maddas Hinsein's coarse hair.

Ask him what will happen if the Americans succeed in assassinating him.

"You know the Americans have sent agents to harm you, Precious One," Kimberly prompted. "Do you not fear the consequences? You say they do not want war. Could that be because they expect to unhorse you through skulduggery?"

Maddas glowered. "It will do them no good."

"No?"

"My defense minister has instructions in case of my death. Deadfall commands, they are called. If I fall in battle, he is to launch an all-out attack on Hamidi Arabia and Israel."

Kimberly's violet eyes brightened like twin novae.

"You are willing to go to war dead," she pressed, "why not alive, so you may enjoy the fruits of victory?"

"Because I may be a crazy ass, but I am one smart Arab. I know the Americans will reduce all of Irait to cold, sifting ashes if I launch war." He shook his head. "No, not now. In a few years, when we have nukes, I can do what I will. I must survive until then."

Tell him he cannot survive until that day. His generals are plotting against him.

"I hear it whispered in the *souks* that your generals are plotting against you," Kimberly said. "They saw you vomit into the coffin of your ambassador, and took it as a sign of weakness. All of Abominadad is buzzing that you are chary of war."

"Let them buzz. Flies buzz too. I do not listen to flies either. My subjects will fall into line the moment I order them to. They know, as does the entire world, what a crazy ass I am."

Tell him they denigrate him with each hour.

"They denigrate you with each passing hour."

Maddas sat up, frowning. "They do?"

Tell him that they call him Kebir Gamoose.

"They are calling you *Kebir Gamoose.*"

"Big Water Buffalo! They call me that?"

"They say you are a spineless hulk masquerading as an Arab."

Good touch.

"I will not stand for it!" Maddas Hinsein shouted, shaking a fist. "I will have every man, woman, child, and general in Irait executed for this!"

"Then who will do your fighting for you?"

"I have all the Arabs of Kuran as my new subjects. They will be loyal for I have liberated them from Western corruption.

"No, you know what you must do."

"And what is that?" asked Maddas Hinsein sullenly, as he sank back into his bed, his arms crossing again.

Kimberly Baynes smiled. She toyed with a lock of his coarse brown hair, thinking how much like the fur of a water buffalo it was.

"You must publicly execute Don Cooder and Reverend Juniper Jackman in retaliation," she said flatly.

"I must?"

"You must. For if no one wants war, no one will attack you over a mere newsman and a failed presidential candidate."

"It would be good for my polls," Maddas Hinsein said slowly.

"Your people will respect you again."

"As they should," Maddas said firmly.

"Your generals will not seek your head."

"My head belongs on my shoulders," Maddas shouted, "where it should be—housing the keen brain that will unite all of Araby!"

"Your path is clear, then."

"Yes, I will do this."

Kimberly laid her blond head on Maddas Hinsein's shoulders. It needed support anyway. "You are truly the Scimitar of the Arabs, Precious One."

The big gamoose *is putty in your hands, my vessel.*

"I know."

"What is that, my sugar date?" Maddas murmured.

Kimberly smiled sweetly.

"Nothing. Just talking to myself."

43

The water roiled and bubbled. Harold Smith could discern the rust flecks swirling in the water lapping at the foot of the stairs like a disturbed subterranean sea. They made him think of glinting specks of blood.

The bubbling grew agitated and a diver's mask broke the surface. A rubberized hand reached up to throw the mask back and pluck the mouthpiece from the navy diver's teeth. He spit twice before speaking.

"Nothing, Colonel. If there's a body down here, we can't find it."

"Are you certain?" Smith asked hoarsely.

The diver climbed to the lowest dry step. He stood up, shaking water off his wet suit like a sleek greyhound.

"There are eight floors underwater. A lot of territory to cover, but no body that I can find."

Smith's prim mouth compressed.

"I can't accept that."

"Sir, we'll keep looking if you order it, but I can assure you that every room has been searched. Twice."

Smith considered. "Step out of your wet suit."

"Sir?"

"I'm going in."

"Colonel, the environment down there is pretty hairy. Rotting beams. Floating wood. I wouldn't. At your age. I mean—"

"Step out of the suit now," Smith repeated.

Without a word. the diver handed Smith his flashlight as Smith helped him off with his oxygen tanks. Smith stripped to his gray boxer shorts and T-shirt. The suit was a snug fit. The tanks felt like booster rockets on Smith's spare frame.

Smith blew into the mouthpiece to clear it, and trying not

to trip over his flippers, simply walked down the steps into the coldest, blackest water he could imagine.

He thumbed on the light. The water closed over his head. He could hear his own pounding heart, his labored, ragged breathing, and a faint gurgling. Nothing else. The world he knew was replaced by an alien environment that pressed its swirling cold fingers into his ribs. Steeling himself, he launched himself from the security of the steps.

There was a heart-stopping moment of disorientation. The floor and ceiling became indistinguishable.

Smith had done demolition work for the OSS during his war days. Long ago. His underwater craft came back to him. He pushed after the cone of light he held before him.

He swam the length of the ninth floor—actually the twentieth, counting down from the desert—going from room to room, his light probing. Fortunately, the Condome project had not reached the furnished state when it had been stopped. There were few floating objects to navigate around. Just wood flotsam and algaelike jetsam.

Other divers joined him, adding their lights to his. Not wanting to be distracted by their activity, Smith motioned for them to follow his lead.

The ninth floor proved disappointingly empty. He swam past the elevator door to the propped-open fire doors and enjoyed the eerie sensation of swimming down a long flight of stairs.

The next floor was devoid of even floating detritus. So was the floor beneath it.

Smith persisted. He glanced at his borrowed chronometer, then realized he had not asked the diver how much air remained in his tanks. Grimly he pressed on. He must be sure before he abandoned the search. Although the thought crossed his mind that if the Master of Sinanju truly lay in this watery realm, he had been here for nearly three months. Smith's heart sank. What did he expect to find? Perhaps only a corpse whose spirit demanded proper burial.

That and no more. Meanwhile, the world marched toward the Red Abyss of Kali. And if they went over the precipice, there might be more dead to bury than living. But since he was powerless to affect the situation otherwise, Harold Smith pushed on.

In the end, Dr. Harold W. Smith gave up only when he found himself gasping for oxygen. Frantically he reversed course and swam for the stairs. His heart pounded. His ears rang. Then his vision turned as red as the roaring in his ears.

Smith broke the surface gasping, his mouthpiece ejecting like a throat-caught bone.

"I'm sorry, Colonel," Lieutenant Latham said, leaning down to pull him up to a safe step.

"I had to see for myself," Smith said hollowly.

"Shall I call off the search?"

Smith coughed a dry rattling cough.

"Yes," he said quietly. His voice was charged with defeat.

Two engineers assisted Smith to the surface. His lungs labored. His breath came out in wheezes of agony. He carried his uniform and shoes.

"Maybe you'd better rest a few moments," one of the pair suggested.

"Yes, yes, of course," Smith gasped.

They all sat down on the steps, saying nothing. The divers continued on in their bare feet.

"Too bad the elevators aren't working," one grumbled to the other. "Save us the climb."

Smith, in the middle of a cough, looked up.

"Elevators?" he gasped.

"The're not working," Lieutenant Latham told Smith. "We might be able to jury-rig a stretcher if you don't think you can manage—"

Smith grasped his arm. "Elevators," he repeated hoarsely.

"Sir?"

"Did . . . anyone . . . check the elevators?" Smith wheezed out.

"I don't know." The lieutenant looked up. "Hey, Navy. The colonel wants to know if you checked the elevator shaft."

"Couldn't," a diver called back in the murk. "All the doors are frozen shut below the nineteenth floor.

"The cage," Smith croaked, "where is it?"

"We don't know. The unsubmerged section of the shaft is clear, so it must be down below."

Using the engineers for support, Smith clawed himself to a shaky standing position.

"We're going back down," he said grimly.

"Sir?" It was one of the divers.

"We must investigate that elevator."

They returned to the dry tenth floor in silence. Using pry

bars, they separated the elevator doors. Smith looked in. He saw dancing water with rust specks floating on top less than four feet below. The cable disappeared into the murky soup.

"Check the cage," Smith ordered.

Lieutenant Latham gestured to the open doors. "You heard the man."

Without protest, but with a noticeable lack of enthusiasm, two of the divers donned their breathing equipment and climbed in. Slithering down the cable, they disappeared with barely a splash.

Their lights played down below, faded, and then disappeared entirely. Time passed. Throats were cleared nervously.

"Either they found the trap," Latham ventured, "or they're in trouble."

No one moved to investigate.

It was the better part of ten minutes before a sudden hand reached up, like a drowning man returning to the surface. Smith's heart gave a leap. But the hand was encased in rubber. A rubber-encased diver's head popped into view next. The hand peeled the scuba mask back.

"We found something," the diver said tensely.

"What?" Smith asked, tight-voiced.

"It's coming now." The diver returned to the water.

He was back in less than a minute, joined by his teammate.

They bobbed to the surface in unison, cradling between them a small bundle wrapped in wet purple cloth. Flashlights came into play.

"My God," Smith said.

Reaching down, he touched a cold, bony thing like a slime-coated stick. It was as white as a fish's underbelly. The surface slipped under his grasp with appalling looseness, considering it was human skin.

Resisting an urge to retch, Smith pulled on the dead thing. Other hands joined. Using the heavy cable for support, the divers lifted their burden.

As they wrestled the soaking cold bundle to the floor, Smith saw that he had hold of a pipestem forearm. The hand attached to it was clenched into a long-nailed fist of anguish. The skin over the finger bones was hung slack and transparent. It reminded Smith of a boiled chicken wing.

"It was in the elevator," one of the divers muttered as he climbed out. The other joined him, saying, "He was in a fetal position. Just floating like a ball. Isn't that weird? He went out the way he came into the world. All curled up."

Harold Smith knelt over the body. The head rolled, revealing a face that was stark in its lack of color. The wrinkles of the Master of Sinanju's face were deeper than Smith had ever seen. The head was like a shriveled white raisin, the lips parted in a grimace, exposing teeth that looked like Indian corn. His hair clung to his temples and chin like discolored seaweed.

It was a corpse's face.

Still, Smith put one ear to the sunken chest. The wet silk was clammy. He was surprised that the muscles had not gone into rigor mortis.

"No heartbeat," he muttered.

"What do you expect, Colonel? He's been immersed for the last three months."

Smith looked back at the face.

"Just a body," he said huskily. "I came all this way just for a body."

Behind Smith's back, the others exchanged glances. They shrugged.

Silence filled the dim corridor deep in the sand.

Smith knelt with one hand over the body's head.

Under his fingers he detected something. Not a heartbeat—exactly. It was more on the order of a slow swelling, like a balloon. It stopped, or paused. Then the swelling retracted with studied slowness in the next breath.

Without warning, Harold Smith flung himself on the body. He threw it over on its stomach. Leaning one hand into the other, he began pumping away at the Master of Sinanju's back.

"Sir, what are you doing?" It was the lieutenant.

"What does it look like?" Smith hurled back savagely. "I'm doing CPR."

"That's what I thought," the other said in a small voice.

"Don't just stand there," Smith snapped. "You have a medic standing by. Get him down here!"

There was a moment's hesitation. Smith pushed again, using every ounce of his strength.

"Do it!"

The team broke and ran. They climbed the stairs like Olympic runners fighting to be the one to light the torch.

Smith threw himself into a rhythm.

He was rewarded by a sudden expelling of rusty water from Chiun's tiny mouth and nostrils. He redoubled his efforts, not stopping until the water slowed to a spasmodic dribbling.

Taking the frail shoulders in hand, Smith turned the body over. He found no heartbeat. Prying the teeth apart, he dug his fingers into the tiny mouth. It was like putting his fingers into the cold dead innards of a clam.

The tongue was not obstructing the windpipe, he found. There were no chunks of vomit or phlegm lodged below the uvula.

"Where the hell is that medic!" Smith called in the emptiness twenty floors down in the California desert.

"Here he comes now, sir," a diver offered.

The medic took one look and said, "Hopeless."

Smith climbed to his feet with arthritic difficulty and put his face into the medic's own. He spoke one word.

"Rescuscitate."

"Impossible."

Smith took the man's khaki tie in one trembling fist. He pushed the knot up to uncomfortable tightness.

"Do as I say or lose your rank, your pension, and possibly your life."

The medic got the message. He got to work.

A scalpel parted the fine purple silk of the kimono, exposing a chest whose ribs could be counted through translucent bluish-white flesh. The heart-starting paddles came out their box.

"Clear!"

He applied the paddles to the chest. The body jerked.

"Clear!" the medic repeated.

This time the body jumped. As everyone held his breath, it settled back—sank, really—into macabre repose.

Three times the galvanized corpse spasmed, only to settle back into inertness.

After the fourth try, Smith got down and pinched off the nose. He blew air into the dead mouth.

The medic joined in, somehow inspired by Smith's determination. It was impossible, ridiculous, and yet . . .

The medic manipulated the chest. Smith blew in the air.

After an eternity of moments, Smith felt a return breath—foul and distasteful. He turned away. But in his eyes tears welled.

Everyone saw the sharp rise of the naked chest. It was repeated.

"He's breathing!" the medic choked out. His voice was stupefied.

"He lives," Smith sobbed, turning away, ashamed of his display.

And in the dimness pierced only by crossed underwater flashlights, a rattling voice spoke up.

"You . . . understood."

It issued from the paper-thin lips past discolored teeth like Indian corn.

The lids split open, revealing filmy reddish-brown eyes.

The Master of Sinanju had returned from the dead.

44

The dawn that shook the world began like any before it.

The sun lifted over Abominadad's storied minarets like a resentful red eye. The *muezzin* wailed out their ageless cry, calling the faithful to prayers, "*Allaaah Akbar!*"

God is Great.

In this hot dawn, Remo Williams' thoughts were neither of dawn nor of God nor of greatness.

The darkness had borne witness to his despair. He had not slept. His mind was a frozen eye of fear.

Then a crack of light. The ironbound door creaked open on his cell deep in the Palace of Sorrows.

Remo looked up, shielding his sunken eyes against the unwelcome light.

And was struck by a cold shower of water thrown over his body. Another followed. And soon he was drenched.

"Dry yourself." a voice commanded.

It was Kimberly Baynes's voice, no longer breathy and childish, but strong and confident.

Remo removed his soaked kimono, now heavy as a rain-soaked shroud. He dried himself slowly. He was in no hurry.

Something landed at this feet with a *plop!*

"Put these on," Kimberly instructed.

In the raw light, Remo struggled into the strange garments, not fully aware of what he was doing, and not caring. The pants were gauzy. He saw that. The shoes soft. What he mistook for a shirt proved to be a sleeveless vest. He looked for a matching shirt, and found none. Shrugging, he donned the vest.

"Step out, Red One."

Remo entered the light, which was coming through an

iron-barred window high in the stone basement wall of the palace.

"You look perfect," said Kimberly Baynes in approval.

"I feel like . . ." Remo looked down. He saw that his purple slippers curled up at their tips. The vest was purple too. He wore scarlet trunks with gauzy reddish leggings. His bare sunburned arms almost matched the color of the gauze.

"What is this?" he asked, dumbfounded.

"The proper costume of the official assassin of Abominadad," Kimberly said. "Now, come. You have victims to claim."

She turned with a swirl of her *abayuh*, drawing the hood over her head and restoring her veil.

"Who?" Remo asked, following her with wooden steps.

He was ignored until she let him out a side door to a waiting armored car. The door slammed shut behind them. Remo took a fold-down seat.

"The very ones you came here to save," she told him then.

"Oh, God!" Remo croaked in disbelief.

Maddas Hinsein stood before his Revolting Command Council, attired in a splendid green burnoose, Nebuchadnezzar's heroic portrait behind him.

"I have made a decision," he announced.

"Allah be praised."

"Reverend Jackman and Don Cooder must be liquidated before all mankind so that the world knows that I am a crazy ass not to be trifled with."

The Revolting Command Council blinked in stunned silence, eyes like fluttering, frightened butterflies.

As hot-blooded Arabs, they understood the need—no, the absolute necessity—of repaying the stinging insult the United States had inflicted on Arab pride by shipping home the murdered and desecrated body of their patriotic ambassador, along with the bald lie that he had drowned in a car accident.

But as rational men, they knew that this could, more than anything else, put them under the cross hairs of the American fleet lurking in the Arabian Gulf.

"Are there any here who think this is not the proper response?" Maddas demanded. "Come, come. Speak truthfully. We must be of one mind on this."

A lone hand was raised. It was the agriculture minister. Maddas nodded in his direction.

"Is this not dangerous?" he wondered.

"Possibly." Maddas admitted. "Are you concerned that the U.S. will retaliate?"

"Yes, Precious Leader. It concerns me deeply."

At that, Maddas Hinsein drew his pearl-handled revolver and shot the worried minister full in the face. He fell forward. His face went *splat* on the table, breaking like a water balloon. Except the water was scarlet.

"Your fears are groundless." Maddas told him, "for you are beyond their bombs now." He looked around the room. "Are there any others who are concerned about falling before a U.S. bombardment?"

No one spoke.

"You are all very brave," Maddas murmured. "We meet in Arab Renaissance Square in one hour. After today, we will know who stands with us and who against."

Polite applause rattled the wall hangings, and Maddas Hinsein took his departure.

No more would they call him *Kebir Gamoose.*

Selim Fanek's visage was known throughout the world. His was the official face of Maddas Hinsein. When President Hinsein wished to give a speech over television, it was Selim Fanek who gave it. He had been chosen because, above all others, he most resembled Maddas Hinsein. It was an honored post.

So when Selim Fanek received a personal call from his beloved Precious Leader to officiate at the public execution of Reverend Jackman and Don Cooder, he took it as a great honor.

But as the official car whirled him to Arab Renaissance Square, he realized that this could be a double-edged honor.

For this made him a participant in what the Americans might call a war crime—and suddenly Selim Fanek had a vision of himself swinging from the end of an American rope.

Since his options swung between the rough bite of American hemp and the blistering wrath of Maddas Hinsein, he swallowed hard and beseeched Allah to strike the U.S. forces dead from thirst.

* * *

When the door opened on their Sheraton Shaitan suite, at first Don Cooder took the uniformed intruders for an American task force sent to personally liberate him. He had counted on his network to pull strings. He was paid whether he broadcast or not.

The grim mustachioed faces of two Renaissance Guards, like cookie-cutter Maddas Hinseins, stopped his shout of triumph in his throat.

"You . . . you guys aren't Americans," he blurted stupidly.

"We are the execution escort," he was told.

Ever the newsman, Don Cooder asked his question first and thought about it later. "Who's being executed?"

They seized him roughly, and two more went in after Reverend Jackman.

"I knew they'd free us," Jackman whispered as they were hustled down the stairs.

"They say they're the execution escort." Cooder hissed.

"Yeah? Who's being executed?"

"I think it's us."

"Is it us?" Reverend Jackman asked tightly of one guard.

"You have been condemned to die before all the world."

"Does that mean cameras?" Reverend Jackman and Don Cooder said a quarter-second apart.

"I believe it is called simulcasting," the guard offered.

The Reverend and the anchorman exchanged glances. The glances said that the news was bad, but at least they were going out as the centers of attention.

"Is my hair okay?" asked Don Cooder.

"Am I sweating?" asked Reverend Jackman. "I don't want my people to remember me all sweaty."

Then together they asked the escort if they had a final request.

"Yes," they were told.

Reverend Jackman requested a good makeup man. The best.

Don Cooder asked if he could go first.

Reverend Jackman decided going first took precedence over a good makeup man. "Let my people see me sweat. Sweatin's no sin."

They argued about who would have top billing at their mutual execution all the way to the crossed scimitars of Arab Renaissance Square.

* * *

Remo Williams, dressed like a scarlet-and-purple genie out of *The Arabian Nights*, stepped from the overheated armored car. His hair was wet, and the sweat crawled down his exposed and sunburned chest between the loose wings of his purple vest.

Kimberly Baynes led him past the crowd that surged on either side of the broad throroughfare that ran through Arab Renaissance Square like a sea of mustaches. He passed under the shadow of the upraised scimitars. It felt like the cold shadow of death falling over him.

Kimberly stopped at a wooden platform like a reviewing stand positioned in the middle of the thoroughfare, directly under the apex of the crossed sabers.

"Ascend," she commanded.

Remo mounted the stairs, his legs wood, but his Sinanju-trained feet as silent as a whisper.

The reviewing stand was awash with Renaissance Guards, AK-47's at the ready. They stood between the Revolting Command Council, who wore condemned expressions, and a knot of people at the front of the stand.

Still blinking the light from his eyes, Remo raked that group, looking for Maddas Hinsein.

He discerned a tall Arab woman in an *abayuh* surrounded by several persons who might have been Maddas Hinsein: one wearing an all-white suit that made him look like the Bad Humor Man, another in a khaki uniform, and a third in a green burnoose. Remo squinted, trying to identify which was Maddas.

He gave up. It was like trying to distinguish among dates.

The man swathed in a green burnoose abruptly stepped forward and, lifting his hands in the familiar palms-up benediction, faced the crowd. The crowd roared their response.

In the shadowy folds of his headdress, the familiar brushy mustache of Maddas Hinsein quirked in a cold smile. He spoke into the microphone. The crowd roared and the brown hands emerged from his robes to gesture toward Remo. The crowd went wild.

"The Iraiti people are very proud of you," whispered Kimberly Baynes, hovering behind Remo and translating. "They think you are the only righteous American in the world."

"Where'd you learn Arabic?" Remo thought to ask.

"Your future bride taught me." And she laughed.

Remo said nothing. A short impatient snapping sound came to his ears. He glanced around and he saw Kimberly's *abayuh* rustle. Of course. Her other hands. They were worrying a hidden rumal, the ceremonial strangling scarf of the Thuggee.

"I'm not strangling anyone," Remo said tightly.

"You will do as you are bidden," Kimberly returned. Then, "You will use the Sinanju blow known as the floater stroke."

Remo flinched inwardly. It was the most dangerous blow in Sinanju. The unforgiving blow. Once unleashed, the pent-up power of it rebounded on the attacker with fatal results if the blow did not land. And as the scent of Kali choked his nostrils, Remo knew that he would deliver it upon command.

He also understood he had the option of missing—and thus executing himself. Kimberly's muted laughter told him she appreciated his dilemma too.

The crowd was settling down now, assisted by Iraiti crowd-control police wielding kidney-punishing truncheons.

And then, from a grumbling APC that braked before the reviewing stand, came Reverend Jackman and Don Cooder. They were arguing.

"I go first," Reverend Jackman insisted.

"No, me. Me. Me. Me."

They were brought up to the reviewing stand, where the burnoose-clad figure of Maddas Hinsein turned to greet them. He smiled widely. His dark eyes sparkled.

The cameras strategically positioned around Arab Renaissance Square zoomed in for the moment of high drama to come.

The victims were made to halt before the burnoosed figure. Muttered words came from under the shadowy *kaffiyeh*. Brown hands lifted as if to bless the dead.

"With all due respect, President Hinsein." Don Cooder pleaded, "as the highest paid network anchor in the world, I respectfully, humbly, and sincerely request the right to die first."

"As a fellow third-world brother," Reverend Jackman piped up, his eyes protruding like turtle eggs emerging from a mudbank, "I claim that right."

"I don't think he understands English," Cooder whispered.

"I'm with that," Reverend Jackman said. He lifted his orator's voice. "Any of you folks speak English?"

The Revolting Command Council maintained their stiff, full-of-dread expressions. They, too, were picturing themselves swinging on the ends of U.S. ropes. The big woman in the *abayuh* standing directly behind the man they took to be Maddas Hinsein faded backward, her feet clumping like a soldier's.

Then, under the prodding of the guards, Reverend Jackman and Don Cooder were made to turn around until they faced the phantasmagoric figure of Remo Williams.

"Address your victims," Kimberly Baynes whispered to Remo.

Remo stepped forward. The crowd went still. Even the birds in the sky seemed to go quiet.

Remo stood nose-to-nose with Reverend Juniper Jackman.

"This isn't personal," Remo said stiffly.

"Amen."

Remo stepped sideways until he was looking into Don Cooder's worried face.

"But you," he growled. "You, I'm going to enjoy."

"What'd I do!" Don Cooder demanded, suddenly scared.

"Remember the neutron bomb you had built?"

Cooder's mouth fell open. "How'd you know about that?"

"That's why."

And then Kimberly spoke up. She hovered very near.

"Execute!"

Remo stood frozen for a full minute.

Deep within him, he fought to resist the order. Sweat broke out on his brow and trickled coldly down the gully of his spine. He lifted one hand, forming a spearhead with fingers and thumb.

He drew back. The power of the sun source that was Sinanju began to build within the column of bone and sinew that was his arm. His eyes flicked from Don Cooder's trembling face to the shadowy visage of Maddas Hinsein towering by a full head behind him.

"Now!"

Remo released the blow with a vicious snap of his forearm.

The energies, coiled like a viper, rippled down his arm as Remo drove hard fingertips toward the unprotected throat of his intended victim. There was no stopping it. One of them would die.

Remo's mind froze. *If there was ever a time I needed you, Little Father*, he thought wildly, *I need you now.*

What happened next happened too fast for human eyes to ever comprehend, and although it was recorded on video and broadcast throughout the world, no one saw it clearly.

A millisecond from striking the blow, long-nailed hands reached out to snatch Don Cooder from the path of Remo's strike.

The speed was blinding. Elegant. Hauntingly familiar.

Chiun! Remo thought, even as Cooder faded from his sight and the force of his blow continued traveling in a straight line—through the empty space where Don Cooder had trembled and directly for the exposed breast of Maddas Hinsein, tyrant of Irait.

The burnoosed figure took the blow like a scarecrow shot with an elephant gun.

Arms jerking crazily, he was jolted backward, his burnoose flying like green wings. He fell backward over the railing to land with a mushy *thump* on the pavement below.

Grinning, Remo turned, joy in his heart.

"Little Father . . ." he began.

His grin washed away like a sand castle before a dam-burst.

For standing there was not the Master of Sinanju, but the *abayuh*-clad figure of Kimberly Baynes, holding Don Cooder with two long-nailed hands as two more pairs emerged from the ebon garment, snapping a yellow scarf between them.

"But I thought. . . ." Remo began. And he remembered. The Master of Sinanju was dead.

With a careless fling of yellow-nailed fingers, Don Cooder was thrown aside, and the silken scarf snapped around Remo's exposed neck. Kimberly wrenched. The force was quick and brutal.

Remo heard the brittle snap of breaking vertebrae. He staggered on his feet, his head lolling to one side brokenly.

As the reviewing stand shrank back in horror from the momentary impression of the human spider in an *abayuh*, the scarf was whipped away, revealing a blue bruise around Remo's neck. Remo's eyes snapped open. They were like burning coals.

Gathering his precarious balance, he faced Kimberly Baynes, who jerked off her garments, revealing blood-red eyes that were like twin suns in her face. Her neck tilted left. Remo's tilted right.

And from Remo's mouth issued a thunderous voice.

"I am created Shiva the Destroyer; Death, the shatterer of worlds! Who is this dog meat who stands before me?"

"I am Kali the Terrible; the devourer of life!" a voice that was no longer Kimberly's shrieked. *"And I claim this dance!"*

Their feet began to stamp the reviewing-stand flooring.

And in that moment, the world fell into the Red Abyss.

Epilogue

As if a small comet had struck a lake, Arab Renaissance Square exploded outward in circular waves of fleeing humanity as the reviewing stand was reduced to wood chips and splintering boards.

The great overhanging crossed scimitars trembled as if in an earthquake, while in the settling maelstrom of wood that had been the reviewing stand, two figures drummed their feet in violent discord, their heads thrown back, their voices roaring to shake the very sun from the sky.

It was from that hellish roaring that the assembled citizenry of Irait fled—unaware that they were but insignificant specks of bone and gristle and plasma in the Caldron of Blood that had begun churning.

One insignificant speck of bone, gristle, and plasma who plunged through the retreating multitudes wore a flowing black *abayuh* over shiny black paratroop boots. With his thick arms, he beat and elbowed helpless Iraitis out of his path, cursing in fluent Arabic.

He paused in his flight to glance back. Under the trembling scimitars—held aloft by massive replicas of his own mighty arms—Maddas Hinsein beheld an awesome sight.

The naked four-armed figure of Kimberly Baynes faced the American called Remo. She howled. Remo howled back. Their feet stamped the planks and joists under their drumming feet with such fury that the wood gave up tendrils of friction smoke. Their hands were about each other's throats.

If this was a dance, Maddas thought, he would hate to see them at war. For they looked as if they were intent upon strangling each other.

As they surged to and fro, their earth-shaking feet inched

toward a prostrate form in a green burnoose, who lay before the wreckage, where he had fallen.

One foot—Remo's—stamped the *kaffiyeh* once. The green cloth turned red to the accompaniment of a horrible melon-pop of a sound.

And Maddas Hinsein knew that no one would ever identify the fallen man as Selim Fanek, his official spokesman. The world would think the Scimitar of the Arabs dead. He grinned with dark humor. Not even the Americans would think to hang a dead man.

But then he remembered his defense minister, Razzik Azziz, and the deadfall commands that would soon go into effect. His grin became a scowl. He faced a hard choice. Perhaps the most difficult of his presidency.

Gathering his all-concealing *abayuh* about him, he plunged into the fleeing crowd, taking care to inflict as much damage as he could on those who dared impede his flight.

"Call me *Kebir Gamoose*!" he muttered darkly. "If I allow the American bombs to obliterate you all, it will serve you right!"

TO BE CONCLUDED IN DESTROYER #86
Arabian Nightmare